R3NEGADE IN TIME
Book 2
The Red Mesa

WRITTEN BY COSME DUARTE (SKYWALKER)

ISBN: 979-8-218-24559-7
Ebook ISBN: 979-8-218-24560-3
Edited By Annie Chi and Astera Duarte
Cover Art by Cosme Duarte and M. Waqas

PROLOGUE

"Agents of evil are escaping through every portal in this Earth and it is only getting worse by the day. The deeds of men are dark, massacres, wars, genocide, its all adding up. Building and building until there is nowhere left to build, growing and feeding until there's nothing left to eat, nowhere left to grow. By that time humanity in general will cease to exist. This is why I tell you that your mission is far greater than just one or two friends. No matter how close they are, no matter what they have done. If they knew what you know, they would make the right choice... As you must do."

The Wise Man...

DEDICATION

To The Almighty, The Father, Hachem, Elohim, The Great Spirit , Creator of Heaven and Earth, The Ancient of Days, The Maker of Humankind, Lios, Dios, The Most High.

YHWH

The Great I Am

To The Son of God, The Son of Man, The Son of David, The Savior, The Redeemer, The Good Shepherd, The Lamb of God, Immanuel, The Messiah, The Lion of the Tribe of Judah.

YEHOSHUA

YESHUA

JOSHUA

I pray that this work brings glory and honor to you in some way shape or form, It is by your will that all exists and I choose to acknowledge, honor and follow you until death and then life to come. Amen.

SGT. Jose Julian Gallegos
U.S. ARMY - WW2

Though I only met you once, I have spoken with you many times in my life and have always found strength by looking at the examples you left behind. I love you and pray that I will see you someday on the otherside.

The Character of The Wise Man was Based off of Jose Julian Gallegos. A full blooded Native Warrior who served valiantly in

North Africa as well as in France, Belgium, Austria and Germany. I chose him because he is who I see when I thought of the character years back and I wanted to honor him as well as the Anasazi by creating such an important character for both. To their descendants, I pray that you will understand that this story is purely fictional and though I based much of it off of your ancestors' homelands, I worked hard to honor it and them with my writing. Thank you.

The Meshica or Aztec. My GrandFather whom the character of the Wise Man is based off of was a full blooded Warrior from the D.F. area. His family migrated North just before he was born and he ended up being born in New Mexico. Though my GrandFathers true tribe is not known, I chose to base the punto Cinco Chapters of both Book 1 and 2 around their pre-invasion culture and lifestyle. I am by no means an expert in Meshica culture nor do I claim to be but I did work hard to represent their way of life with honor.

Language and translation of the Nahuat or Aztec Language was provided by, NoPaltsin The Aztec Translator via Lingo Jam. All rights reserved.

R3NEGADE

ABOUT THE AUTHOR

I am just a poor boy from nowhere doing my very best to help bring some of YESHUA's Light to those who have not seen it yet. I grew up a dreamer with nowhere to go but down, books were a way for me not only to escape my own circumstances but to grow and learn. I read more Hardy boy books than I can count, not to mention the daily newspaper and every magazine around. Mysteries were my favorites but so were adventure stories that took you to different places that only you as the reader could visualize. All of my life I was interested in writing my own stories, tales of Good VS Evil and everything in between. Star Wars helped me visualize the spirituality and the battle that rages on over our souls. Lucas, whether he knew it or not, helped many of God's Warriors see the evil that surrounded them on every side through his storytelling. My reason for writing this novel is because it truly was there, inside of my being, waiting to be told. I simply was unable to write it until that fateful day just before my 40th birthday. 5 years later, I present a tale as original as they come, written by a Man from the heart. I pray you all find His Light...

COSME DUARTE (SKYWALKER)

TABLE OF CONTENTS

R3NEGADE IN TIME
Book 2
The Red Mesa

CHAPTER UNO

The Midnight Ride

"Yeah, that sounds like a terrible shortcut, but if it's the only way we can beat them soldiers to Lupes house then we are already wasting time. Lead the way my friend!" said the Stranger as Lee jumped onto his horse and turned it around.

"We will ride down slowly to ensure we are as quiet as can be, as soon as we hit the bottom we find Washee and break left, not right. Understand?" Lee asked as he snapped the reins, kicking the horse into action! The Stranger nodded and followed Lee down the mountainside trail keeping an ever watchful eye out for other riders. Over the horizon a large pale moon was about to break its boundaries and cast its light upon the entire valley.

As beautiful as it was, both men knew it could get them caught so they needed to be extra cautious.

They picked up a little speed while moving down the trail hoping to get to the bottom before the moon broke free from the Earth's grasp. Once they hit the bottom Lee broke left as he said he would and the Stranger followed close behind him. They rode for a hundred yards or so when they saw the silhouette of a man on a horse. They rode up to him and stopped,

"Washee, we are headed back to Lupe's casita, are you

coming?" asked Lee as his horse moved around ready to run.

"Yes, I am! Let's go!" smiled the young man as he answered. Lee nodded and kicked his horse into action again riding as fast as his horse would go. The Stranger motioned toward the young sharpshooter and he followed Lee with a snap of the reins. The Stranger realized that he just might get left behind if he didn't get moving himself so he gave his horse a nudge and off he ran!! He followed the other two as best as he could though it was not easy for him. He tried hard to keep up but was far too scared to be comfortable riding at that speed so he slowed the horse down a little and kept a good pace.

Lee was out front and although he rode fast he held back to ensure that the Stranger didn't fall too far behind and so did Washee. This is where the moonlight became their friend for if not they would indeed be riding blindly in the darkness and not making much for progress. The Leader had a head start on them by a few hours and depending on the rate of speed they rode it was gonna be a close one to the finish line.

Not knowing what the intentions of this Jackson were, made this whole situation bad, he was after the stones that was for certain but was he really after Lee and his family also? The Stranger knew that he was different, even the dying Soldier knew he was not of this world so he could understand why he was being hunted. But Lee? He was just an old man who helped the wrong guy and now he was a part of it too. This was hard for him to handle, knowing he caused all of this trouble. He was hoping that it would not affect anyone else, especially Lee's friends and family.

That beautiful little girl Onley with the bright smile, Lee's daughter Olivia, never did he want any harm to come to them. Though it wasn't exactly his fault, he felt like it was and therefore he needed to do all that he could do to help ensure that everyone was safe and accounted for. He just had to.

Thinking about the cruelty of this, Jackson made things worse for if he could murder his own men for simple mistakes made, it was obvious that hurting regular people for a wanted possession would be an easy task. All of these thoughts filled his mind as he rode as fast as he could to keep up with Washee and Mr. Lee. Hoping that they would make it in time, praying that they could stop the madmen from hurting anyone else. This was all that he could think of.

Riding hard through the rugged desert landscape in the bright moonlight, felt familiar to him somehow. It was like something out of a dream yet real life…

The feeling of speed combined with power underneath him stirred up feelings from deep within his core, visions of riding through a different desert suddenly came to him, the path that his horse was riding began to change before his very eyes.

It was as if the desert began to peel away on either side of him, exposing a smooth black surface. His horse was different also, it was loud in a whole different way and seemed faster than before, not so rough in its movement. The reins were replaced by strange handles that sat in front of him, one on either side of the saddle and he held onto them tightly. His vision was suddenly filled with the blinding brightness of lights zooming by him at high speeds!!! The pressure from them passing by almost pushed him off of his strange horse though he held on as if it were normal to him. Now that the lights had passed, his eyes readjusted and he could see the path in front of him more clearly than before.

It was as if the eyes of his horse lit up like the stars of the sky allowing him to see into the darkness ahead with ease. Yellow and white lines flashed before his eyes and he tried hard to follow them as he rode along, then suddenly, more lights were coming up ahead, brighter ones. As they got closer, he looked directly into them causing him to lose sight of all else and then everything disappeared!! The lights were gone, the smooth marked path turned back into the rough dirt trail they had been riding.

The loud rumbling sound turned back into the rhythmic trotting of hooves on the hard ground and the lights in front of his horse faded back into the moonlight once again. For the first time since awakening, he felt in his heart that he had just experienced… A memory! His very own memory! It was brief and only lasted a few moments but the feelings it allowed him to feel were different.

Unlike any kind of feeling he has experienced since he woke up in that cave. That is why he believed that what he had just witnessed was in fact part of his life… Life before the cave, before this place. It was good for him to know that he had some sort of existence before but it also hurt knowing that there was so much of it that he had already lost. So much of it that he may never get back and that made his heart sink. He thought of these things for hours as they rode on through the night, soon the faint glow of the oncoming day was visible on the horizon.

And as the night began to lose its battle to the coming of the dawn the three men became weary from the ride, The Stranger noticed that the two men in front of him were slowing down so he did also. Once he caught up to them, they all came to a stop. Lee looked at his companions and said "I know a stream that is near here we will ride on until we reach it then we will stop for a rest."

The Stranger asked, "A stream out here in the desert really? Sounds like a dream to me my friend but I go where you go." Lee smiled and they continued riding into the morning light.

After an hour or two more of riding, when the Sun had cleared the eastern horizon, they came upon the most amazing sight for it was just as Lee had stated. There was a small stream that came from out of nowhere and it broke the desert into two halves. It was a Godsend for they had very little water left and no food with them since having to leave the wagon behind.

Therefore this water was more than special, it was a miracle. "This water is sacred my friend, the stream I mean, it is called La Vida because it has saved many lives from certain doom in this place," Lee told the Stranger as they approached the stream's edge and dismounted from their horses next to its bank.

"My Pops always told me about this water but I have never seen it myself, I often wondered if it were true... He is always right!" said Washee with a smile on his face. They all stretched out their bodies like kids after a nap before they grabbed their bags. The Stranger removed his water bag from his saddle as he stared wildly at the running waters of La Vida.

It truly was a sight to see and the Stranger was as a child would be, all smiles as he led his horse to the water for a drink. "From here we follow the stream into the Mesa, it has many canyons and is one of the most dangerous places to attempt to pass through. I would typically never come this way but passing through the Mesa saves us one whole day of riding and considering our circumstances, we need every moment that we can get." said Lee as he removed the saddle from his horse's back.

The Stranger turned to him and asked, "This Mesa you speak of, wouldn't happen to be the very same Mesa the soldier mentioned would it?" Lee put the saddle on the ground and then walked his horse down to the stream and allowed it to drink from the clear fresh water.

He knelt down and removed his hat from his head.

"If he was referring to the Red Mesa then yes my friend, I am afraid it is one and the same. It has an ancient history and most of it involves a great deal of evil, madness and disappearances.

Lupe and I had to pass through there back when we were younger men, I almost didn't make it out. If not for him I'd be lost in that place still. We have to get through it and get to Lupe before they do. There is no other way."

The Stranger couldn't help but to wonder about the Mesa and its possible connection to the riders and their leader, Jackson.

"What do you think this place has to do with those men and their leader, this Jackson guy? What kind of history does it have and why is it so evil?" asked the Stranger curiously.

Lee stood up and faced the two men, "Lupe told me that one of the earth's portals lies there, a gateway to other dimensions and realities. He said that long ago an Indigenous nation we only know by the name of Anasazi, lived there and during their time there they somehow learned to live harmoniously with it.

They were capable of understanding its language, its seasons, mysteries of the Universe it is said! The Great Spirit communicated with them through this portal and they were chosen by it, to guard the Mesa from outsiders and invaders. The Anasazi Warriors had powers and devices like no other nation had seen before, the other nations nearby tell of flying birds without wings and weapons of light."

"Sounds alot like the weapons of them Soldiers wouldn't you say?" said Washee. The two older men agreed. "The Mesa was a holy place for them, it was here that they were blessed while others suffered. Their hearts were pure though and they often shared food and water with the neighboring tribes in times of famine or war. They spent their lives serving as protectors and providers, not just of the people but of the elements. They built their cities inside the cliffs of these canyons and knew how to exist in perfect harmony with the natural flow of life, even though they had these great powers, they still lived without luxury, the way the Great Spirit intended them to live."

The Stranger and Washee took a few moments to absorb the information given to them by Lee about the Mesa and then Washee asked, "If the Anasazi were good people, why do you say that the mesa is filled with evil? What happened to them that changed everything and where are they today?"

Lee looked back at the stream and said, "Lupe told me that one day the Sun became black as the night and in that darkness the Anasazi disappeared from this reality defending this dimension from some sort of danger.

Whatever it was that was trying to get into this world was not successful in its attempt because of the power of The Almighty and the efforts of the Anasazi people. Though in the process they themselves were lost into the abyss with it, fighting forever. Who knows?" The Stranger looked downstream and began to feel the energy of the story and its importance. He knew it was his destiny to pass through that Mesa and he was prepared to face whatever he had to face to help his new friends from possible danger.

"When the Spanish first invaded this land centuries ago in the South, small tribes told them about the great Kingdoms that existed in the North. After torturing, raping and murdering almost every tribe they came into contact with, they received inside information as to how those kingdoms operated. Information that allowed the Invaders to gain the advantage over the Native populus as there was not much that was known about the invaders other than what could be seen.

It was not only their weapons nor their greed that allowed them to prevail, it was the sickness they brought with them that truly won the war. The Indigenous people had no immunity to Smallpox or even the slightest of the Europeans diseases and that is what turned the tides. The first lands to fall were those of the Arawak, they lived on Islands far from here in the sea. The next to fall were the mighty Mexica! They, like the Anasazi, had knowledge and wisdom above and beyond the comprehension of the Invaders and for the most part were a just society built on wisdom and art.

Unfortunately none of this could overpower the Greed that fueled the Spanish Invaders as their appetite for destruction was unsatisfiable and after receiving the pity of the Emperor and gaining access to the sacred city. The kingdom soon fell to the darkness that lay within the invaders' hearts.

All of the secrets that were entrusted to the Natives by the Great Spirit were exposed like dirty laundry for anyone to see and used to perform Evil deeds of every kind. The city became a center of evil and the men who commanded the Spanish forces became possessed with those demons, bound to do their wills and fulfill their blood soaked plans, performing horrible surgeries and mutilations on the people of the city. It is said that their cries of agony could be heard hundreds of miles away. Once they were done with that Kingdom they traveled South in search of the City of Gold.

It was a decade after the fall of the Mexica that the Pizzaro brothers stumbled upon another great Kingdom. This Kingdom was just as magnificent as the Mexica but it was at war with itself at the time of the Invaders discovery. Needless to say the Inca fell just as hard as their Northern family did, losing everything to the Spanish. The brutality of the Pizzaros is legendary, millions upon millions were murdered along the way.

Once the South was dry of gold and blood, it didn't take their Son's long to head North again, this time in search of another sacred city of gold and treasure.

During their journey North they did the very same thing to every nation they came into contact with. Slaughtering and pillaging everyone and anyone in their way. What they found was that the majority of the nations they encountered did not live the way the Mexica and the Inca did. They chose the ways of the simple and cared little for the material life but were highly advanced in the ways of the spirit.

The invaders heard about the Mesa from one of those nations, they were told about the power that the Anasazi possessed and how it was even mightier than that of the Mexica and Incan kingdoms combined. Of course the commander could not resist but to have what the Anasazi had, the weapons of light and wingless birds. It was told to them that the Anasazi lived in a great complex, one with riches beyond all imagination, one with secrets and power that no other kingdom possessed.

This information led them on a great quest, a quest for the golden city they called Cibola. This city of Gold had many rumored locations, many legends tell of its hiding place and the Spanish spared no expense searching for it. They came through here, murdering everyone they could until they reached the Mesa. It was said that the people tried to warn them of the dangers of the Mesa but only ended up having their tongues cut out before being burned alive for their mistake.

The Natives knew that the powers of the of the portal were not to be messed with and that its earthly guardians were never replaced with another, it was for a reason.

The Spanish cared not for the words of the Natives and the entire Army entered the mesa, prepared to battle the Anasazi for their gold and treasures but they were never seen or heard from again. Anyone that passes through the innards of the Mesa must face the evil spirits within, along with the evil that the Invaders carried with them into its cracks."

The Stranger sighed and said, "I feel like I know the power you speak of, the portal, maybe that is how I arrived here in the first place. This whole story seems so familiar and the connection with the Mexica, it's all too close, Lee. I want to act like it has nothing to do with me but I know it is my destiny to see this through to the end, whatever that end may be. So let's roll into this freakin Mesa and kick some ass!" The words of the Stranger shocked Lee and made Washee laugh! The expression on Lee's face was like no expression he had ever expressed before!

"I'm not even sure what you mean, must be some sort of portal talk, yes? We have only horses, Mijo." said Lee humorously.

"Hahaha! I'll explain later my friend, for now let's replenish our water bags and get moving, this Mesa doesn't sound like the kind of place we want to pass through in the dark." suggested the Stranger. Once he filled his bag he stood up and began checking all of his equipment, making sure they had everything they needed before mounting up again.

Though the majority of their supplies were left at the wagon they had what they needed to survive, so the three of them jumped back on their rested horses and began riding down the creek toward the Red Mesa and all of its mysteries. What they would find inside those canyons is uncertain but what was certain, was their need to get to the other side as fast as possible, before Jackson arrived. If he was indeed after them in the first place.

The whole thing sounded like some sort of a story, one that Grandfathers scare their Grandkids with. He was hoping that it was all just a story but he knew that most likely, it wasn't. He truly wanted to believe that things weren't as bad as Lee was warning them about but he figured Lee wasn't much for exaggeration. He was also hoping that this whole Jackson thing was just some big mistake but he knew better. Then he remembered the fact that they had to kill three soldiers just to get to their horses and that made it all as real as it gets. Not to mention the addition of young Washee and his help killing two of them.

Even if it were two other men that Jackson and his men were searching for they would now be hunting them also because of the situation. The only choice was to continue onward without wavering, without second guessing or doubting themselves, they had but one chance to get ahead of this Madman and they could not fail.

"We must be strong and faithful in ourselves in order to pass... Remember this," said Lee as he rode.

The Stranger and Washee looked at each other and then back to the path in front of them. Washee said, "Pops told me all of them same stories growing up but I never believed they were true. What do you think Stranger? You remind me of someone by the way, I just can't put my finger on it."

The Stranger looked over at the young man and said, "I feel the same way about you Kid. I feel the same way... What do you think, Lee? About the Mesa I mean... Is it really like you said?" asked the Stranger.

The only sound that was heard was the sound of their horses in motion. Lee gave no reply, he simply rode on... the Stranger and Washee looked at each other with concern as they both understood what Lee's silence meant. From that point onward they proceeded without communication, no more questions, no more answers. Aside from all there was to worry about, the morning was beautiful, like none he had seen before.

This was something the Stranger found himself saying a lot these days considering his circumstances as every day was a little lovelier than the last. The sky was filled with every color you could imagine and if the sky didn't show a particular shade then the landscape that it revealed surely did. The sound of the precious water rolling over the rocks and bed of the desert felt like a long lost tune to the Strangers ears as it filled them up with its melody. He couldn't help but to think of the crystal clear stream he and Lee stopped at while on the mountain pass.

How beautiful it was though it was super cold to the touch. A few hours passed as they rode next to the bed of the river called La Vida, just as the beautiful cool morning turned into the hot deadly day it suddenly began to present itself on the horizon.

The flat top of the Mesa was visible from where they rode and the further they rode down river the bigger it became. There was a large crescent shape that was carved or blasted into the front of it, almost as if it were hit by an asteroid at some point in its long legendary history. It was hard for them to see the details of the mesa due to the trotting of the horses but it seemed to change every time the Stranger looked away. The heat of the day began to slowly cool down and a small chill creeped into the bodies of the three men as they finally reached the last stretch of road before reaching its face.

They rode side by side the entire way and simultaneously came to a stop as the river seemed to just dry up and die off.

"This is it, my friends, the Red Mesa. Not even the waters of La Vida enter this place. Lupe said that long ago when the Anaszi watched over the portal, that this river ran all the way through the mesa and its waters enabled their entire civilization to thrive. Since the darkness came and the guardians disappeared, the waters stopped right here. It is another mystery if you weren't tired of them yet. We must stick together if we are to make it through this place, no matter what it is that we see or hear, We must stick together."

The Stranger looked at the Mesa with sudden hesitation in his face and after a few moments he looked over to Lee and replied, "If this place is a test of one's heart, I can not make any promises, Lee. I don't even know who I am or where I came from for truck's sake.

I could turn out to be one of them, remember what the soldier said? He said I was one of them."

Lee looked at the Stranger and with a loud shout he interrupted saying, "You are not one of them! That is what this place can and will do to you if you do not focus your energy and your heart! You know deep within yourself what the truth is, you are a Warrior like none I have ever met and I am honored to make this journey with you by my side." He looked at Lee and then over to Washee. He then looked back to the Mesa for a moment as he nodded in agreement.

"I am honored to call you my friend, Mr.Lee, thank you for your help, I won't let you down "

Lee then gave a smirk and said, "Now let us go into this Mesa and kick some ass!" he shouted as he snapped the reins of his powerful steed and darted off straight in the Mesa's direction! The Stranger and Washee couldn't help but laugh out loud before snapping their horses into action as well!

As they caught up to Lee the Stranger yelled over at him, "Was that some kind of portal talk Lee?!" Lee laughed as he rode on...

CHAPTER DOS

Three Men Enter

As the three men approached the ancient windswept face of the Mesa, dark clouds began to roll in from nowhere and as they thickened, so did the caution of the three men who approached. Soon, the clouds began to rumble with thunder as bright flashes of lightning began to explode within them. The sharp blue sky that once filled their sight was quickly being overtaken by the darkness and as he looked back, he could see the once welcoming color further itself from them with every trot.

Turning back toward the Mesa, the Stranger asked Lee, "This can't be a good thing right?" While motioning his head toward the sky above the Mesa, Lee looked at the Stranger but made no comments as they finally reached the base of the plateau.

They slowed down until they came to a stop, Lee looked around carefully at the face of the Mesa and then pointed to a trail a few hundred feet before reaching the Crescent shaped portion of the Mesa. "There it is… That is the entrance that we seek. Let us hurry." he said with all seriousness.

The Stranger squinted his eyes and searched for the opening that Lee was pointing to when Washee asked, "Are you blind? Haha… I mean, can you see anything?"

He looked over at the youngster with a harsh kind

of glare and replied, "I can see just fine Kid, thanks."

Washee lowered his head and answered lightly, "Just asking cuz, you sure don't look like you can see very well."

"Oh really? What, are you some kind of eye detective? How do you know what I can or can not see huh? Damn kids, they are all the same Lee, ya know?"

Lee chuckled at their conversation before adding, "I have seen the way you look at things my Strange friend. I often wondered if you were blind also."

Washee began laughing with Lee as the Stranger gave them both a stern look before chuckling himself. "Yeah well, I see enough. Anyway, instead of making fun of the blind guy, we should be moving our asses, yeah?"

Lee looked up at the dark clouds as thunder rolled from a distance and replied, "What is it with you and asses? I have told you already, we have only horses. Do you not know the difference between the two?"

He motioned to his horse as if to prove his point before positioning it into the desired direction and then he began trotting over to it.

The Stranger and Washee looked at each other and then the Stranger replied, "I don't think that you and I are talking about the same kind of ass Mr. Lee...

That's alright though, because soon we will be on the same page. Don't even worry about it." he smiled as he followed behind Lee. He was riding over to what seemed to be a hidden entrance to the mysterious mountain and the closer they got to it, the more confused the Stranger and Washee became. Though they were close to Lee, they still could not see the entrance that Lee was headed for.

Lightning and thunder made themselves known once again as the three men reached a thin trail that ran alongside the Mesa. Lee led the way and it appeared that they were riding around the Mesa looking for a way to ascend its steep slopes or so the two younger men thought.

The Stranger looked back at Washee and shrugged, Washee shook his head in agreement but neither of them questioned Lee, they just kept riding behind him in silence.

Then, out of nowhere Mr. Lee pulled back on the reins of his horse and came to a stop. "Here we are amigos. This is the way in." The Stranger and Washee stopped next to him and as they set their eyes upon what Lee was looking at they couldn't help but to marvel a bit. It was almost invisible to the eye, especially while riding but once you saw it, it was unforgettable. It was a small thin crack in the side of the Mesa, just large enough for a man and his horse to get through. Lee motioned for them to follow him as he entered.

The Stranger looked at Washee and smiled at the youngster just as he entered into the opening not far behind Lee.

Washee followed the Stranger and once they were all inside of the opening to their surprise they had just entered into a strange looking canyon. The sound of thunder cracking like a giant whip bounced off of the stone walls of the canyon suddenly!! The sound hit with such power that all three of the men could barely withstand it!!! Their horses upon hearing the thunder, began bucking and kicking out of sheer fright! The Stranger tried holding on as long as he could but was kicked off rather easily, once again landing on his back with a thud! "UGGHHHH!!!" he grunted upon hitting the ground!

Lee on the other hand, was able to dismount without being thrown but it was only due to his extensive experience with horses over the years. Washee rode it out for a while but ended up having to jump off also for if he didn't, he would be thrown off too. Once he was on the ground, he rushed over to the Stranger as he saw him get thrown from the horse and asked, "Are you ok amigo? That was a nasty fall you took there!!" Lee jogged over also and knelt down next to him, inspecting him for injuries.

The Stranger said painfully, "I think I am ok Lee, I landed on my back but I think I am ok. How about you, better luck on the landing I see… that's nice."

Lee replied, " Yes, much better luck for me but we are at a loss either way, all of the horses have run off sooo…"

The Stranger flipped over from his back onto his stomach and witnessed the ass of his horse exiting the canyon with no apparent remorse.

"Aye, that is freakin awesome guys! I guess this is why people have such a hard time getting through this place eh? It has already earned its reputation as far as I am concerned."

Lee stood up and offered his hand to the Man, "Let's go amigo, now that we are on foot, it will be more difficult."

The Stranger reached up and grabbed the hand of his friend and pulled himself up. He straightened himself out and checked his belongings. "Good thing I didn't leave my water bag in the saddle!" He said with enthusiasm. Lee also had his bag along with a few other things such as a knife and some other weapons made from wood and string. He couldn't quite see what they were but if Lee carried them, then they were deadly and that was certain. Washee had his long weapon, his pistol and his water. So for the most part, each man had what he needed.

Lee slung his bag over his shoulder and turned toward

the innards of the canyon, "We will continue straight into this canyon for a few kilometers until the canyon walls begin to close, there are many twists, many turns and the trail is hard to follow but if we remain together we can make it. At times the trail seems to move around you, like a serpent. One minute you're right on track making good time, then suddenly you're lost and unable to find your way.

This place has power over one's mind and if we are not careful we can end up lost as well. My memory isn't as sharp as it once was, last time I passed through here… Haha! Lupe and I were just Kids. He saved my life… He got me through. If not for him, I would not be here today."

The Stranger reached over and placed his hand on Lee's shoulder. "And now we have you to guide us through!! We will save each other's lives, we will get each other through my friend. You are not alone… Right Washee?"

The young man smiled and said, "Damn right Stranger man! I won't let anything happen to either of you old guys, you have my word!"

Lee laughed as the Stranger replied, "Who's this other old guy you refer to? Can't be me.. I mean, I'm probably just a few years older than you young man."

Washee laughed and said, "Ya know how I can prove that you are an Old guy???"

Lee interrupted by saying, "Yesss, this I would like to know. Go ahead Washee, tell us?"

"Yeah Washee, tell us! How can you prove that I am an old guy? Tell me Young One, I am waiting."

Washee laughed again and then replied, "Only an Old Guy would call me a young man or young one!

Sorry Sir, but you've been made!! Hahaha!!"

The Stranger laughed along with the two of them for a few moments and then he stopped suddenly and said, "I see this is gonna be a real long walk…" He then turned back toward the innards of the canyon and began walking into them.

The other two guys followed suit, Lee walking on the right side of the Stranger and Washee on the left. After walking silently for a few hundred yards or so, the Stranger asked Lee, "Any other info about the path? It might be useful…"

"Yes, there is much about the path that we need to be wary of, as I have said, it seems to move, almost as if the canyons are alive and plotting against you. There are many different levels and valleys in there, remnants of ancient civilizations along with all of their paths and trails. Before any of that is important, we first need to find one specific trail that Runs along the Northern wall, not the Southern. It will take us up to the summit of the Mesa…

Once there, we must find our way over it and then down the other side. As simple as that seems, it has proven to be the opposite as many have gone missing in this place, I can not stress that enough."

After a moment Washee said, "My Dad used to tell me stories about that place, He said that there are so did Pops. He said beings from another world lived up there. Little grey beings with big black eyes."

"Wait, what did you say?" asked the Stranger curiously.

"What, about my Dad?" replied Washee.

"No not about your Dad, though I'd like to learn more about him to. For now, you said he saw little grey beings up there or that somebody else saw them? asked the Stranger curiously.

Washee's demeanor changed suddenly and after a few moments of awkward silence he replied, "My Dad said that he saw them . He said... that they took him when he was young and that they did things to him. Bad things. I never thought I'd have to cross through it too. But I'm Ready!! I'm not scared..."

The tone of his voice said otherwise and the two older men heard it easily. "It's not about being scared or not being scared, it's about being smart. Right Lee?" asked the Stranger. He looked toward Lee and awaited a response.

Lee then looked at both of his companions and said, "If we are smart, we will make it through this place... You are right, Stranger. Yes."

The two younger men looked at Lee curiously before Washee asked, "So why did you ask me about what my Dad saw?"

The Stramger looked at the young mans soft face and said, "I saw some beings like that myself a while back but it was nowhere near here. Little green turds in suits of somekind. They tried to kill me in the desert one night but I took them out first! Did your Father tell you anything else about his experience with them?"

"Nah." said Washee coldly. He then turned to Lee and asked,"

"Tell us some more Mr. Lee, I mean about the wierd stuff that happens up here. I would but you can do a better job, plus... you've been here before and you made it out." Just then, a huge flash of light shot through the inside of the dark clouds causing them to stop in their tracks, each man cringed as if he were about to get struck by one of them bolts but they awaited the thunder that followed.. They all covered their ears and prepared themselves for the, "" Booooom!!!!!!!"

The sound was so overwhelming that the Stranger could feel it rattling within his bones! He opened his eyes and saw Washee yelling at the top of his lungs into the sky. Although for the most part what he was saying was inaudible, the Stranger assumed that he was yelling out in fright. Lee, although he covered his ears, was anything but fearful and seemed to have a great respect for the power of the Creator's designs. Once the rumbles rolled on and the echoes passed down through the canyon they uncovered their ears and started walking again.

"Wow, that is some serious sound right there! I don't think my ears can take much more of that," exclaimed the Stranger while shaking his head.

"It's because your old guys, ya know? Can't handle things like you used to maybe...?" said Washee playfully.

He looked over to the youngster and replied sharply, "Weren't you the one who was just screaming Washee?"

The youngster looked at them with surprise on his face, "No... I wasn't screaming!? Really... I wasn't."

The two older men looked at each other and laughed. "It is ok young one, lightning can be very scary. No matter how big your rifle is!" said Lee as he reached over the Stranger and patted the young man on the shoulder.

They all chuckled a little and then continued onward deeper into the Mesa's interior. "Anyway, fires have been seen on the flat top at night, or so they appear to be fires anyway. Few have witnessed the lights up there, lit by weary travelers attempting to pass but they are never seen again. There are other kinds of lights that appear up there also, strange colored lights that move around, no one knows what or who they are as few have made it out to talk about it."

"You and my Pops made it out though... a couple times, right?" asked Washee excitedly.

"Yes, when we were younger men," answered Lee in a somber tone. That was it, that was all he said, from that point. He started walking a little faster and his mood changed dramatically, maybe he was concentrating on remembering the path or maybe he was feeling something inside that he didn't share with his fellow travelers. The Stranger and Washee took note of this and followed closely behind him in silence. All this talk of lights floating around in the night, reminded him of the small discs and the little dude with the shank.

"For some reason, I have a bad feeling about those lights Lee is talking about. But I'll keep quiet about it for now, I don't want to speak anything into existence," he thought. Satisfied with that conclusion, he continued on, scanning the walls of the canyon with careful eyes as he watched the other's backs, looking for anything out of place as Lee led the way. Their mood changed also after Lee started acting strangely, something about the whole situation was beginning to feel creepy the further in they went. Both of the younger men walked in silence for a while as did Lee. The sound of their feet hitting the ground as they traveled was all that could be heard.

Just then the Stranger realized that for the first time, the footsteps of Lee could be heard also. He smiled like a kid and said, "Heavy steps Mr. Lee, I always wondered what they sounded like!"

Lee turned his head back slightly and gave the Stranger a weird look, "There is no way to conceal oneself in this place my Strange friend, it is a spiritual place. Therefore I will waste no time giving it the effort."

The Stranger was caught off guard by Lee's response though it made complete sense. "So, you don't think we need to keep our profile low, just in case?" asked the Stranger.

Lee replied, "We are here for one reason alone... to get to the otherside, not for ourselves but for our friends. This should give us what we need to be successful in our mission."

"Yes, exactly. That is exactly what I was gonna say Lee. See, you and I, we are on the same level." The Stranger pointed his index and middle finger at his own eyes and then toward the eyes of Lee as if suggesting that there was a mental connection. Lee couldn't help but laugh at the man and all of his strange talk. "Even though your answer completely sidesteps my question, it's cool, no worries. I'll just take it as it comes Mr. Lee. You know," said the Stranger as turned his attention back to the path and then continued on.

Lee finished chuckling and then he also concentrated on where he was going. Washee was amazed by the way the Stranger talked and couldn't help but to smile as he followed behind his elder companions. The entrance to the canyon along with the crisp blue sky could no longer be seen as they were deep enough into the Mesa that all they could see was dark gray clouds and flashes of lightning above. The smooth sandy path that led them into the canyon soon turned into a thin, rocky trail surrounded by thorny shrubs and sharp pointy cactus.

Though it was only midday the sky had already become dark from the storm clouds that hovered above. The path started to shift over to one side of the canyon as the steep canyon walls began to grow closer together, forming a dead end up ahead or so it appeared. The trail, just as Lee previously said, began to steepen along one side of the canyon wall , leading to what appeared to be the top of the Mesa.

"Jive Turkey!" yelled the Stranger as he stopped to pull some cactus pins from his leg. "I swear I didn't see that sucker!"

Washee stood next to him looking around at the walls of the canyon. "I got the nasty feeling that we are being watched but I don't see anything anywhere."

Lee stopped a little ahead of them and said, "This is because we Are being watched young Washee, we Are… But by whom or what, this, We do not know." They waited as the Stranger struggled to pry the pins from his leg. "Yeah, you really gotta watch out for cacti around here, amigo. Not sure if I mentioned that one but uhhh," said Lee in a comical kind of way.

The Stranger rubbed his leg furiously as if to rub the pain away but it didn't work as well as he had hoped. "I feel like I know this feeling," he said to Lee as he shook it off and started walking again. "I feel like I've been poked with that stuff before, it's an annoying kind of pain, ya know?! I guess the body doesn't forget as easily as the mind does eh?" He nodded at Lee as if looking for an approval of sorts.

Lee only shrugged his shoulders as continued scanning the landscape ahead.

"What do you think Boss?" asked the Stranger as he walked over to where Lee stood.

"I am uncertain about this my friend, do you recall when I told you we must only take the trail that was was long the North wall?"

"Yeah why? Is there a problem?" replied the Stranger.

Lee looked at him and then motioned to the dead end ahead He then pointed at the only trail leading up either wall. "There is only one trail now."

Washee chimed in and said, "Looks like its safe to me, what do you guys think?"

The Stranger took a few moments to see if maybe he was missing something. After all he didn't have the greatest vision and the Mesa was known for illusions. But he saw nothing, no trail on the opposing wall just smooth rock. "Maybe the two trails were in another part of the Mesa Lee? Do you remeber climbing twice?"

The three stood shoulder to shoulder as they pondered the path ahead, the two canyon walls came together a kilometer or two ahead of them and there was only one trail visible. Seemed pretty simple but it was not.

Lee shook his head and began walking forward, he turned and said, "I still feel all my years of training though I may have forgotten the days, this is life amigo. Just be happy that you finally recall something from your past" Lee said as he continued forward. The Stranger shrugged in agreement and proceeded onward without a reply.

Washee said nothing either as he was busy scanning the walls of the canyon for signs of anything unusual. "Very uncomfortable, you have become my friend. Just remember that Mr. Lee here is an expert guide, he will make sure you get back to your Grandfather and so will I! Don't even sweat it…"

The young SharpShooter smiled once again at the way the Stranger spoke, "I could say that this is cool right?" asked the young man.

"For sure bro, for sure. Too cool as a matter of fact!" replied the Stranger happily. Washee smiled and then began whispering words to himself as they continued forward. The trail was rough alright, obstacles seemed to suddenly appear from nothing blocking their path, making things more difficult than they should be. It was as if the terrain was challenging them by constantly changing itself around. It was madness!

Once they made it to the trailhead, it was as if boulders had suddenly been thrown down onto the path making it harder and harder to get around and over them. The Stranger kept looking at the trail ahead memorizing every pebble of it with his mind yet every time he had to focus on something else, when he looked back to the trail, it was different again.

"I dont know about you guys but I am starting to think that I am insane. Where the hell are all these rocks coming from? This cant be real!" Lee stopped and looked at the Stranger in agreement he then looked around as if he did not recognize where they were.

He crossed his arms and placed one hand on his chin, pulling on his goatee while he thought. "Hmmmm, it is as if the trail has been destroyed," he said. The two younger men walked up next to Lee and looked at what he was looking at carefully. The path that they were following for the last few hours had suddenly disappeared?!

"Wait, what the hell is going on here? What happened to the trail?" asked the Stranger confusedly.

Washee said suddenly, "See I knew that someone was watching us? I told you guys!"

Lee looked at them both and said, "It has nothing to do with being watched, Young One. The Mesa… It is altering itself to throw us off track, or it is highly possible that we are imagining this. We must not let ourselves become lost."

"Okay, what do you suggest we do Boss?" asked the Stranger. Lee stood in silence as he studied the terrain ahead. They were just ascending a thin trail along the side of a canyon wall, it hadn't led them that far off of the ground even though they traversed it for hours. Now, instead of a path leading them to the top of the Mesa, there was a dead end. "Wait just a minute Lee. How long have we been on this trail? Cuz it seems like we just started up it but if you guys look back, you will see thats not the case. Tell me what you think." said the Stranger.

The two men looked and saw that they indeed had walked more than a few kilometers and were way to far to go back. "Whoa, what the hell is goin on here fellas? It was like we just climbed a couple of boulders, no big deal right? How did we get this far along? Don't make sense to me." said Washee confusedly.

"This doesn't look good... It's like we are going in circles... right?" asked Washee as he evaluated their position.

"It is definitely not good, my young friend. We should be much higher off the ground than this, especially since we have apparently come such a along way. Not only that but the top of the Mesa is a long way up. This is just not right." answered Lee.

"Okay, okay. Let's not freak out now, I'm sure there is a way to explain this. It may not make any kind of sense but I'm sure there is a way. Lee, do you remember running into this dead end before?

I mean, is there a possibility that we are not on the correct trail? Or maybe it's been so long that the trail collapsed... Though it doesn't look that way does it?" asked the Stranger.

Lee looked down at the ground as if he were struggling to recall his steps from decades before. "I do not remember this at all," he said as he tried hard to search his memory for clues but came up short. "I guess... I am not feeling so well at the moment. I don't seem to remember any of this.

I... remember Lupe... he was leading the way up and we were on a thin trail, just as this but it led to the top of the Mesa, just as this one did. I am sorry but I do not remember anything else from this trail. I just don't remember, I am sorry my friends..."

The look upon Lee's face was lined with the pain of failure. Though it was not his fault though he seemed to take it as if it were.

"Don't sweat it Lee, we will find a way through this alright, I promise. Okay, let's think for a minute, old friend... How long has it been since you last set foot in here?" the Stranger asked.

"Well... I was a young man not much older than Washee here. Lupe and I both," Lee replied.

"See, there you go, I mean how old are you now? That was a long time ago.

You guys were kids when you were faced with getting through this place. Obviously, it has changed since then, hell, it changes with every step! It isn't your fault, mentiendes?" he said with a smile.

Lee looked at Washee and saw that he had a faint look of fear in his eyes. "Let me think on this for a few moments, I'm certain that it will come to me."

"I;m certain that it will amigo, take your time. We could use a break anyway," said the Stranger as he took a knee in observance of the obstacle ahead.

The sky was dark and the winds were blowing just enough to give them all the chills. Lightning and thunder continued as the men looked around for a way past the dead end they encountered.

"Maybe we should go back the way we came," suggested Washee.

Lee shook his head in disappointment and replied, "We do not have the time to go back young one. We must find a way around. I am sorry my friends, I have failed you. Now we have no horses, no supplies and are lost inside of this place.

Please forgive me." Lee said as he stared at the dead end in front

of them.

CHAPTER TRES
Dead ends

The Stranger looked around but saw only the two walls of the canyon on either side of them with a small valley below. The Stranger knew that it was a long walk back to the start line and none of them really wanted to do that unless there was no other choice.

So the Stranger looked around as if he were searching for clues to a crime and while he searched, his companions did the same. "You know... something's just not right here... it's like..." He rose up from his crouched position and walked curiously toward the rock face that ended the trail.

"What is it, Mijo, what do you see?" Lee looked at the Stranger and then ahead of him at the rock face in wonder.

"What are you guys looking at? Is there a way around" asked Washee?

The Stranger looked back at both of them with a mischievous look. He then continued cautiously walking over to the rock face, looking it up and down as he went.

Lee and Washee looked at another and shrugged in confusion. " What do you suppose he is doing? Is he gonna climb it?" Lee asked curiously.

" I don't know Sir but I think he's missing a few pieces... ya know?" said the Young Man comedically.

Lee nodded in agreement before returning his focus to the Stranger as he inspected the wall in disbelief.

The Stranger approached the stone wall cautiously, almost as if he were sneaking up on someone. Once he got to it, he stopped and peered at it intensely. After a few moments of this, he slowly reached his hand out and went to place it on the wall but instead of making contact with the rock, his hand passed right through it! His companions caught up to him just in time to see what had happened.

"Whoaaaa!!! How did you do that, your arm... It's gone!?" exclaimed Washee.

The Stranger paid little attention to what the young man was saying and concentrated on what he was doing. He closed his eyes tightly and when he did, a strange vision passed through his mind, one of a bridge in between two canyon walls that was camouflaged so well that it could not be seen until it was stepped upon. Forcing whomever it was that needed to cross it to basically step forward in faith. He saw a man, wearing a brown hat with a brown leather jacket and he was standing on one side of the canyon with confusion on his face, then...

He put one foot forward and stepped into oblivion or so he thought. Just as his body started to lean forward, his foot hit a solid surface!

The bridge suddenly became visible underneath his foot. It was an illusion... Just an illusion!!! He opened up his eyes and stepped forward. Just as his face was about to pass through the rock, to his amazement, the wall that stood in front of them miraculously flattened out and turned back into the trail!

"Hahaha.... It was an Illusion, it was just another

Illusion!!" he exclaimed as the trail became visible
for them to not only see but to continue traversing!
Lee and Washee looked at each other in amazement
as they both started laughing in relief.

"You did it amigo, you did it!!"
exclaimed Lee in excitement.

The Stranger stopped and looked back to Lee and said.
"Indiana Jones Mr. Lee... Indiana Jones." he then turned
forward again and started back up the trail following the
thin path revealed to them in their moment of doubt.

"Who is Indian Jones?" asked Washee as
he and Lee began walking up the trail.

"Never heard of it. Might be one of His relations, one
can never tell when it comes to our Strange friend.." said Lee.

"Sounds pretty cool to me," Washee said
as he followed closely behind Lee.

"I still do not understand how I could have forgotten
such a challenge as that," said Lee in a sad kind of way.

The Stranger looked back and saw trouble upon
his friend's face so he stopped walking and turned
around, "Don't worry about it amigo, like I said, it was
a long time ago. Hey, if it makes you feel any better,
I don't remember anything at all hahaha..."

The Stranger, seeing that his attempt to make his
friend laugh had failed, changed his tone and said, "I know
what you mean, about this place now. It is very strange
indeed. If you think about it Lee, you probably never faced
that challenge before, if this place is as you say it is, and so
far, it has proven to be just that, then it probably doesn't
use the same trick twice. Know what I mean amigo?"

Lee looked at the stranger and nodded, "You are right Mijo, thank you for helping me to understand the situation. I came to be a help, not a burden and not being able to remember that obstacle, created a lot of doubt in my ability. I must remember that doubt in itself is one of the tests... We must beware."

The Stranger and Washee looked at each other then the Stranger said, " You are correct my friend, it was never you. That is what this place does I guess, that little obstacle back there could have stopped us in our tracks or sent us back to the entrance. We are fortunate this time. We really need each other here guys, I mean it. It's gonna take everything we have to make it out of here." The two nodded in agreement as they listened to him.

"Now, I kind of lost track of time as we were walking. Can't tell where the Sun is through the clouds but I am assuming that it is close to night time, which means we need to find a spot to make camp. Why don't you take the lead Lee, you are still the best guide we have through this place.

Washee, you stay right behind Lee Ok? I'll watch our backs, make sure nothing comes running up on us." said the Stranger.

Lee and the Stranger switched places and then Washee and the Stranger switched also. Now that they were in order they started back up the trail in silence, though each of them felt the need to speak, none of them said anything.

As the three followed the thin trail up the canyon wall they hoped to find a place where they could set up camp and rest for the night but the trail was far too thin for even one person to lay down safely. Some portions of the trail widened a few feet but nothing big enough for the three of them unless they all laid along the trail single file.

That was a decent idea but there was no shelter just in case the storm clouds decided to start shedding their tears down upon them. Just as he evaluated that scenario, the weather was beginning to get worse as the winds were blowing harder and faster. "We really need to figure something out here buddy!" yelled the Stranger to Lee who was marching up the trail ahead of him.

Lee looked back and nodded his head then proceeded up the path a little faster than before. Flashes of lightning followed by ear bursting blasts of thunder became so frequent that the men began to get used to jumping from the shock of it all. Just as their situation had become challenging enough the sensation of water hitting their faces reminded them that it could always get harder.

The droplets of rain that gently fell upon them soon became large heavy drops that began to pour down from the sky as if it were being hurled down at them! As they made their way along the thin dirt trail, the level of difficulty increased by ten with every passing moment as the water severely limited their ability to see and walk.

The trail quickly became saturated with water and little streams started flowing down the canyon walls across the trail in spots, turning it into a slippery mess. The Stranger knew it was time to figure something out and fast but what?

There was no way off the trail unless you fell off and that wasn't the way he wanted to travel. Just as he was thinking this, the young man in front of him slipped right off of his feet and was going over the side in a hurry!! "Aaaaahhhhhhhhh!!" yelled Washee as he grasped at the trail in an effort to stop himself from falling to his death.

"Washeeeee!!!" yelled the Stranger as he lunged

forward to try and grab the youngster before he fell off the side of the cliff! Lee quickly turned around and saw what had happened, he also rushed to try and grab Washee as he fell but was too late. The Stranger was able to grab onto Washee's arm but his grip on the young man was weak, "Grab my arm Washee!! Pull yourself up a little so Lee can grab you too!"

"I... Can't... I'll lose my rifle!!!" said the Youngster as he dangled off of the Stranger's grip.

"If you don't grab my hand, you're gonna lose more than that damn rifle boy!! Now reach up and grab ahold of my hand!!!" yelled the Stranger angrily. The young man looked down and then back up at the Stranger. His rifle hung from its sling and he carried it over his shoulder but in the process of falling, the sling slipped down to his arm and he was afraid that if he reached up he would not be able to hold onto it.

"Washee!" snapped the voice of Lee. "You must understand that your life is worth more than that rifle, now reach up and if it falls, then it falls. Let it be what it is going to be... Do you hear me? At least your life will be saved." The youngster finally did as the Stranger and Lee commanded him to do and he reached up allowing Lee to grab hold of his second hand securely. His rifle strap fell back onto his shoulder and it was secure for the moment. Then they both pulled the youngster back up onto the muddy trail safely.

"Thank you, thank you!!! I thought I was a goner!!" exclaimed Washee as he tried to catch his breath.

"You really need to watch your step, Washee, this trail is treacherous! Though now at least, I don't need to remind you," said Lee in a fatherly tone.

"Yeah man, that was a close one Kid! Too close. I'm glad you made the right decision but next time... Let go faster, alright?" said the Stranger as he patted the young man on the back.

"We really need to get inside somewhere, this trail is way too thin for us to walk it safely." The Stranger raised his right hand to block the rain drops from his eyes as he searched up the trail for shelter. Just as their need was great, he saw what appeared to be a natural enclave up ahead just off the side of the trail inside of the canyon wall.

"No freakin way!! Do you see that Lee? Look up ahead, it looks like a little cave on the side of the trail, can you see it?" asked the Stranger.

Lee turned around and looked ahead at what the Stranger was pointing to. "I see it, my friend but I do not remember such a spot on this trail. It could be a trick or another illusion of some kind."

"Yeah well it's kind of the only option we have right now, don't you agree?" Lee looked at the Stranger and then to Washee and nodded reluctantly.

"Okay, so are we gonna go?" Washee asked curiously.

"Yes, let's go. Get on up young man and this time, watch your step. Next time you may not be so lucky. Or any of us for that matter," said the Stranger. They rose to their feet and started back up the trail cautiously, watching their every step as they went. It seemed like the storm was worsening the closer they got to the enclave, it appeared to be close in proximity it was taking forever to reach.

The water washed away a lot of the soil exposing smooth rock underneath, this made it all the more difficult for them to ascend the trail up to the cave. Upon arriving, they were pleasantly surprised to find that it was far bigger than it appeared to be from the trail.

It was dry and there was a small spot near the wall with a couple of logs! "Whoa this is nice!!!" said the Stranger excitedly! "And there's even a few dry logs. Can you believe that? Huh?" asked the Stranger happily. He looked at his companions with a smile on his face but they did not share his enthusiasm.

He shrugged his shoulders and then motioned for them to step into the enclave. They did but were careful not to get the inside of the cave wet, so they removed their boots and hats, setting them down near the entrance of the cave as they entered.

The Stranger went straight for the logs and began organizing what wood was there so that he could begin performing the steps necessary for making a fire. The other two sat down, each in their own place and paid the Stranger no mind as he methodically worked on creating a flame to keep them warm.

Lee kept a constant eye on the trail in both directions but it had become dark outside and the rain was too thick to see through. It didn't stop him though, he was steadfast that way, a true Warrior.

Washee on the other hand was still recovering from his near death experience. Patting himself down trying to remove mud stains from his clothes. "That was a really close call, guys. I am very lucky to have you guys as my friends. Really." he said thankfully.

Lee looked over to the young man and said, "That is what family is for, young Warrior. Always remember that."

Washee looked at Lee and smiled. The Stranger said nothing as He was busy working on the fire, too busy to hear what the young man said. Washee and Lee were both rather silent after that. They just sat there and observed the Stranger in the darkness working hard until finally... a spark! It was small but inside of that little enclave, in the darkness, that spark was a huge burst of light and soon the Stranger turned it into a warm little fire.

"You are the best fire maker I have ever met, my Strange friend, " said Lee as they all huddled around it, rubbing their hands together.

"How did you do that so quickly?" asked Washee.

"I'll have to teach you sometime, young one. Wait, you mean you don't already know?" asked the Stranger in a condescending tone.

"Uhh, yeah. I know how to make a great fire, just not that fast," replied the young man defensively.

"Agghhh!! I'm just messin with you Kid! Don't take it to heart okay," said the Stranger in a humorous way as he turned and shoved the young man a little.

Washee looked up at him and smiled. "Still, as you say, it would be cool if you would show me."

"Ayyyee, orale vato, check you out A!! Cool? Damn right it would be cool bro. Hey you know what homie? You are a cool kid, don't forget it!" exclaimed the Stranger.Washee smiled happily with a hint of confusion on his face as he obviously didn't understand everything the Stranger was saying.

Lee also smiled awkwardly at the Stranger as he finished speaking. "I really don't know where you learned to speak Mijo but the things you say are soo..."

"Cool! Hahaha!!" exclaimed Washee with a laugh. Lee looked at the young man with a sideway kind of look but then he smiled a little also.

"See vato, you got it down man! Good work holmes." said the Stranger with a smile. As they talked amongst themselves the rain poured down from the dark gray skies harder and harder but did not enter the cave. It was as if it were all planned out somehow, the cave, the wood.

No matter how hard things have gotten, the Stranger always felt that something was watching out for him. These thoughts kept his mind occupied as he and the other two huddled inside close to the warm fire. They sat and watched as the water formed little streams along the trail, one of them flowed right around the edge of the cave almost as to suggest that it was used to gather water.

The Stranger saw this and placed his hand into the little stream filling his palm with fresh rain water. He brought it up to his face and slurped it down. "Ahh, that is some serious water right there guys. So clean!" he said enthusiastically before repeating the action a few times.

Once he got his fill he then dried his hand off next to the little flames of the fire satisfied for the moment. Washee did the same thing and then Lee followed suit, drinking from the little stream that flowed along the rim of the cave.

"This really is a blessing. Now we do not have to drink from our bags. You both should drink as much as you can... while you can," said Lee as he continued to drink palmfuls of water. The Stranger nodded in agreement and leaned back against the cave wall relaxing his spine from the day's travels. Their clothes began to let off steam as they dried next to the crackling flames and the look of exhaustion had become apparent on each man's face, after all they did ride all night and all day.Not to mention that they had been traveling since dawn on foot, it was enough to make even the toughest of humans weary.

Washee rolled up into the fetal position on the edge of the cave while Lee did the same on the opposite side of the youngster. The Stranger didn't really have the option of laying down but he did have the wall of the cavern to lean against and that was something he was accustomed to.

It didn't take long for his companions to fall asleep as the little fire crackled inside of the cave. He looked at both of them with great happiness in his heart knowing that they were in it together, "We will make it through this place my friends... We've got to." he said as he closed his eyes for the night, hoping that tomorrow would produce better fruit.

The sound of the rain drops falling to the ground mixed with the crackling fire were the last things that he heard before falling asleep...

CHAPTER CUATRO

Enemies or Friends

Suddenly, he woke up with a jolt!! "It's soo freaking cold!!" he said angrily as he crossed his arms and hugged himself in an effort to get warm. His eyes remained closed as his intentions were to remain asleep for as long as possible but a feeling grew inside of his heart telling him that something was not right. He then opened his eyes and saw that the little fire was all but ash, he leaned forward to inspect it when the other two men crossed his mind. He looked up to where each of them were laying and saw that neither Washee or Lee were present.

"What the hell? They were just here… I mean, I wasn't asleep for that long was I? Where would they have gone in the middle of the night without me?" he asked himself with concern as it was still raining outside and very cold. He got up onto his knees and reached over to where the young man was when a flash of lightning exploded above him illuminating an empty enclave with no sign of his companions at all. "Here we go again… Shit, what am I gonna do now?" he thought as he looked around for his friends.

The ear shattering power of thunder caused him to retreat back into the shallow enclave in fright! He sat there in the dark covering his ears from the sound, he realized that he didn't know what to do, he was tired and confused about what happened to his friends. "Why would they just wander off and leave me behind like that? It doesn't make any sense... wait... maybe they were taken?" As soon as the words left his lips another blast of lightning lit up the sky causing him to jump within himself! "Gosh damn it man!!!" he exclaimed as he tried to get ahold of himself.

The idea of something abducting Washee and Lee without him even noticing began to send little waves of fear up his spine! "Drug off by some unseen creature in the night? That's all I need is some demon running off with my friends in the middle of the night." Aside from the fact that he was afraid, the thought of them in danger was more than enough incentive to overcome the slight fear he was experiencing and motivate him to take action.

He took his hands off of his ears and scooted to the end of the enclave. Once there, he looked up and down the trail, hoping to see some kind of evidence as to where they may have gone but he saw nothing. His vision was not strong enough to penetrate through the rain and the darkness combined so he waited patiently. Hoping that another flash of lightning would come and allow him to get a glimpse of the ground as there may be some tracks that he could follow. But as he waited there silently, the storm suddenly seemed to dissipate and he got no such favor. "Just my luck right?" he said sarcastically.

Just then he remembered the fire and it gave him an idea. "Maybe I can light one of the smaller logs and use it as a torch. If I can at least see their tracks then I can follow them, now that the rain is coming to a stop" He turned around and reached for one of the logs but all that he found was a pile of ash. Though it made no sense, he was not surprised by any of it. The ground where the fire was hours earlier was not even warm, it was as if it had never even burned. "This is all so weird, how could the stone not be warm? It's almost like

I never had a fire burning in here at all." he said curiously.

He turned his attention back to the outside, the sound of the rain was all but gone and all that he could hear was the breeze as it blew through the canyon next to him. He could not tell how long he had been asleep nor could he tell how far off the dawn was, it was as if he were lost in time once again. Not to mention the fact that he was all alone in the dark. "I've got to find them, I've got to. They are my friends and I am sure that they need my help but what do I do?" he thought.

The thoughts ran through his mind at the speed of light yet none of them produced any viable ideas. He knew he could just sit tight and wait for the dawn to come but if his friends were indeed in trouble and needed his help then every second he waited was time lost. "Almighty, whoever you might be, wherever you are. Please shine your bright light for me so that I can find my friends and get them out of here in one piece..." Just as the words left his lips a bright light flashed in the darkness up ahead on the trail somewhere.

It was soo bright that it seemed like a Star had fallen to the earth and exploded on the ground. A loud booming sound followed behind the light and then as the eyes of the Stranger tried to focus on the origin point of the light, a blazing hot projectile hit the cliff wall behind him exploded into pieces!! Shards of rock flew everywhere barely missing the Stranger's face as he turned his back just in time. "What the hell was that?" He looked back at the cliff wall and saw there was a huge chunk of rock that had been blasted off. Then another flash followed by yet another boom and then, ZZzzzzzzip!

"Whoa, something just flew by my head? Wait a minute, somebody's shooting at me?!" he exclaimed as the realization of what was happening sunk in. He dropped down low to the ground and kept quiet wondering who was out there and more importantly, why they were trying to kill him! "How the hell can anyone even see me in the dark like this?" he asked himself angrily! "Next time they fire, I'll be able to see where the shots are coming from, then maybe I can sneak up on them and end this madness." Just as he formulated his plan, all fell silent.

The echo from the two shots fired still bounced off of the canyon walls as he laid quiet hoping to see some movement in the darkness. After a few minutes he decided that the only way to find the shooter's location was to draw him out, so he rose to his feet slowly. All while keeping his eyes open for the flash, knowing that if he did not react accordingly once he saw it, he could very well lose his life. Just as the thought passed through his mind, there it was, the flash he was waiting for!

It was followed by another booming sound as the projectile zoomed past the Stranger's body at lightning speed. "He's on the trail!!" shouted the Stranger deep in his mind!! "Just ahead of me about 100 yards or so. Now all I need to do is find a way to make that distance as fast as possible without getting myself killed." He sprung forward, exiting the little cave and began running as fast as he could up the dark wet trail. He kept as low to the ground as he could to avoid being seen by the shooter. The only issue with that train of thought is that he had no real idea of what the shooter could and could not see.

It was obvious that whomever it was that was shooting could see the Stranger where he sat in the enclave. Therefore it would be fair to say that whomever was shooting, could also see the Stranger as he was charging up the slippery darkened trail blindly. "Perhaps this was not the wisest of decisions on my part but I have to get this fool before he gets me and I can't afford to just let him shoot at me all night!" he exclaimed just as another flash and bang broke through the silence!!!

Then, "ZZZZZpppppppp!!!" The sound of a red hot projectile whizzing past his arm filled His ears. "That was too close!! The flash seemed like it was in a different location this time. Maybe he's on the move!? That wouldn't be good for me!" He ran harder and faster, careful not to make too much noise or run too slow, afterall, he still had no idea where the shooter was, especially now that he had changed firing positions

The upper hand was not his but he couldn't let that stop him, he had to get this guy and stop him before he himself was killed! Time slowed down inside of those strange moments where the line between life and death blurred out and disappeared. The sound of his heartbeat took over as he ran up the trail searching for the mysterious gunman with his eyes, his ears and his heart. He ran as hard as he could up the trail until the ground suddenly evened out, causing him to stumble and slow down for a few moments.

He tried to evaluate the situation as quickly as possible but when he realized that the trail had come to an abrupt end, "Whoa, what the hell?" he thought as he realized that he was in trouble. His run came to a stop just before the dead end but his momentum continued to carry him forward into the wall with a thud. "Agh shit!!" he thought as he turned around and placed his back against the cliff wall. Deep inside of his body a strange feeling emulated bringing his attention back to the fact that someone was still out there trying to put a hole into him. Just then, a blast of light followed by a familiar whhizzzzz, then, smash!!!

The cliffside exploded into pieces next to his head, sending slices of rock in all directions!! "Agghhh!!" he exclaimed as he raised his arms in an effort to protect his face from the razor-like pieces of rock flying by. It took a few moments for his mind to process all of the information that it had just received. Once complete, he came to the conclusion that the shooter had found some way to climb up the wall and had now flanked him from the upper right.

Making him a, "I'm a sitting duck here, what do I do, what do I… Come on man think!!?" He told himself as he tried to locate the attackers position hoping to see the path he may have used to get to the top or at least to see the face of the man who was about to take his life. Then… another blast of light. Like before, time seemed to slow down in that moment, allowing his mind to process what was happening, while it was happening.

When the blast of light left the barrel of the rifle, it illuminated the unknown assailants position. The problem had been that the blast of light traveled at high speeds not allowing the normal human eyes the ability to see anything other than the light itself. Turns out, he was able to not only see the shooter's position but the face of the shooter himself. "Washeeeeeeee???? Nooooooo!!!!!!" he yelled out, but by then it was too late. The revelation of the identity of the shooter distracted the Stranger allowing the blast of light past his guard and into the left side of his rib cage.

"Uggghhh!!!!" he yelled as his body slammed into the cliffside wall and then onto the ground. Things had gotten pretty blurry by that time but he swore that Washee was still firing shots into the wall, even as he fell. He knew that the young man would not continue to miss for very long so he started crawling toward the cliffside to his right. Hoping to try and get out of the shooter's line of sight as the shots kept raining down near his position. It took some shuffling but he made it there safely, placing his back against the wall.

"Awww man that sucks!! Why would he do this? Did he kill Lee also? I don't know what the hell is going on anymore but I need to find a way to get his long weapon from him before he finishes me off for good." he thought as he looked down and inspected the wound in his side, it was bleeding badly and he knew he had to do something to stop it but how? He literally had no time to move much less work on himself. Just then the firing stopped… He sat silent trying to catch an earful of movement but the only thing he could hear was the sound of his own heart beating within his chest. "Okay, I need to think quickly now… What can I do to get this kid off of my back!

If he spots me again, it's a big game over and that's for sure," he said to himself as he struggled to catch his breath. He looked at his surroundings and saw that he was at the top of the trail that he and his friends were following earlier except it had reached another dead end, this one was real though. To the left of the trail was the cliff wall that the trail was carved into. This is the very same wall he currently had his back up against. Now that he was situated against the wall he looked across the canyon to the opposite cliff wall and saw how high he actually was. If the cliffside he rested upon was the same elevation as the opposite side then he had made it to the top of the Mesa!

He turned his head up and to the right, where the shooter had been seen and realized that he was firing from a fixed position at the top. "I made it! I can't believe I made it! Just got to find a way to lure this kid down to my level.

Then, I think I have enough strength to take his weapon and just maybe I can get him to snap out of it." Then there was a loud Thud!!! The sound of the young man's boots slamming onto the ground right in front of the Stranger's face caught him off guard! Washee pointed his long weapon directly at the Stranger and just as he was about to fire, the Stranger cocked his legs back and pushed them upward and out, hitting Washee directly in the midsection with force! "UUUGGHHH!!!!" The young man blurted out in pain as the force of the Strangers kick knocked the air out of his thin framed body.

He fired the rifle just as he was kicked but the projectile passed just next to the Stranger's left ear and into the cliff wall. Once again the shards of rock went flying everywhere, cutting the back of his head and shoulder up like razor blades. The kick knocked the shooter clear off of his feet and as he flew backwards, it became apparent that he was going right off of the edge of the trail down into the canyon below!! "Washee, wait, Noooooooo!!!" the Stranger yelled as he lunged forward in an attempt to grab onto the young man's foot even though he knew that he was already too late.

To the Stranger's surprise, the young man made zero sound as he fell, it was as if he were not the same young man the Stranger had come to know. He reached the edge of the trail on his belly and looked over hoping to see that the young man had somehow caught himself on a tree branch or something but what he did see was anything but the silhouette of a body laying on the ground a few hundred feet below.

It wasn't moving or squirming around. He just laid there... still. His mind flashed back to the first time he had seen the young man a few days earlier and how he had come to like him since then. He thought of the young man's hat and how he meant to ask him about it soon, he thought about Lupe and how he was now responsible for the death of his grandson. It was a heart breaking event in his short life and he wasn't sure how he was going to handle it. He didn't know what was going on or why, but he was losing his way and fast.

"Washeeeeee!!!!" he shouted into the canyon at the top of his lungs while he layed helpless on the ground. After a short period of time he rolled over onto his back and looked up into the sky, tears were rolling out of his eyes down the sides of his face. Though he had been through alot of things since he awoke inside of that cave, nothing had broken his spirit like the death of his friend. Knowing that he was the cause of it was too much for him to handle and he felt like giving up on it all, right there and then.Lee was nowhere to be seen and now... now Washee was dead.

There was no Light to be seen this time around, no friendly faces, nothing. Even the stone that hung from his neck had been dull for days and as a matter of fact, he almost forgot that it was special at all. Something had to give, "Can't just lay here and do nothing. Besides, I'm bleeding to death and there's still a chance that Lee is out there. If he is, I need to find him." he thought. He placed his hand over the wound and cringed at the feeling of it.

The air smelled of earth and wood mixed with the undeniable aroma of blood, the sky began to show signs of the Sun's arrival with a low glow in the east and he hoped to see it, even if it were for the last time. He tried to focus on what he was going to do next but he kept getting distracted by the will to give in and die. His thoughts were running slow and his vision started to blur out. Silence ensued, followed closely by darkness and then there was nothing...

Then, out of the darkness, "Mijo... Mijo, wake up!! Wake up amigo, we need to get going. Can you hear me?" What was this sound and where was it coming from? The depths? It was a voice, a familiar one, calling to him. Bidding his return to the world he had found himself stuck in. It was the voice of... Lee!!! The Stranger's mind returned to his body and as it did he opened his eyes to find the face of his lost friend Lee! "Oh man, am I happy to see you!" he said to Lee as he tried to sit up.

"Careful Mijo, you are right on the edge of the cliff. Move over here and tell me where you have been? Washee and I have been searching for you for three days!" said Lee.

"What? You and Washee? But.. It can't be. He tried to kill me and I kicked him off of the cliffside. Look, he shot me!" the Stranger exclaimed as he sat up.

"I don't understand... Why would Washee try to kill you? He is our friend, remember?" said Lee in a sad tone.

"Yeah, I know he is but that doesn't change the fact that he tried to kill me bro... Okay... so where is our friend then?"

Lee looked troubled when he was asked about Washee but he replied, "We were separated last night while we searched for you on the Mesa. One minute he was walking next to me, the next, he was gone. I know this place... and it is separating us... testing us. Our hearts. We must find Washee at all costs, can you travel?"

The Stranger shook his head in confusion, "You are not listening to me Lee... he tried to kill me and I kicked him off of the cliff!! Just look!"

Lee gave the Stranger a stern look and then he stepped closer to the edge of the trail and peered over. A few moments passed by awkwardly before Lee pulled himself back and then looked to the Stranger with that same look and said, "As I said before, you are under the influence of this place. Washee is not down there and you did not kill him. Whatever you think you saw was simply... an illusion. Do you understand?"

The Stranger shook his head and replied, "If I am just hallucinating then how do you explain this!?" He said as he moved his hand from his side exposing his wound to Lee as a reminder. The look on Lee's face was one of confusion and sadness as he did not believe that the Stranger's story was possible, until now.

He knelt down next to the Stranger and inspected the wound closely while the Stranger held his shirt up. After a few moments, Lee looked up at the Stranger with shock upon his face, "This wound... It is from a rifle. A powerful rifle. The kind that a sharp shooter would use... The same kind of rifle that Washee carries..." Lee sat down next to the Stranger with disbelief apparent on his face. "Why? I... don't understand why." he said.

The Stranger sat upright with a grunt. He then reached over and patted Lee on the shoulder. "It's like you said, boss, this place... It's separating us. Dividing our forces, as if it knew we were planning on staying together to make it through."

Lee nodded and said, "If you kicked him off of here then he would not have survived that fall. There is no body down there, no blood, no trace. That could mean that whoever shot you may not have been Washee... Maybe it was someone else."

"Yeah or something else. This place is filled with spirits or something. I can feel it," replied the Stranger as he removed his hand from Lee's shoulder and asked, "You said that you and Washee had been searching for me for three days now? Where was the last place you guys saw me?"

Lee looked over at the Stranger with another weird look, One that made the Stranger a bit uneasy. "I... I don't seem to remember. That is very strange, don't you think?" Lee said in a tone that the Stranger had not yet heard.

"You mean you don't remember the last time you saw me? Well, when did you notice I was missing? Where were we?" The eyes of Lee seemed weak in a way, not sharp like daggers as the Stranger was used to seeing them. Lee's mind seemed to be stuck on the questions that he was asking him for some reason, though they were not difficult, Lee seemed to have forgotten.

"I... Don't seem to recall... I am sorry. We really need to get going. We have to find Washee before nightfall. Things get very strange around here at night." Lee stood up and offered his hand to the Stranger. He looked up at his friend and thought back to all of the things they had been through together up until that point. He had no reason whatsoever to doubt Lee or his intentions but for some reason he just couldn't shake the feeling that something was wrong.

"Amigo? It is time to go... Isss everything alright?" asked Lee. The Stranger decided to let it go and trust that his friend was just experiencing the effects of this place just as he himself was. After another moment of silence he shook his head and reached up for Lee's hand.

The older man pulled him up to his feet and helped to stabilize him. "You ok amigo?" Lee asked.

"Yeah Lee, I'll be alright. The bleeding has slowed down alot, guess that nap kind of helped. I'll follow you," said the Stranger as if nothing were wrong. Lee gave an awkward smirk and then he turned around and faced the cliff wall that the Stranger was leaning up against and stepped up to it.

To the Stranger's dismay, an old dirt covered rope that blended in with the cliff wall appeared as the hand of Lee reached up and grabbed ahold of it.

"Son of a monkey, that's how he got up there?" said the Stranger.

"Who?" asked Lee curiously.

Once again, the Stranger found fault in his friend's question and so he replied sternly, "Washee... Remember him?"

Lee turned awkwardly toward the Stranger and said, "Yyyess. Of course... Washeee. How could I forget my friend. Haha." He turned back to the rope strangely and started to climb it.

The Stranger watched Lee as he ascended the

rope studying his every move as if he still did not trust his friend. Lee's body disappeared over the top of the cliff wall leaving only pebbles and dirt falling behind. It was now his turn to climb the rope but for reasons that were starting to mount up, he was unsure of what would be waiting for him at the end of that rope. Would it be the hand of his friend or the barrel of a rifle? "Well, I can't just stand here and wait to slowly bleed to death. Can't go back either… Guess I just need to trust that the Light has my back and proceed onward." He walked up to the rope and looked up at where it led to before grabbing ahold of it.

Just then a voice rang out, "Amigo!! Are you coming?" shouted Lee just as the Stranger was grabbing onto the rope.

"Yeah buddy, I'm coming," he replied as he started pulling himself up high enough so that he could secure his footing on the cliffside. Once his footing was secured, he began reverse repelling himself up the cliffside. "Aaaagghhh… Gosh damn that hurts!" he exclaimed as the wound in his side tore due to the strenuous movements of the climb. The ultra warm feeling of his blood wetting the front and back of his shirt before streaming down both sides of his left pant leg reminded him of the severity of the situation. He didn't let it stop him though, he knew that there was no going back, no resting.

Not until they found Washee. So despite the sound of his blood splattering on the trail below he continued to ascend until he was at the top. Just as his eyes were about to clear the cliff wall his mind stirred up thoughts of what awaited him, but once again, he had to shake it off and face it! Once his eyes cleared the horizon, the hand of Lee was right there waiting to help him over the edge.

"Come on amigo, I got you," said Lee with a welcoming smile. The Stranger, relieved at the sight of Lee, reached up and grabbed Lee's hand allowing him to pull the Stranger's weary body the rest of the way over. Once on flat land he sat down and tried to catch his breath while attempting to put a little pressure on his wound.

"Man that hurt, bad! For some reason, I still feel ok though. Good enough to finish this trip... I hope anyway...

Now that we are at the top, it shouldn't take long to get over and back to Lupe's right?"

Lee turned around robotically facing the East and then he said, "In the direction of the rising Sun. Yessss, follow me amigo... Follow me." Lee then started walking eastward as if he had no companions, almost as if he was blindly obeying someone's orders. But who's? None of this made any sense to the Stranger yet he knew that something was off, especially with Lee but then again... Maybe it wasn't Lee. Maybe it was him. "Remember all of the things Lee told you... This place and all the tricks it plays on the mind. I know that Lee is acting strange but he is still my friend.

I just need to focus on finding Washee and getting out of here in one piece. I'll keep my eyes peeled in the meantime," he told himself. He reluctantly rose up onto his feet and walked over to the edge of the cliff peering down into the canyon where he saw Washee lying motionless, presumably days earlier. Just as Lee said, there was no body down there, no blood. Not that he could see anyway. Whatever was happening to him was also happening to his friends, they just needed to stick together and that is why he decided to continue following Lee. He walked for a while, still holding his side hoping the bleeding would stop before he looked around at where he was going.

One thing was for sure, the top of this Mesa was anything but desert.

There were trees everywhere and the wild grass covered

its expansive top like a fine hand woven rug. It was truly a beautiful sight and it eased his mind a little even though things had been difficult. His side was hurting and the blood was slowing down again but he was still losing it and that was not good. "At some point I am gonna have to deal with this wound boss, I won't make it too far like this. How far do you plan on traveling today? Where did you and Washee get separated? Are we going to that same area to try and find him?" asked the Stranger. Lee continued walking almost as if he had not heard a word the Stranger was saying to him.

"Lee!! Hey man, I'm talking to you!!" The Stranger sped up to Lee and grabbed his shoulder. Lee spun around with a quickness catching the Stranger off guard a bit.

He stood back a couple of feet and asked, "Lee? Are you ok? I'm talking to you. Are you just ignoring me?" asked the Stranger angrily. The look upon Lee's face was disturbing to say the least. It was almost as if he were excited about something. His breathing along with the look on his face said it all. He was awaiting something, something ahead and it was showing in his behavior. It was juvenile, almost kid-like. Lee's eyes were wandering around as if he were unable to look at the Stranger eye to eye.

"Lee, you're acting weird bro, I don't know what is going on with you but hopefully you are ok."

Suddenly Lee stopped looking around and a serious demeanor overcame him. He then looked the Stranger right in the eyes and said in a strange tone, "I am more than ok amigo... Don't worry, no. Because we are close... Yess... Very close." Lee turned away from the Stranger and continued onward as if he was programmed to do so.

"This is not right, not right at all. I shouldn't follow this guy!" he thought. "Problem is, I don't think that I really have a choice. I mean, yeah. He's acting weird but I can't just bail out on him, not like that. What if he needs my help? With all that he has done for me, I could never leave him like this. Especially when he may be in danger..." he said as he reluctantly continued following behind his friend once again though this time with a sense of suspicion. He tried not to take his eyes off of his companion but he needed to look around also in order to better know where he was positioned.

The top was anything but flat, there were many little mounds and valleys everywhere. Valleys of lush green grass and trees that filled in all of the cracks. After a while the Stranger started to forget about the odd behavior of Lee and only thought of Washee and where he could be. The trail seemed to blend in with itself and all the surroundings. It was dizzying somehow the further they walked. Maybe he was starting to feel the damage from his wound, maybe it was the lack of water.Maybe he was just tired and losing his grip over his senses and reality.

He didn't even seem to notice Lee anymore or what he was doing, the heat that was cast down from the Sun made it seem like they had been walking for days even though he knew better. Or did he? At this point he wasn't sure anymore, about anything. Just then, as he was losing it, the voice of Lee brought him back to where he was.

"This isn't at all as I remember it amigo, the walls seem to have changed somehow and the terrain is a lot tougher than before. Stay close," Lee said as he stood still and waited until the Stranger caught up to him. He nodded at Lee in agreement before continuing forward along the beaten path. Lee then followed suit but this time he wasn't walking at the same speed as before, he was moving much slower and it was giving the Stranger a bad case of the willies. After walking for an extended period of time the Stranger started to feel the effects of his wound as well as the hot sun beating down on his body even more. He kept seeing flashes of his time in the desert, alone without water, food or friends.

Even though he was no longer there the feeling he felt deep inside was the same somehow. "I thought we just got off of this damn trail!!" the Stranger blurted out as his mind returned its focus back to where they were. He looked around and saw that they were descending back down into another canyon with cliff walls on either side of them.

"How did we end up going back, Lee? I mean... Why are we going back?" asked the Stranger passively.

"You are mistaken amigo, this is not the way we came. It is another valley that we must cross. I think you are suffering my friend, it must be the loss of blood... Maybe you are hallucinating," Lee said strangely without even turning around. He just continued forward down the trail whispering to himself as he went. The Stranger looked down to the bottom of the trail and saw what appeared to be a lush little valley. Though he couldn't be certain of it as it was a long way down and his vision had seen better days. The idea of a green valley filled with trees and grass brought him some comfort but it was soon overrun by the ugly feeling that he was being watched.

Just then, Lee started walking faster, furthering himself from the Stranger as if his ability to remain calm had reached its limits. That juvenile spirit about Lee had returned and it was weird for the Stranger to see Lee act in such a manner as to cause suspicion toward him.

"I feel like we are not alone here boss, not sure what it is but it feels like someone else is here with us," said the Stranger boldly.

Lee continued walking down the path for a few steps before he stopped and replied, "It is because we are not alone, there are many here with us. We must be..." Lee stopped abruptly and waited for the Stranger to catch up before saying, "The deeper we get... The stranger things will become. Prepare yourself for the heart is tested in ways that you can not imagine nor can you expect."

The look in Lee's eyes was one of excitement, it was as if he knew where they were going and he was excited about it. Not once did he actually look at the Stranger while he spoke, in fact, he seemed like a whole different person. It had become so obvious that the Stranger started to think that maybe he wasn't Lee at all and if he were leading him astray, he wouldn't know it until it was too late.

"Maybe I should take my chances on my own... I don't think this guy is Lee..."

CHAPTER CINCO

Friends and Enemies

"I am not sure about this guy again… he seems soo different, maybe I should get ahead of him so I can keep an eye on the path ahead or maybe it would be best if I remained behind him. Not sure that I can keep ahead of anyone in my condition. I don't want to get caught up in any bad situations with this guy and I sure don't want to get lost but… I got to do something," he thought to himself. He then smiled at Lee and said, "I'll lead the way amigo, you watch our backs ok?" Lee shrugged his shoulders robotically and let the Stranger get in front of him.

As he passed by Lee, he kept his eyes on him the entire time and once again, Lee didn't look at him not once. He just stared off into the valley below with the strangest look upon his face. The Stranger took the lead and as he began walking down the trail he realized that allowing Lee to follow him was probably not the wisest of decisions as he ended up having to turn back constantly to ensure he had Lee within his sight. So much so that it became obvious that the Stranger no longer trusted his companion. The trail was filled with obstacles and the more he paid attention to his friend the more he began to stumble around, almost falling a few times.

"Gosh damn it, I should have let him lead the way down. There's no way he doesn't suspect me of suspecting him for something by now." He looked back at Lee who hadn't shown a single sign of expression the entire time that the Stranger was in front of him, not one. His eyes looked even more blank than before yet he still maneuvered the trail without stumbling. He did the best he could to keep an eye on him but he also needed to watch out for himself too. His wound was still bleeding and he had gone without water for who knows how many days now. It would be unwise to suffer anymore damage than he already had, especially now not being able to trust his only friends.

He was definitely in a bad spot but he tried hard to keep it cool and not be too obvious though he felt that it was too late for that. So he let it go and walked down that windy trail without worry until his exhausted mind started to forget about it. A few hours had passed but it seemed as if they made no progress, it was like nothing in this place made sense as they were just going in circles without ever turning left nor right! They could plainly see their destination but for some reason, they just couldn't seem to reach it.

Then suddenly, as they rounded a curve in the trail, the canyon walls opened up wide exposing the rest of the lush little valley below. It sure was a sight to see, filled with trees, bushes, shrubs and green grass everywhere! They both stopped and looked upon it in awe while they took a break from the long walk thus far. The Sun was high and the ground was hot, he was tired and bleeding though not as bad as earlier.

From where they stood the valley was close, maybe another 45 minutes walk down the trail and they were there. Then they could rest, maybe find some food and a little water so that he didn't have to drink from his bag. The Stranger looked back at Lee and gave him a childish smile before he started down the trail, picking up the pace as he went along. Suddenly, a brilliant flash of lightning lit up the sky!! The Stranger cringed as he continued down the trail, expecting to have his ears blown out by thunder but when it rang out, it did not penetrate the canyon walls as it had before. "Wait a minute, where did that flash come from? There are no storm clouds out today?"

He thought about the strangeness of the matter but like everything in that place it was a mystery and he soon returned his attention back to where he was going. They seemed to be declining in elevation as the trail winded downward but it was getting harder to tell where they were, on it. "I'm not sure if I am well or not… I feel soo strange, it's like we're getting nowhere. Madness!!" he thought. He looked back again at Lee as they continued down the trail and Lee did not seem to share his concerns in regards to their lack of progress, in fact he still had no expression at all.

Other than a creepy hint of excitement that the Stranger had noticed a couple of times now. Aside from Lee and all that was going on with him, it was starting to seem as if the trail was another illusion and he started to feel as if they might never reach the end of it. To add to it all, he began to feel a very small but powerful feeling building up within his spirit.

It was a small sense of panic. He started walking faster and faster down the winding trail as if it were about to be removed from in front of his feet at any second and then he began to run! He thought not about how it would affect his wound nor did he think about Lee. All that he could think about was getting somewhere… Anywhere! He just needed to reach a destination so that he could rest. He concentrated only on his own pace and speed as he ran down the trail, knowing that Lee may or may not be behind him.

For some reason, he didn't want to look back at Lee. He didn't care if he was there or not, even though it was not in his nature to leave a friend behind, he ran and ran, without looking back. When he finally got tired and decided to stop for a rest, down came Lee, right behind him as if he didn't miss a step. The strange thing about it was that Lee did not appear to be tired in any way. He wasn't trying to catch his breath nor did he break a sweat, it was eerie to say the least.

"I think the Mesa is starting to mess with me Lee! This isn't right, we should have made it to the bottom by now... You know what I mean?" After a moment of waiting for a reply, he turned around to find that Lee was gone!

"Oh Shit!?... Leeee!!!" the Stranger shouted sharply. "Hey, where are you?" The only sound that he could hear was the sound of his own voice as it left his mouth. "This is some serious crap man! Seriously..."

Just then Lee's voice came from the bushes, "It's okay amigo, I had to pee, I didn't run off on you... see?" said Lee in a strangely different tone. His voice seemed altered somehow, he sounded mean, almost challenging in a way but the Stranger let it go once again due to the circumstances. Besides, he didn't want to start trouble, not in here and damn sure not with Lee.

"I never said that boss, I just got a little worried about you, that's all. No need to be annoyed with a brotha."

Lee looked down and then up but never at him. And, once again he felt very uncomfortable at the way Lee was behaving. The Stranger gave a smirk and then began to walk down the trail once again, trying not to let the strangeness of the situation get to him. Once he got twenty or thirty feet down the trail he could hear the footsteps of Lee behind him but they did not sound the same. Lee's foot steps were different, his pace was fluid and his steps were solid, as if every one of them were carefully planned and then executed with precision. The sound that was coming from the feet of the man walking behind him now, were sloppy, uncoordinated and heavy.

The feeling of panic that he felt earlier, elevated a

level within his spirit upon the realization that the man following him was either a tired and weary Lee or not Lee at all... They had been traveling hard for the last couple of weeks without much rest so the first assumption could be true but then again, so could the second.

Afterall he wasn't feeling his best considering all he had been through so the same had to be taken into consideration for his friend Lee. "I'll just shut up and continue onward. I won't trip unless he gives me a reason to," the Stranger thought to himself as he continued walking down the never ending trail, pondering all of these things as if he could no longer control the flow of his mind. He started forgetting about the footsteps behind him and began moving faster and faster down the trail once again. Angrily his pace moved up to a running speed and he no longer thought of anything else aside from reaching the valley.

"This is a freakin trick! I know it is, this trail has to have an end and I'll get to it if it's the last thing I do!!" shouted the Stranger as he rushed down the trail. The sound of his own echo threw him off course a bit and as he began to try to correct himself, he found that his legs had somehow gotten tripped up on something causing him to lose balance! He started falling forward until his body hit the dirt with a huge thud, throwing him violently down the trail! His body was bouncing off of the rocks and shrubs as he spun like a tornado, unable to slow himself down until he finally hit the flat ground of the valley floor!

It took a few moments for his mind to catch up with his body but when both realigned with each other, the feeling was not pleasant. He groaned in pain as he rolled over onto his stomach and looked around at where he had found himself.

"Freakin A! Haha!! I was beginning to think that I was never gonna reach this place!!!" he exclaimed as he tried to catch his breath. He then rolled over onto his back and looked up at the sky. "What about you Lee… ?" he asked, assuming that his friend would also be there, but after Lee gave no response, the Stranger quickly noticed that Lee was once again nowhere to be seen. He thought back to the last time he had heard Lee's footsteps and remembered the uneasy feeling that he had experienced at the notion that it wasn't Lee following behind him. He slowly rose up to his feet and looked back to the trail that they were walking down only to find that there was no trail.

"Wait, what the hell? Where did the trail go? Where are the canyon walls that we just walked through?" he said curiously. He was literally standing in the middle of the lush green valley with only the two cliff walls in sight on either side of him and they were both a good distance away from where he stood. There was no slope, no trail and most importantly, there was no Lee. Still breathing hard from all the running and falling he just done, he was still trying to catch his breath while looking around at where he was at.

"I'm not even gonna sweat it, I'm just gonna concentrate on finding a way out of here," he said as he studied the valley in all directions, trying to decide as to which direction he would take. He reached back for the sword for some reason but remembered quickly that it was gone, then his mind thought of the stone so he quickly put his hand on his chest to find that it was gone also!

"Son of a bitch! I lost both of them!? Ooh what am I even talking about? I mean I lost all of them, the sword, the stone Washee and Lee!! What the hell am I gonna do now?" he asked himself knowing that he already knew the answer. After a few moments of belly aching he calmed down and focused on tending to his wound as he seemed to forget about it once again. He looked around for anything that he could use to help clean the wound up but there was nothing in sight. He looked down to his feet and noticed that the soft green grass rose up out of the soil to his knee.

He reached down with his hand and touched it, "It's so soft, it almost doesn't feel like real grass," he said as he brought his hand back up to his side in pain. It was uncertain, like everything in this Mesa, how long he had been standing there. For out of nowhere the smell of the trees nearby overwhelmed his sense of smell. "Wow, that smell is soo awesome! It makes me feel like I am close to home," he said to himself sadly. Then… drip, drip… The sound of his blood dripping off of his clothing onto the blades of grass below reminded him that if he ever wanted to see his home again, he needed to get moving, find his friends and get out of here.

He looked down once again to his left side and saw that a pool of blood had accumulated under his left foot. The sight of the dark red liquid that carried his physical life force falling on the grass helped him realize something. "Whoa, how long have I been standing here? Wait… None of this is right, none of it. I'm lost but I am still alive.

Plus, I already know that this place is going to test me, this is just part of all of that. I just need to focus and remember what I am here for and why. To get to the other side, not for myself, not for glory but for my friends," he said to himself as he checked his wound once again. Confident in the words that he had spoken unto himself, he looked up at the valley ahead of him and then at the valley behind him. He wasn't exactly sure what direction to travel in as he had gotten turned around while falling down the trail but either way, he was lost. Even if he was still on the trail it could not be trusted!

As frustrating as it was, he kept his cool while trying to look for the sun. If he could find it, he could use it to help guide him but it was hidden behind the dark stormy clouds that crept over the sky above. "Soo strange, it was clear as crystal just minutes earlier. Why now is it dark with no sign of the sun?" he asked. As for Lee... he was still nowhere in sight. "I guess I have but one choice, go back or go forward, either way I'll be moving and in the end that is what is important." he thought. Though he said these things confidently to himself, he really didn't believe in them.

He knew he was lost, plain and simple. If he chose the wrong direction he could end up back at the beginning again and that wasn't an option. He needed to find Lee and the young sharpshooter before he could find a way out and that presented a challenge unlike any he had faced to date as it meant that he would die trying.

He scanned the canyon walls looking for anything familiar, a marking or a cavern, a tree even, anything that could help him pick a direction but he saw nothing. Everything seemed to blend into itself, there were no real landmarks or trees that caught his attention. Just a serene little valley that seemed to never end. "Alrighty then. Guess I'll just get moving and see where I end up." He closed his eyes and thought of the cave where he woke and of the times when he was afraid, all alone, in the dark. The Light, it always seemed to comfort him somehow.

Even though he didn't always notice. So he concentrated on his connection with that Light, honing in on the warm powerful feeling that he had become so familiar with on his journey thus far. After a few moments passed he was saddened to find that the feeling he sought, evaded him. The Light did not shine for him nor did his heart fill with warm electric power. He realized that he was all alone this time around, no tools to help him out, no weapons or stones of light.

Heck, he didn't even have his only friends to count on, nothing but the sound of his own heart mixed with falling drops of rain and blood. He opened his eyes and looked forward into the valley with uncertainty as the rain continued to fall. He took a deep breath and took a step forward. It started with one and then a second step. Soon he was moving through the valley at a solid pace, weaving himself around the rocks and dips as best as he could.

The valley was filled with trees and his ability to navigate through them had diminished as he had to constantly stop and check his positioning. Aside from the small challenges, the day was cooler now that he was in the valley and this helped his mind knowing that the heat was not an issue this time around. Raindrops would fall then stop as if the Almighty was turning on and off the faucet. Flashes of lightning began to light up the dark clouds once again and thunder clashed in the sky, shattering the interior of his ears as before!

"Whoa, what the heck?!! One minute it hurts, the next nada... This place is really getting to me." he said as he shook his head and continued forward or at least what he perceived to be forward. Soon the clouds began to cry again, sending their teardrops down onto the earth, covering the red cliff walls and the valley's grassy floor under his feet. Making the journey a bit more difficult for the Stranger to traverse as the rain poured down, this time with little sign of letting up.

It didn't take long for his clothes to become soaked all the way through but he didn't seem to get cold, the climate was warm and he was in motion which in turn kept him warm. The branches of the small trees provided cover from the rain but soon they dumped more water on him than did the clouds. "Wow, not sure I've ever seen so much rain before," he said in disbelief. His body ached from getting shot, not to mention all of the falls he had taken. He needed rest desperately, but the day went on and on.

He was also still bleeding pretty badly from the gunshot

wound in his side. "Aggghhh… I'm getting tired from the constant movement… I'm not sure how long I can keep this up." he thought as his mind traveled back to his time in the desert, the feeling of utter loneliness. Helplessness… he soon forgot about the weather as he struggled more and more just to make his way through the valley. It was hard enough to see through the falling water combined with raindrops hitting his eyes but throw in the lack of food, real water, a wound and he was starting to look like a goner.

There was no real shelter nearby and the rain only became worse as time went on. He had already stopped looking for his friends but he remained aware of them, just in case he happened to see them.

He looked up into the sky and saw that the daylight was fading fast… Although it sucked, it helped him to realize that it was just too dangerous to continue, he had to stop and search the area for some kind of refuge before it was too late but he just couldn't see anything. He walked closer to one of the cliff walls and scanned the trees and area in front of it, looking for anything that he could use to cover himself up with and that is when his eyes saw something… Not on the ground but above it, on the cliff wall itself!

"Can it be? Is that what I think it is?" he asked himself as he tried to clear the water from his eyes.

He started walking toward the cliff wall as fast as he could, avoiding the rocks and dips that filled the spaces in between the medium sized trees. He couldn't help but to adore the smell that filled the air as he struggled to get to the cliff wall. The aroma was so strong that it did something to him… His world suddenly felt thin. Just as it always did when he traveled to other places, it was a feeling he had become accustomed to.

"This smell makes me feel like I am home somehow but I don't even know where it is that I come from. Such a head game!" he exclaimed as he got closer and closer to what he had seen from the interior of the valley. Putting the amazing aroma aside he was approaching the cliffside wall and when he cleared the last of the trees, what he had seen from the valley moments before turned out to be exactly what he thought it was. A circular opening in the cliff wall! He gazed at it for a few moments to ensure that it was big enough for his body to fit into and as he looked closer, it seemed to be more than large enough for him to rest in.

"Thank the Creator!! Now, I can finally rest." he said in absolute relief as the day seemed to finally come to an end, leaving only a soft glow of light behind in the distance. He began trying to scale the slippery cliff wall to get to the opening which was up the wall about 20 or 30 feet but the climb was extremely difficult and he was already injured.

He tried climbing it anyway only to slide down multiple times nearly injuring himself more but after a few attempts, he was able to reach the edge of the opening with one hand. Once he had a solid grip on it, he then reached up with the other hand and grabbed ahold of the edge also. He hung there for a few moments to gather up the last of his remaining energy and just as he was about to pull himself up into the dry opening, he lost his grip and slid down the wall just a foot or two... Then, Boom!!!!! The small portion of cliffside that his head was just in front of, exploded into shards right above him!!!

"Washeeeeeeeeeeeeeeee!!!!!!!" he screamed out in anger as he turned around quickly to try and spot the shooter before he fired another shot. Just as he turned his head, another flash illuminated an area from within the trees near the center of the valley. Then Bam!! The blast hit the cliffside just underneath his right foot, almost blasting it right off of his leg! The Stranger wasted no time in getting off of the cliff wall as he pulled himself back up to the edge and into the opening just in time. Just as his legs cleared the cliff wall, another blast hit just outside of the entrance!

"Gosh damn it that was close!!! Why the hell is that boy trying so damn hard to kill me anyway?" he asked as he crawled deeper into the tunnel to avoid being shot at. "Ahh man, do I need a freakin plan! This kid is gonna kill me if I don't… That's for sure." He struggled to catch his breath as he sat against the round wall of the tunnel.

He looked into the blackness of it but could not see further than he could reach out and though he wanted to venture further into the tunnel he knew that it could be even more dangerous than the danger he already faced outside.

"What if it's a dead end and the Boy catches up to me, then I'll have nowhere to go? I can't put myself into that kind of position, not with this kid on my ass the way he is." Despite all of his thoughts and ideas, he knew that the only real way to stop Washee from killing him, was to stop Washee from killing him. It was that simple.He just needed to figure out how. After a few short moments of resting he laid down on his belly and crawled back toward the tunnel's opening. "I need to get a fix on his position or he will be able to pick me off anytime he has a clear shot," he thought as he cautiously got closer to the opening of the tunnel.

He obviously didn't want to get too close to the edge as the young man had already proven himself to be a decent shot and the Stranger could attest to that fact. Rain drops continued to pour outside, limiting his ability to hear and limiting his ability to see out into the night but he had to try. He tilted his head to the side to limit the shooter's ability to see him as he tried to get an eye on where the youngster might be. Once he reached a point where he could see the majority of the valley outside, he stopped and remained as still as he possibly could. His body began to shiver, slightly at first but after laying still for an extended period of time, it started shivering harder and faster.

Soon he was shivering so badly that he was no longer able to focus his vision due to the constant shaking. Just then, a small flash of light could be seen about 50 yards from the cliff wall. Though it was not a blast from the kid's long weapon, it was faint and small. He waited patiently to see if the light would return and after a few moments it did! "That's no rifle blast, the kid is trying to make a fire! He's actually giving up his position to try and stay warm." It was in fact very cold now that the sun was gone and the night reigned free, not to mention he was probably just as wet and miserable as the Stranger was...

"Maybe he's injured too," he said to himself with a certain sadness as he once again thought about his young companion. He could tell that the young man was struggling to start the fire as the flash of light kept dying out. "This would be the perfect time to try and get that weapon away from him. Yeah, now that I can see where he is and the rain is masking my steps, it's a perfect time to strike. Besides, this may be my only chance to try and talk some sense into him before he ends up killing me. Maybe Lee too and I can't let that happen... not while I am still able to do something about it anyway," he said as he rolled over to check his wound.

A small pool of blood formed on the tunnel floor where he was lying which meant that his wound was still torn but at least the bleeding was not excessive. Even if it were, he had no choice but to go after the young man. "Do or die homie... It's do or die," he said as he waited for another sign that the young man was still there.

Once he saw it, he slid out of the tunnel almost head first! Grabbing onto the edge as he passed it, catching himself as he completed a frontal flip out of the opening. He then let go of the edge with his right hand and turned himself around, placing his stomach against the smooth cliffside. The cliffside had just enough of an angle that when he let go of the edge, he simply slid down the already wet cliffside to the earth, almost without making a sound. Strange he thought to himself, "How do I know how to do stuff like that? Maybe I used to be in the circus…"

Once his feet were on the ground he set his sights on the area where he had seen the young man attempting to light a fire moments earlier. He then lowered his body into a half crouch and began moving forward through the trees as fast and as silent as he could…

CHAPTER SEIS

The Sharp Shooter

His heart was pumping adrenaline through his veins but his mind remained still and focused on the mission at hand. "I don't want to hurt the boy, I just need to make sure I disarm him before he gets a shot off. That's all! I know he is not in his right mind, he would never try to kill me if he were... It has to be this place. It has to be," he said to himself as he moved around and in between the trees, careful not to slip or make too much noise.

For if he alerted the kid, he would surely end up dead. While he made progress through the medium sized trees he searched for any sign of the light in hopes to zero in on the kids position but he did not see anything. He started to slow his pace down just enough to allow himself to expand his visual search for the shooter's location but still, he saw nothing. He decided that it would be wise for him to stop and hide out behind one of the trees for a while so that he could try and zero in on the kid's position. He figured that if he waited around patiently, the kid would end up trying to spark a flame again, giving up his position.

Then, he would close in on him, secure the kid's weapon and control the situation! The sound of the pouring rain was all that could be heard as he waited quietly for a sign.

"Is it just me or do I hear a voice out there somewhere?" he asked as he thought he heard someone yelling off into the distance. He repositioned himself and placed a hand around his right ear, hoping to amplify the background noise. Drip, drip, drip. Multiplied by the millions, that is all he could hear and after minutes of waiting, he decided to forget about it and refocus his attention back to the kid's possible location.

Just then, a flash of light breaks through the night no more than 50 feet from where the Stranger was hiding!! He waited to make sure that what he saw was indeed what he was waiting to see and when the flicker of a small flame began to steadily burn, he sprung into motion! Quietly making his way through the trees over to the light his eyes searched for the silhouette of the young man's body so that he could attack him with precision but he was unable to do so as the darkness combined with the rain and his movement hindered his vision.

At that point he was committed to his approach and if he tried to change course due to his inability to see the target, it would only lead him off into the trees and make him vulnerable to flanking. This is not where he wanted to end up but if he continued on, straight toward the little flame, without being able to identify the target, he could also end up in a vulnerable position. "What should I do? I am running out of time!!??" he thought! Inside of those moments, his mind began to stir itself crazy with doubt from the realization he had just experienced and even though he was already in motion, he still had a slight moment to make a different move if he absolutely had to.

"But where? This whole thing could have been a trap!!!" he exclaimed inside of his mind with frustration! Just as he had reached the small flame's range of light, he came to find that it was just as he was afraid as no one was there!! No Washee, no Lee, No one. He came to a sudden halt and as he did, the silhouette of a person off into the trees broke the plane of his peripheral vision!!! Through pure instinct, his body jumped back into action faster than he thought possible and he sprinted toward the figure with all of the speed and power that his tired, injured body could muster.

Not knowing if the figure had spotted him yet, he pushed on and closed the distance between the two individuals in a matter of seconds! The Stranger leaped into the air, extending his right leg out in front of himself like a missile! Before the figure could react he took a devastating kick straight to the side of the head!!

"Yeeeeeaaaaaaaaa!!!!!!" he screamed out as his foot made contact with the unknown figure's face, knocking him to the ground like a rock off a cliff! The figure hit the wet earth with a splash and laid as still as a forest log. Meanwhile the Stranger remained in his fighting stance as prepared as a warrior could be while he scanned the area for other possible enemies. Once he was satisfied with the results, he turned to the figure that lay unconscious on the ground and grabbed him by the feet. He then drug the figure into the light of the little flame and rolled him over.

"Gosh damn it man!!! Why bro, why??" he asked the sleeping Washee with sadness and disappointment, "I tried to get myself to believe that I was just crazy but, I guess it really was you trying to kill me. How did you survive the fall though? I saw you dead on the rocks... I saw you," he exclaimed with emotion as knelt down next to the young man and began searching his pockets for any unseen weapons. He found a knife and a few large rifle shells that he tossed on the ground.

"No pistol and no rifle, Wait a minute... Where would they be? Where have you been this whole time?" he asked as he grabbed onto the young man's vest and shook him with anger while he repeated the same question again and again. The young man groaned a few times but did not wake up. His right cheek bone was swollen and already turning blue from the power of the Stranger's kick. He looked upon the young man's soft face and he couldn't help but to remember his smile, the innocence he exuded. Even though he tried not to. The Stranger's heart welled up with feelings for the kid almost as if the boy were his very own son.

He released the kids vest from his grip and through guilt, he straightened the kids body out so that he could sleep comfortably. "Not without a little restraint though," he said cautiously as he removed the young men's belts and then proceeded to use them to tie his feet and hands together with them. "There, now it's time to tend to this dying little fire." he said as he got up and searched the nearby area for something dry to burn.

He walked around but was unable to find anything due to the constant rainfall. He also searched the nearby woods for a cache of weapons that the youngster could have stashed but found nothing. He walked back toward the dying fire disappointed that he had nothing to feed the embers on a cold wet night. "Aye, Almighty. I really could use a little." Just as the words came from his lips a huge blast of lightning hit a tree a few yards away from where he and Washee were positioned!!!

"CCCRRRAAAACCCCKKKK!!!!! It went as it sliced directly through a nearby tree!!!

"Oh shit!!!?" he exclaimed as he ran back and jumped over Washee protecting him from the shrapnel of wood that flew in all directions. He looked back toward the tree and saw that it was about to fall over directly on top of them! "Come on boy, time to goooo!" he yelled as he grabbed Washee and threw him away from the tree as it fell to the ground with a loud, bam!!! The snapping sound of the branches breaking off as they hit the ground echoed throughout the valley! Mud and twigs went flying into the air, splattering the two men as the Stranger covered Washee and himself up as best as he could!

He remained in place for a few extra moments trying to absorb what had just happened, "Talk about being careful what you ask for... Haha, sheesh!" he shouted before he rolled over and looked at the aftermath of the lightning strike.

"Well, I'll be a monkey's uncle, would ya look at that? Thank you Almighty, thank you! Hahaha... Now we have something we can work with!" he said as he looked into the sky above, then over to a small but intense fire that burned inside of the stump that was just struck by the bolt of lightning. He looked over and made sure the youngster was ok before getting up and trying to secure the flame, they needed to try and get warm fast or else they could get sick. He knew this as if he had been educated in such things or it just made sense, either way he understood the importance of keeping the flame alive and burning.

The rains began to die down, turning into a light sprinkle and soon after that it stopped all together helping him to dry off a little. He moved some debris around as best as he could while Washee was still unconscious and made a bench of sorts next to the burning stump. He grabbed the young man and carried him closer to the fire, setting him down carefully. Positioning him just close enough to the flame that his clothes could begin to dry off yet far enough away that he wouldn't get burned in the process.

He didn't have the heart to be angry at the youngster though he sure wanted to! "Maybe I should try to get some sleep while I can, at least no one will be shooting me this time around," he said sarcastically as he leaned against the downed tree to check his wound. It was something he had gotten used to doing at this point, almost instinctively. The water made it hard to tell how much blood he was losing but it didn't seem too bad, either way it was lost and he had to find a way to stop it.

He closed his eyes for a few moments and tried to think of something... "Come on man, think of something. Okay, okay. What do I have around me that I could use to close this wound?" Just then, he realized that he had a knife! "Okay, what do I do with the knife?" he thought. Then, it came to him. He rose up and walked over to where he had dropped the knife and shells on the ground and he picked it up. He pulled the blade from its sheath exposing a rather large blade that appeared to be decently sharp and then he walked over to the burning stump with it.

He stuck the blade of the knife into the flames and sat patiently watching the heat from the fire warm the blade. It was hypnotic in a way, watching the flames dance around the steel. Sometimes it was as if they avoided it just to spite him, making him wait longer than he wanted to. Anticipating the pain to come, the burning pain of the hot steel on his side. He was fixed on it, so much so that when he heard a voice, it didn't startle him nor did it bring him joy, in fact it hardly attracted his attention at all.

"Hey... what are you doing to me? Hey now Mr. What are you doing to mee!??" yelled Washee!! The sound of his voice broke the trance that he had fallen into with an angry and confused tone. The Stranger moved his head around the flame exposing his face to the youngster but to his surprise the Young man didn't seem to recognize him.

"Washee, it's me... The, um...Stranger? You know?? We came here together...? Remember?" said the Stranger in a somber tone.

"I don't know who you are Mr. but you best let me loose and I mean now!!" Yelled the young man as if he truly had no idea who the Stranger was.

"You have got to be shitting me kid! We rode here

together, I am a friend of your Pops, Lupe!! Does that ring a bell?" asked the Stranger wholeheartedly.

"I don't know how you know my name, or my Pop's name… but I don't know you Mr. and if you're the one who stole my rifle, I'm gonna get you! Now let me out of these belts!!" he exclaimed!

The Stranger rose to his feet and turned away from the young man placing his hands upon his hips. "How could this be? Is he really so far gone that he doesn't remember me or is he just bullshiting? Is there a possibility that he is only playing stupid so that I let him go, then he can try to kill me again? Gosh damn, I don't know anymore… I just don't know." he thought. The sensation of a heavy warm liquid trickling down his side caused him to suddenly remember the knife.

He turned to the stump and saw that the blade was nice and red so he walked over to it and grabbed the handle carefully. Washee looked at the Stranger with the glowing red knife in his hand and he started saying,

"You better not hurt me Mr. I… I,
Didn't do anything wrong I swear!

Please Mr. I don't even know where I am… I am lost okaaay! I didn't try to shoot you, it was him…"

The Stranger looked over to the young man and asked, "Who? Who then?" He stepped a few feet closer to the youngster out of pure curiosity forgetting that his appearance was rather frightening to the kid.

"I don't know who it is… I… I woke up and I was lost. I lost my friends and my rifle. He has been chasing me too! I just wanna go home, you don't have to hurt me. I swear, I'm telling you the truth!! I swear I am!" The Stranger saw the young man's anguish and because of it, he turned around and walked back to the stump, lost in thought. He then stuck the knife back in the flames while he removed his shirt. The wound was bad looking,worse now that it was exposed. It was a hole the size of a coin in his side with a constant stream of blood leaking from both sides. He set his shirt on the fallen tree and then grabbed the knife out of the fire again.

"What are you gonna do Mr.?" asked the young man with a tremble in his voice as he struggled against his restraints. The Stranger held the blade up to his eyes and as he peered at it he whispered something unto himself as if he were saying a prayer of sorts and then he lowered the blade down to his wound. He did not hesitate as he placed the blade on top of the wound searing his own flesh closed. The sound of the blood and skin sizzling was strange enough but the smell of his flesh burning was a bit hard to handle.

"Gggggrrrrrrrrrrrrrrrraaaaaaaagggggghhhhhhh!!!!!!!!!!!!!!" he yelled as the pain from the burning blade shocked his senses back to life! He pulled the blade away from the front side of his wound and before he could lose heart, he switched hands and proceeded to use the other side of the blade to burn the exit wound on his back. The sound of burning flesh infiltrated into his ears, followed once again by the smell of burning meat. He held the blade in place until he could take the pain no more and then he dropped the knife and fell to his knees in relief.

Suddenly the sound of rustling followed by footsteps alerted him that something was wrong. He turned to where Washee was tied up and saw that the young man had freed himself from his restraints and was now running off into the darkness!!

"Ahh man!? I can't catch that kid, not now anyway." he said as he shrugged his shoulders in defeat. He looked down and inspected the wound closely to ensure that it was closed. "Looks like I got it alright. Can't really see the back side but I think it's good to go… I don't think I can do that again though so it better be!!" he mumbled as he looked around for any signs of Washee in the trees but he saw none. He then looked up into the sky and saw that daylight was coming soon and the last thing he wanted to do was be out in the open valley where anyone could see him.

"I really need to rest, I can't sleep comfortably out here. Maybe I'll go back to the tunnel and rest there, at least it's somewhat safe. Just need to make sure no one sees me going in." he thought. He knew it was easier said than done but he had to do something, his body had been through alot and it was long past time to rest. He rose back onto his feet, grabbed his shirt and put it on. He grabbed the knife and its sheath and joined the two of them together. He looked at it for a second and then he put it into his front pocket, the warmth from the blade could be felt through the sheath as it rested against his leg.

He started walking away but before he got far, he suddenly remembered the shells that he tossed on the ground. "Maybe I shouldn't leave those behind… Ahh, he probably won't find them anyway." he said. He shrugged as he turned toward the cliffside and began walking back to where he thought the opening was. The flames from the burning tree stump were starting to give way to the wet trunk and was now turning into a pillar of smoke. That'll be visible for a long way, maybe I'll spot Lee… Yeah, maybe he will see it and come to investigate… Then, we can get the kid and get out of this place." He said as he trudged along the forest ground.

He kept searching the trees for any sign of the young man but saw nothing, though the aroma from the wet trees kept bringing up feelings that he didn't know he had. It was like being home somehow even though he knew not where he had come from, he could not help it. Then, there it was. The Sun was beginning to glow in the eastern sky and he knew that he had to hurry.

He couldn't afford to take another shot, not in his condition anyhow and this, he knew. The cliff wall grew larger and larger behind the trees as they became thinner with every tree he passed. As he was concentrating on getting to the cliff he started noticing that the world had become alive again as the sounds of the birds singing and chirping in the background filled the fresh morning air. The sound of the world always comforted him, even in the worst situations. His mind took him back to the time that he and Lee were traversing over the great mountain pass as their wagon had been destroyed by a mysterious flame.

The feeling of fear worked hard to overwhelm him with all that they saw in the forest that night but he did not give in to it. The sounds of the wildlife kept him rooted somehow, helping his mind remain in a state of reality versus dark imagery. He finally cleared the last of the trees and reached the face of the cliffside. He stopped and turned around, intently scanning the trees, ensuring that no one followed. After a few moments of searching, he turned back toward the cliff and looked up to locate its opening.

Once his eyes were fixated on it, he moved accordingly along the wall until he was directly underneath it. He looked back a few times ensuring it was clear before dedicating himself to climbing the wall. Afterall, it was a compromising position to be in and He had already had a near death experience the last time around so He wanted to be cautious.

Even though the sun was upon them, the darkness still gave him sufficient enough cover and since the rain had stopped, the climb should be a little easier than last time so he decided to make his move.

"Here we go, here we go!" he said as he faced the cliff

wall and began climbing it as fast as he could. It was at this time that he began feeling that strange sensation again... That buzzing feeling, like something was about to go very wrong. It was hard for him to understand how to take the feeling, it was intoxicating and sickening at the same time.Though he got the idea that the feeling was a warning of some kind, he knew not what to do about it so he simply continued upward, pausing to look back every few seconds

All that he knew was that he had to get to that tunnel, he desperately needed some rest and as far as he could tell, the tunnel was gonna be the safest place to do that. He didn't try to look around anymore as he was almost too exhausted to care and he was worried that he would lose his balance and fall so he focussed only on getting into the tunnel safely. Nothing more.

"That's all I care about right now is resting..." he said as he struggled to climb up the last few feet of the smooth cliff wall. It was looking like he might not make it as the entirety of the last few days had suddenly dropped down on him like a hammer! "I... I, Have to make it!! I have to get therrrrrrrreeeeee....." he said as he desperately clung to the cool smooth stone.

He could see the edge of the tunnel but he didn't have the strength to hold himself with his left hand securely enough to let go of the wall with his right and reach upward with it.

"I may only have one chance to grab it... Got to get up there!!!" He mustered up all the strength he had left and he jumped up, barely grabbing onto the ledge of the tunnel with his right hand! Once he had a hold of it he had to search himself for more... More energy to not only grab onto the edge with his left hand but to also pull himself to safety... "AAAAaaagggggghhhhhh!!!!!" he yelled as he used the last of himself to grab onto the ledge with his left hand and then to pull himself up to the opening.

As his head cleared the edge of the cliff wall he threw his right arm into the tunnel and then his left also, enabling him to pull his upper body into the dry, safe tunnel. He was so tired that he laid still, face down with the upper half of his body in the tunnel and the lower half still hanging out of the opening. He knew He needed to get himself all the way inside but he was so tired that he was just unable to do so, he needed a second to rest before he had the strength to move again. So he took it… As he lay silent in the tunnel and the seconds passed by, he finally caught his breath and when that happened he noticed something strange.

The world he had heard come to life minutes earlier was suddenly dead silent.

The alarm feeling that he had experienced while climbing the rock face had dissipated momentarily but was suddenly ringing in his heart like a bell.

"Ooooohh, what now!?" he muttered angrily as he lifted his head and opened his eyes to the darkness of the tunnel. As he peered into the tunnel curiously he thought for a moment that he saw something moving around back there… In the darkness. "Wait… Did something move back there or am I seeing things?" he thought curiously. Then, out of the darkness of the tunnel, the face of Lee with beast-like features appeared as he came toward the Stranger!!!

"Whoa shit!!" he shouted as he pushed himself back to the edge of the tunnel with a quickness!!! He looked down at the valley floor and then back to Lee in disbelief! Lee opened his eyes and the very same dark red color that the Darkness showed him was now in Lee!? His lips were dripping with saliva and his teeth were like those of a wolf!! "I knew you would come." he said to the Stranger, snarling as the words left his mouth. Then with a surprise move, Lee lifted his hand, exposing bear-like claws at the end of his fingertips! He then started clawing the Stranger's arms and face, opening his flesh up with every swing!!

"Ahhhhh, freakin Leeeee!!" he yelled as he tried to pull himself away from the beast!!! Just as he moved backward, he realized that there was nowhere for him to go!

He had no choice but to throw himself backward from the ledge onto the wet cold ground or try and fight on his belly with his ass hanging out of the tunnel's opening. Falling was his only chance to get away from the vicious attacks of the beast and maybe, just maybe, he could pull the beast out with him!? "Yes, that's what I'll do! I'll take this fool with meee!!!" he shouted as he grabbed onto Lee's arms and pulled him toward himself with all of his might!!! He looked Lee right in his evil red eyes and let out a battle cry that seemed to shake his very own soul, right in the beast's face!

"AAAAaaaaaaaggghhhhhhhhhh!!!!!!" he shouted as he planted both of his feet onto the side of the cliff and used the extra leverage to pull that sucker right out of the cave!!! He threw him over himself with all the power he had down onto the ground below! As a result, he too was now falling to the earth! His eyes were still fixated on the horror that had become his friend Lee, he just could not fathom that something like that could have happened to him yet, the proof was falling before him at that very moment.

It was undeniable. Despite all that was going on at the time, he felt free for a few moments as he fell through the cool morning air. He felt no regret nor did he feel fear, just freedom. Even if it meant that his life was over, even if it meant the end. His body making contact with the ground was the last thing that he experienced before the darkness once again overcame him…

CHAPTER EL SEVEN

Two Worlds Collide

"Hurry up Choco everyone is waiting for you!" A voice rang out of the darkness as he opened his eyes to find himself standing on a strange wooden ladder that is tied to a cliff wall on the side of a canyon!?

"Whoa, what the heck!?" he exclaimed as he grabbed ahold of the rung and hugged it in complete surprise at where he had found himself at this time. He looked around and saw that there were other people around him, most of which stood at the bottom of the ladder looking up at him as he was not moving.

"Hurry up dude! You're always the slow one I swear..." the voice of a young man once again called out to him as he looked around to see where it was coming from. He then looked up and saw that ten rungs or so above him was a circular opening in the cliffside where the ladder ended. Just as his eyes saw the opening, the body of a young man in a blue and black checkered shirt could be seen disappearing into it.

"Wait, who are you?" he asked the young man as he let go of the rung and climbed up to the tunnel's opening.

"Quit being stupid man. Let's go already!" the boy replied. He could see the silhouette of the young man in the back of the tunnel but not in detail due to the dark.

"Washee? Is that you? Wwwaait, don't leave! I've been searching for you bro, don't go!" he shouted to the young man. The voice of the mysterious kid sounded strangely familiar to the young sharpshooter's voice and it made him question his sanity once again for he had found himself inside of yet another mysterious place though familiar somehow. Even the sound of his own voice sounded strange, it sounded as if he were a young man again!?

He looked at his hands for the first time and saw that they were soft and much smaller than previously. "Whoa, what the? It's like I'm a kid again!" He looked himself up and down in amazement until the voices of people down below could be heard saying.

"Hurry up Kid, we don't have all day!" shouted a man from the bottom of the ladder. Snapping out of it, he then looked down at who was speaking but he could not see anyones faces, strangely all of them were blurred out. He turned back to the opening and climbed over the last rung of the wooden ladder pulling himself into the tunnel. As he made his way through the tunnel, he focussed his sights on what he perceived to be the center of the dark circular tunnel in front of him. After making his way through the dark for a while he noticed that it had become so dark, he could no longer see his own hand in front of him.

He turned around and found that the entrance that he had climbed into a few minutes earlier was no longer visible!?

"What is Happening now?" he said as the uncertainty of it all began to attack his courage. He turned back around into the direction that he was originally walking in and cautiously took a few steps forward. He hesitantly stepped forward again then again until he felt comfortable moving in the dark. For some reason, he felt like the tunnel had changed on him somehow, he knew the tunnel was not very large in size but it sure felt big.

He began doubting his ability to remain calm, he wasn't sure where he was nor was he sure of what was waiting for him in the dark. He turned his head in all directions but saw nothing, his feet kept moving but he was unsure in what direction they were moving in. Suddenly, a light appeared down the tunnel in front of him and with it, hope. It seemed to be shining down from above so he hurried toward it as fast as he could until he had reached it. Once he was there near the light, he looked up and saw that it was another tunnel that led to a different room above!

Then suddenly, a wooden ladder tied to the wall appeared, so he reached out and grabbed onto it, climbing it one rung at a time. His stomach began swirling around within himself from the anticipation of what he would find up there.

"What could it be? Hopefully it's not another dark tunnel." he said sarcastically as he continued climbing up the last of the wooden ladder. Once he reached the top and his head surfaced from the darkness of the tunnel below it took a few moments for his eyes to adjust to the light, but once they did, he marveled at what he saw... It was so amazing that he almost didn't believe in the accuracy of his own vision! It was a large naturally formed cave located on the side of the cliff, much larger than any he had seen thus far.

It was completely surrounded by smooth red stone in all directions and it appeared to be the perfect shelter from the elements, enemies or whatever a person needed shelter for.He pulled himself out of the tunnel and rose onto his feet, he looked around at the environment in awe.

"Man that is so cool bro!" the voice of the young

man in the blue shirt echoed out as he walked up to the Stranger and smacked him on the head.

"Check that out over there..." the older kid pointed to what looked like an even larger cave up ahead.

It was visible only through a small doorway at the end of the cave they stood in. As He looked in that direction he saw a couple, they both looked familiar to him but He was not sure why as he could only see them from behind. They were following others through that small doorway as if they were on some sort of tour.

"Let's go punk!" said the bigger boy as he ran along a trail leading toward the small doorway. The Stranger hesitated for a few seconds before following the other boy toward the opening but he soon found himself running behind him trying to keep up.

"Let's go chump, let's go!" he exclaimed as he reached the doorway first. He gave a smirk before turning around and walking through the opening. Once he reached the doorway, he stopped to look around at the interior of the cavern where he stood. After a few moments of observation, he noticed that the cavern was empty, there was no one else inside of it but himself. No one else had surfaced from the tunnel even though there was a line of people waiting for him to get up that ladder, it was strange indeed.

He turned back and faced the little doorway looking through it for a few moments before he stepped into it. If he were a little bit taller he would have had to duck under the doorway in order to avoid hitting his head, he thought of that for some reason. He closed his eyes, holding his excitement in as he passed through it. Once he was on the other side, he lifted his head up and allowed his eyes to behold an ancient wonder like none he could have imagined!! It was a whole other opening that was much larger than the cave he had just come from and it was connected by a large trail that ran alongside the cliff wall.

The other opening was filled with structures, buildings and what appeared to be small yet intricately built homes.

In fact one would not be exaggerating if he said that it was a medium sized city! An entire civilization built inside of the cliff wall with amazing precision. There were more structures than he could count, ingeniously designed and placed together as if they were naturally part of the canyon wall. He ran up ahead of the other boy and the couple, mesmerized by what he was looking at, "I feel like I've been here before." he said to a man in a funny hat and a green uniform as he ran by. He weaved his way through the other people and followed his own lead into the city, peeking around corners and admiring the brick buildings for what seemed like a few hours.

Upon realizing that he had lost track of time, he looked around for the others but no one was there, they were all gone! The older boy, the couple, the man in the green uniform, all of the other people had vanished! He started to freak out a little as he didn't know what to do. He scanned the area where everyone once stood and found no sign of them... no sign of anyone at all. Just himself, all alone. "What am I gonna do, I'm not even sure where I am?" he said to himself in desperation. He ran around the city calling out for help but there was no reply, just silence. He stopped at the edge of the trail and gathered himself together.

"Come on now bro, don't let it get the best of you. I will find my way." he said just before he ran back to the edge of the opening where the large trail began and looked around again, thinking that maybe this time he would see the other boy but he still did not.

"Wait! What is that?" he asked as he suddenly saw something on the other side of the wall through the doorway! "What in the world is that?" he asked again as he squinted his eyes tightly trying to focus on what appeared to be... a man? He was lying on the ground near the entrance on the floor of the cave!? The boy ran down the trail and back up the otherside closer to the doorway so that he could get a better look and sure enough, "It is a man!?" he thought as he stood silent, gazing upon the man from the other side of the doorway.

He was not moving nor did he seem to be conscious, he just lay there still and silent. The Boy slowly walked over to the entrance and hesitantly walked through it, entering the smaller cavern where he was earlier. He wasn't sure what to think, nor was he sure what he was gonna do. This whole place was obviously in the middle of nowhere and that kind of limited his ability to find help. He continued forward and though he was weary about the situation, he didn't let it stop him. He had to see who the man was, he just had to.

He proceeded cautiously toward the body, the closer he got to it, the clearer he was able to see the condition of the man. "Oh crap, just what I needed... he looks like he's hurt pretty bad. What the hell am I gonna do, I'm just a kid right!? Whoever this guy is, he's covered in blood and it looks like he's been burned, his side is charred black! I don't know what to do." he thought as he neared him. Suddenly he heard the man struggling to breathe, "He is alive!?" he shouted aloud. It was then that he saw the man fighting for his life on the hard stone floor.

He was dressed in old style clothing like from a movie but he had tattoos on his arms and that sure didn't match the way he was dressed. His hair was longer and it was black with silver strands powering through. He could not see the Man's face due to the wounds and blood that covered it but he tried to see it anyway as he got closer to him… Then suddenly, he mumbled something… He sounded angry and this caused the boy to stop in his tracks! He began rethinking what he was doing as fear began to take hold of him and he started looking around frightenedly for the other people but was reminded quickly by the silence of the area that no one was there.

For a brief moment, he thought about turning back toward the city and running for it but then the raspy voice of the man shouted something… Something unexpected, something that made the boy change his mind. He stood there for a few moments lost in thought, not knowing what to do next but whatever the man said, it resonated within him. He decided to let go of his fears and at that, he turned and walked over to the wounded man, kneeling down next to him.

He then asked, "Hey Sir, can you hear me? Are you alright?" with concern as he slowly placed his hand on the man's shoulder. When he did, what felt like a bolt of lightning suddenly shot through his mind! When that happened, behold, a series of visions shot through him!! Visions of the cave, the wolves, the Woman… So much emotion was passed into the boy that he was blown back from power of the energy onto the stone floor behind him!

"Whoooooaaaaaaa!!!" he yelled as he slid on his back along the floor! Once his body stopped sliding, he sat up and looked toward the Stranger's motionless body. "What in the hell just happened?!" he shouted!! He looked about in disbelief as he started questioning himself like a madman. "I saw so many strange things… What does it all mean? I ddddon't know what to think!" he mumbled frustratedly as he tried to shake the feeling off. He then turned his attention back to the Strange man lying on the ground. "Hey Sir, cccan you hhhear me? I don't know what I can do to help you Sir but I am here and I will try…

I… I promise." he said passionately as he looked around at the cliffside opening in search of something that he could use to help the man with. Unfortunately there was nothing in sight, absolutely nothing. "I don't know what happened to the people I was with, they just disappeared but I'll find them and get you some help. I promise! Just don't give up and don't go anywhere, okay? You have to stay as still as possible alright? Ok I'm gonna go now. Ill be back though, like I said." He rose up onto his feet and stared at the man for a few moments before he turned around and headed back in the direction that he came from.

He stopped at the doorway and looked back at the man ensuring that he was still there, that is when he suddenly felt an unexpected amount of concern for the man's well being. He redirected himself to the doorway and passed through it to the other side.

Once he was through, he ran down the trail that led to the city built within the cliff opening as fast as he could. His eyes constantly searched for another person, anyone at all who could possibly help him with the wounded man but they saw no one. He slowed down to a walking speed as he approached the first set of buildings, his heart racing, his breathing rapid. Still hoping to find some trace of the other's as he went. He couldn't help but to look at the buildings as he passed by giving each one of them a quick moment of admiration. They looked old and unkempt, empty and cold but they were all in very good condition and remained in place.

Almost as if they awaited their former residents' return at any moment, to be lived in once again as they were designed to be. Suddenly the Sun along with all of its warming light faded away into a dark gray sky. The rain began to pour down onto the cliff walls and into the valley below but it did not enter the city. He looked around as he could hear the sound of water running inside the cavern, but did not see any rain entering into it. He decided to walk around a bit more and widen his search for something he could use to help the poor man but he still didn't know what.

As he reached the second set of buildings, he walked around the corner and saw small canals carved into the stone floor where rain water was channeled from natural openings in the Mesa and collected in small pools near every building.

"Water!" he shouted as he walked over to the small pools in amazement! He knelt down next to them with a smile upon his face and placed his hand into the pool. He collected a palm full of water then he brought it to his face and gave it a sniff before slurping it down. "It smells so fresh!!" he whispered as he got a couple more drinks from the pool with his palms. "I got to give that man some of this water, it is so good. I feel like it will help him… but how?" he wondered as he looked around for something that he could use to fill with water so he could get it to the man safely.

"I can't use my hands, it will spill before I even get there with it." Then, miraculously, he saw a small clay bowl near one of the other pools!! He quickly ran over and grabbed it, he then knelt down next to the pool and after rinsing the bowl out a few times, he filled it to the brim and held it up before his face. The energy he was feeling from being in that place was unreal, his blood was buzzing within his veins, it was like being inside of a dream, one that he had some sort of control over for once. It was hard to describe, even unto himself.

"Maybe it's the water? Cause I feel like SuperMan here, it's awesome!!" he exclaimed. He got up with the bowl in his hand and turned around toward the doorway. He then headed back to it, running as fast as he could, careful not to spill any of the precious water that he was carrying. Once he exited the shelter of the cave he was hit with the falling rain outside of the opening onto the trail that bridged the two openings. It was unreal, being there, seeing the elements from that setting.

"Just unreal." he said again as he approached the little doorway still jogging carefully, cup in hand. He looked through it and saw that the man was still there, lying in the same position that he was laying in earlier when he left him to find help. He passed through the doorway back into the smaller opening, this time paying little attention to the strange feeling in his guts caused by the unusual circumstances that he found himself in. He finally reached the wounded Man and knelt down next to his body with the bowl in hand.

"Hey Mr. I have some water for you... Hey, Mr. You need to wake up and drink some of this. HEEEEEYYYY!!!!!" he yelled as he shook the man's shoulder. The man moaned a little and that was sign enough that he wanted the water so he placed his left hand underneath the wounded man's head and lifted it up ever so gently. He felt all the dried blood in the man's hair and saw it all over his face and body. "This is so bad, I don't think he is gonna make it. Okay Mr. I'm gonna pour some water into your mouth now so don't choke on it! Alright??" he said as he slowly poured a little bit of water from the bowl into the wounded man's mouth.

Strangely, the Man did not choke nor did he spit it out, he seemed to be drinking it without issue! "That's it Mr. Drink it up. I can get more for you no problem ok!?" Once the water from the bowl was empty and the man finished it, he started shaking and moving around violently as if the water were doing something to him!

He started coughing and mumbling something to the young man but the boy could not understand what he was saying. "I'm sorry Sir but I can't understand what you are saying!? Don't worry though, I will help you through this. Just don't give in, ok? Don't give in..." Just then, he started feeling dizzy. His vision began to blur, like a mirror in the bathroom while the hot water ran... His hearing had become muffled and his voice sounded like he was speaking underwater... The light dimmed out and the image of the wounded man faded into black... "I won't leave you, I promise!! I won't leave!!!!!! He shouted with all of his heart as he felt himself fall backward onto the stone floor...

After an uncertain amount of time had passed, he woke up shouting out loud, while laying on the ground at the bottom of the cliff. "Aaaaaagggggghhhhhhh!!!!!!" The feeling of his blood covering his face and eyes stopped him from trying to open them as his echo bounced around the valley. A great and painful sadness took over his heart and as his mind struggled to regain control over his racing thoughts and emotions. He tried hard to process what hell had just happened to him but it was not setting in.

He could barely move as his injuries were extensive yet he pushed himself backward anyway, until he felt his head hit the cliff wall. Then he wiggled himself up the wall until he could sit in an upright position, relieving some of the pressure on his chest. He kept his eyes closed until the rain had washed the blood away from his eyelids then he rubbed them clear and attempted to open them.

The first thing he expected to see was the dead or damaged body of Lee lying somewhere close by but he did not. "That son of a motherless goat!! Where the hell did he go now?" he asked as he looked around for signs of him. As usual, there was no sign of him, "Why didn't it kill me while I was laying here unconscious? Why the games?" he contemplated angrily. "I am way too tired for this shit, I need to find shelter... A place where I can get away from that sucker... At least until I can recoup a little..." he thought.

Either way he hadn't the strength to do anything about

Lee, he could barely believe that he was still alive much less continue fighting. "I don't even know how I am still alive… Shit!" he shouted. He knew that he wouldn't last long out in the elements injured as badly as he was. "Ahhhh, I don't even care anymore damn it! I'm just tired… I'm so tired." he said sadly. He had already lost a lot of blood from being shot, now he was losing even more due to the battle with Lee and as a result he would soon succumb to that loss. He looked at his arms and saw how badly they had been torn up,

"Ayyyee, that's even worse than how them damn dirty mutts did me back in the desert… Sheesh!" he felt the slashes on his neck and face also, they were all pretty water logged. Which meant that he had been laying out in the rain for quite a while now. "None of this makes any sense, I don't understand what is going on here. Almighty… I pray that you give me the strength I need to die well.

I also ask that you take care of Lee, Lupe and Washee as I have already failed them all…" he said sadly as he thought of the sweet face of little Onley smiling at him when he first woke up in Lee's home. He thought about how she had found him in the desert wandering around like a dead man after his battle with the wolves. He also couldn't help but to think of that ghostly Woman…The one that seemed to spark the flames of love inside of his weary heart.

"It all seems like it was for nothing, this whole thing." he mumbled as he laid his arms down at his sides and looked up into the sky. It appeared to be late afternoon or early evening by that point but once again, it was hard to tell for sure. Especially there, it was as if directions, time, and reality were all bleeding into one another's realms. Maybe it was just him. At this point he wasn't sure about a damn thing, the only thing he was sure of was that he was in trouble and there was no one in sight to help.

"It's cool man, I was tired anyway. Been traveling for a while now." he muttered as the rain kept pouring down over him. With absolutely nothing left for him to do, other than to accept the fact that he was more than likely going to die, he found himself doing strange things to pass the time. Every minute seemed like a day. He pondered every sound of nature, the rhythm of the falling drops, even the flow of water rolling down the side of the cliff, where he sat in silent defeat. He turned his head back and looked up at the cliff wall to see where the opening was above, afterall he wasn't sure how far they fell away from it.

Now that it was daytime and he was close, he saw what looked like, "Holes forming a ladder of sorts carved into the cliffside!? Is that really what that is?" he questioned as his mind flashed back to the night before when he climbed the wall twice without ever finding the holes. He never even saw them for that matter."How in the world did I miss those? I swear this place is morphing everyday, always changing."he said as he thought back once again to what may have been a memory from his youth.

That strange man in the green uniform that he saw in his dream, suddenly came to his mind once again, the man was telling him the history of the holes carved into the cliffside, "The Anasazi carved these into the cliff sides and used them as ladders to help them maneuver their way from village to village." he saw himself behind the boy in the blue and black checkered shirt again, the same kid from his dream. After the man stopped speaking, the boy started climbing up the ladder once again just as before. He followed the kid but wasn't able to climb the ladder as quickly this time around, he was tired and out of breath.

As he rested he noticed the holes in the wall, the ones that the uniformed man was referring to. He looked down as if to ask the uniformed man a question but found that the man, just like the others, was gone. He looked up just in time to see the other boy's shoe pass over the top of the ladder and disappear again leaving him alone. He felt the sudden urge to hurry to the top, not sure if it was out of fear or curiosity, the same kind that he felt in his previous dream.

He slowly started to climb up the ladder one rung at a time until he reached the top then, just as his line of sight was about to cross the edge of the cliff into the tunnel, a loud crash of Thunder!! It snapped his mind back to his present situation with a quickness giving him some clarity. He looked around, not being able to tell if this was the same place he had seen in his dream or if it were just this supernatural place driving him Mad!?

"There's no way that I have been here before, not in this exact spot. It couldn't be possible... Could it?" he wondered as he looked up at the holes behind him, shivering from the loss of blood and heat throughout his body. He knew that he couldn't just stay where he was and risk death from exposure but what could he do to get warm? "Come on man! Think of something... I know I can find a way out of this. I just need to think!!" He decided that the tunnel up above was the safest place for him to rest despite finding Lee up there earlier.

"I don't think he would just return to the tunnel and wait, I mean, I was right here all day. He could have finished me off anytime, why wait around and play games?" he thought. He nodded his head in agreement before painfully turning over onto his knees, looking up at where the foot holes were positioned. "It's almost as if the Almighty put these here just for me to climb, I swear they weren't here before. Thank you Great Creator! Thank you." he said graciously. It was hard to see in the rain but it appeared that they went up at least 30 feet or so before disappearing from view.

It looked almost exactly like the dream or memory he just had, but different somehow, once again fogging his mind and its ability to tell the difference between the visions, the dreams and reality. Despite it not looking like the same cliff wall, it had to be the same opening. No matter the differences, "Right?" he asked himself once again with concern. If he truly wanted to know, he would just have to climb it and find out. He had no clue what was true, what was real or what was fake anymore, all that he knew was that he needed to get his ass inside somewhere and out of the rain.

"Not to mention the fact that I can't let Lee and Lupe down, I just can't!" He muttered angrily as he forced a few deep breaths while placing his hands against the smooth stone wall. He then took one knee off the ground pulling it upward so he could put his foot down. Once that foot was on the ground he transferred all the power he had to that leg and used it to push himself up so that he could get his other foot onto the ground also. In the process his body slammed up against the cliffside with a slap, splattering blood onto the wall from some of the open lacerations.

Though it was painful, he used the cliff wall to help stabilize himself as he stood up and tried to gain control over his balance. He was in bad shape and didn't have much strength left, but he decided that to die trying was better than just dying, so he reached up and grabbed one of the holes with his right hand. "Uuugghhh!!!" He exclaimed as the pain from stretching his arm was harsh!

Once his fingers were in place he transferred all of his might to those fingers so that he could pull his left foot high enough to secure it in the lowest hole on the cliffside. Tired and weary, he laid against the smooth red stone for a few moments gathering up what was left of his will before trying to pull himself up to the next hole. The feeling of the smooth red stone on the front side of his body was warming, it comforted him as he had been overtaken by the cold rains. The little stream of water that first caught his attention was broken as it ran into the top of his head and made its way around his body, down the cliffside.

He knew that the clock was ticking and he had to get moving now while he was able to, or risk losing the ability later. He pulled his head off of the cliffside and looked upward at the next hole. "I'm just gonna do this one hole at a time. I can do this, I know I can...With you by my side Almighty One, I know I can make it." he said. With the cold rain pouring down in his eyes he reached up for the next hole, grasping it as tightly as he could with his fingers. He then pulled the other leg up and placed that foot into another hole.

He thought of nothing else but what he was doing, not the rain, not his wounds, nothing but pulling himself up the cliffside hole by hole, until he had reached the top. As he pulled himself up past the last hole, he did it cautiously as he remembered the horrible demonic face of what used to be his friend Lee, waiting there, in the darkness of the tunnel for him like a wolf waiting on a lamb. Lee with his dark red eyes and his snarling face...

But what he saw instead was a long dark tunnel with a light shining down in the distance, exactly like it did in his memory. "If that was even a memory." he muttered as he pulled himself up over the ledge into the safety of the tunnel where it was warm and dry! He lay on stomach first as he struggled to catch his breath, that was when he noticed that his face was in a small pool of warm blood. His own blood to be exact, it was from the previous night when he was scouting the valley for Washee. "How is it possible that my blood is not dry yet, nor did it turn cold? How could this be?" he thought to himself as he rolled over onto his back and wiped his cheek off with his sleeve.

He looked around at the interior of the tunnel, inspecting it for anything out of place but he found nothing of the sort. He then directed his attention back to the opening of the tunnel, waiting silently for anyone that may have followed him but no one came. There was no bad feeling inside of his heart nor did he hear any noises that would suggest someone was nearby. The light off into the distance was a beacon to his weary eyes and to his tired soul. He felt like it was a place where he could rest away from the worries of being out in the open. The visions of the room above filled his mind with wonder as he shook at the thought that it might be the same place.

If it were the same place, that would mean that he had finally found a piece of his past, even though it was without detail. It was still something familiar to him and that made it special. He relaxed his head and laid it down on the floor for a few moments, cherishing the warmth of the tunnel.

He couldn't help but to think about what else he would discover the further into the cliffside he went. Just then, his core started buzzing again like an alarm inside of his heart! He rolled over quickly and sat up, "Looks like I may have spoken too soon..." he whispered as he looked to the entrance of the tunnel, expecting to see the beast's face, but he saw no sign of it, just the falling rain. Partially satisfied, he decided that it would be best if he got out of the tunnel and into the room above but he was unable to get himself to move.

"Come on... Get up... Get up stupid!" he shouted as he reluctantly rose to his feet shaking off the water from his body. He then turned his head toward the light and started down the dark tunnel, constantly looking back for anyone who might be following him as he went. As He got deeper into the darkness his mind wandered as he stopped thinking of the dangers of the beast and started thinking about how fortunate he was to be out of the rain. For one, his wounds had been exposed to the elements for too long making them soft and tender.

He knew it wouldn't be long before infection set in. Now that he was able to dry off a little, the loss of blood could be measured as it was trailing behind him in the tunnel. It was warm in the cliffside though he was cold, his body heat was abandoning him along with the precious life force that he was losing from his wounds. Suddenly he felt a little faint and as he looked back again, to check for Lee, he stumbled and fell to the ground with a thump! "AhhhhhhI... I am not sure... I can make it..." he said as he realized once again, just how exhausted he was.

He laid his head down on the smooth stone of the tunnel floor as he desperately needed a few minutes to rest. So he took them, every second he could get. He just laid there and tried to breath so that he could recuperate just enough to get into the light and up to the next room. Though his will was there, his body was just not able to comply with his requests. It reminded him of the cave where he first woke and how he was unable to move though he was willing to. That cave was more of a home than he had known since. In those few moments while he laid still, he found peace... until...

"Wait... was that whispering? I... Swore, I just heard someone whisper." he thought as he raised his head up and focussed on listening. "They sounded like they were coming from... Outside!!? Oh Shit!!!" he yelled as he looked back toward the tunnel's opening and saw the red eyes and demonic face of Lee snarling wickedly!!! He pulled himself up into the tunnel with ease, planting himself on his hands and on his feet like a beast... He growled violently as he stared at the Stranger drooling from the mouth ready to finish him off.

He then ran wildly toward the Stranger at full speed, howling and screaming as he approached!! He sounded like a tormented beast from the deep and the Stranger couldn't help but to freak out!! "Son of a Bitch!!" he shouted as he scrambled to get back onto his feet!! If he could rise to the occasion, he at least stood a chance to try and fend off Lee's attack but if not he was as good as lunch!!

He threw some kicks at the beast as it slashed and grabbed at his legs and even though the Stranger had boots on, the claws of Lee tore right through them, it was as if they offered no protection whatsoever. He frantically started looking for a way out of the tunnel even though he already knew that there was only one direction he could go in. The very same direction he was headed toward in the first place but that was only if he could escape the deadly grasp of the beast. He wasn't able to run, though he tried, he just didn't have the strength so he kept falling back onto the ground enabling Lee to attack his legs without mercy.

He reached forward and began pulling his way into the tunnel as kicked wildly at Lee's grasp, shuffling his legs and body as hard and as fast as he could! Lee was reaching and clawing his way right behind him, until the Stranger caught him with a solid stomp right to the face! The beast's head was knocked back violently, stopping the Monster in its tracks, giving the Stranger a few extra seconds to create some space between them. As he crawled deeper into the tunnel it became so dark that he could only feel his way around!

Not even the light from the entrance could be seen as he looked for its comfort. "Where the hell did the light go? This can't be happening!!" he thought as he tried not to freak out while escaping the beast and searching for the light all simultaneously. The only thing that he could see were the fiery red eyes of Lee in the darkness behind him though they did not appear to be moving toward him at the moment.

It was more than likely trying to recover from the kick that the Stranger delivered to its face. He used that extra time wisely as he turned his face forward again and quickly began crawling as fast as he could though as to where he was going, he did not know. "I could be crawling into oblivion for all I know! I have no idea where the hell I'm going... Where is that light?" he thought as his eyes desperately searched the darkness for it with no sign of it anywhere. He stopped for a moment and realized that the tunnel not only seemed to be endless in size but it had also become silent. It was a deafening kind of silence, one that had presence and force.

It scared him for he had not experienced such a phenomenon in all of his travels before, not like this. He looked back to see where Lee was but he was nowhere in sight, "Shit! I freakin lost him again! I can't keep doing th..." as he was speaking he turned his head forward and found himself face to face with a snarling Lee!

CHAPTER OCHO

The will to survive

"Mother trucker!!
AAAaaaaaaaGGGGgggggHHHHHhhhhh!!!!!" he screamed
as loud as he could with rage in the face of the Beast and
then he dropped an old-fashioned headbutt directly into
its face!! KRACK!! The sound of their skulls making contact
echoed through the tunnel sharply. Lee's head shot back with
lightning speed and his body rolled over backwards slamming
onto the ground as stars filled the head and vision of the
Stranger!!! Much like the kick he delivered moments earlier,
this gave the Stranger an opportunity to get away if he could.

He could rest for a few moments and gather some
strength to try and continue the fight. Though he knew he
wouldn't last very long no matter how many seconds he
rested for and running was gonna cost more energy than
what he would regain by resting... His vision cleared as he
stood there in thought about what to do. He looked down at
the Beast and saw how it was unconscious, vulnerable even...

"Why run... I should finish him off once and for all!"
he said with determination in his voice. He then jumped
on top of it and started dropping some punches onto the

beast's face without mercy, now that it lay on the ground. Once he felt the spark of life leave the body of the beast he stopped swinging. Tired, he crawled over the demon and scuffled his way blindly through the tunnel as fast as he could, hoping Lee would not wake up and pursue him once again. Then suddenly, slam!! The feeling of hard smooth stone colliding with his forehead, stopped him dead!!

All that he could hear was the sound of his heart beating like a drum. Stunned by this, his mind filled with stars again and he felt as if he were floating on the ocean deep inside of himself. Once the feeling subsided enough for him to focus again, he looked up and saw a bright light directly above his head! Thinking it was the last of the stars in his mind he shook his head a few times to try and clear them all out and then he then looked upward again hoping that the light was still there. Behold there it was, the light of day!

He stood up quickly like a drunk man would, wobbling back and forth a few times until he regained his balance. He started looking for a way to climb up into the tunnel and saw that like the exterior of the entrance, there were holes carved into the wall that lead to the room above! Clearing the blood from his face he reached up and grabbed one of the holes, gripping it with all of his might! After all that he had been through he still needed the strength to get away from Lee and the only way to accomplish that was by going up!

So he pulled himself up far enough to get his foot into the lowest hole in the wall and then he pushed up using his legs. As he pulled himself up with his arms he pushed with his legs and soon, he was climbing it hole by hole! He took no comfort in knowing that Lee was unconscious and as far as he knew, the beast could already be right on his ass. And this time, he might not be so lucky in getting away from it.

The tunnel was short enough that he was able to

get through it rather quickly, pulling his upper body over the edge of the tunnel onto the floor of an unknown room. He then pulled his legs up out of the tunnel onto the floor and rolled over a few times to put some distance between himself and the tunnel opening. Relieved to be out of that situation, even if it were only for the moment, He lay there catching what breath he could. Unfortunately, He didn't get to rest for long, for as soon as he sat up, Lee jumped up out of the tunnel screaming like a maniac!!!

"Whoa!!!" exclaimed the Stranger as the demon caught him off guard once again. As it landed on its feet, it immediately began to search for the Stranger and when it spotted him, it charged at him with haste! As the demon jumped toward the Stranger, the Stranger rolled backward onto his back, raising his feet up so as to catch Lee and stop him from landing on top of him. Once Lee's mid section landed on the bottom of the Stranger's feet, he grabbed him by the collar with both hands and used Lee's momentum against him.

Pulling as well as pushing the demon over and off of himself with one fluid motion! Lee went tumbling along the cavern floor dangerously close to the edge. Just as he was about to roll off, he dug his claws into the rock bed and stopped himself just in time. The Stranger rolled over onto his stomach and pushed himself up onto one knee. He then rose slowly up onto his feet and said sternly…

"This is going to end right here, right now old buddy… I know you aren't yourself and that's why I'm gonna let you live but," before he could finish his heroic speech, the Beast bounced up and charged at him with rage in his red eyes and blood dripping from his lips! The Stranger took a deep breath and got into his fighting stance, he focussed his heart on the Light. It was there within him… Inside of his heart… Giving it strength. He then focussed on his breathing and waited for the right moment… The perfect time… "To Kill this

Sucker!" he shouted as Lee approached with claws poised!

Lee slashed at him multiple times but the Stranger made him miss, he began to swing again and the Stranger was ready and dodged many but soon he tired and began to slow down. He had no power to retaliate or he would have done so by now. All he could do was avoid the razor sharp claws of the beast and try to find some way to overcome it. Amidst the demon's many attacks, it was able to get past the Stranger's guard and when it did, it stuck one of his claws into the Stranger's chest and the other claw right next to it!! The Stranger did not scream nor did give in though his body was about to. He grabbed hold of the wrists of the Beast sternly...

He then looked that Beast directly in its glowing red eyes and let out a battle cry such as not heard before! He then fought against the power of the Demon to pull its claws out of his chest and as the two struggled against one another the Stranger felt the Light inside power up in his core like a flame in the dark! He then yanked Lee's arms backward removing his claws from his flesh and then stepped backward pulling its arms downward toward himself causing Lee's head to drop down low. When that happened, he let go of Lee's left arm and threw a vicious right elbow catching the demon right in the mouth!

"Crrrrraaaaccckkk!!!!" The sound of bone meeting bone once again filled the cavern bouncing off the walls as if it were a voice in song. The blow dropped the demon to the ground and once that happened, he began stomping on its head until it ceased to move. Then he reached down and flipped the demon over onto its back like a fish and used his own claws to stab him in the throat with!! "Aaaaaaaaggggghhhhhh!!!!!" he screamed out in madness as he knew it would be his final effort to destroy the Beast. He dropped the demon's hands and saw that it was gurgling on its own blood trying to breathe.

He looked around for a second and saw a large stone a few yards away from them so he got up and walked over to it and picked it up. He slowly walked back over to where the demon struggled for life and stood next to it. He said a prayer as he raised the stone above his head, "Dear Light, I pray for this beast, I don't know if it is Lee or not... but I pray for its soul..." he struggled with his words as his eyes started welling up with tears.

His voice began to break with emotion as his mind filled with memories of his amazing friend and teacher Mr. Lee. As he stood there watching him die a horrible death, he knew that had the power to end his friend's pain, he just couldn't bring himself to do it. "I... Just can't do it bro... I... I am sorry man!!. Creator, give him peace!!!! he cried out in pain. AAAAAAGGGGGHHHH!!!!" he screamed as he used all of his strength to slam the stone down onto the Demon's head! The Demon's body jerked violently one last time before it stopped moving completely.

Once he saw that the beast was dead he looked up and screamed out once again, "AAAAAHHHHHHHHHHHHH!!!!!!" into the air, releasing the last of his rage out into the world! He then dropped to his knees and fell onto the ground with a slap! He rolled over onto his back and placed his hands over the deep wounds in his chest. "That's it! I don't have anything left to give. I'm sorry Lee!! I couldn't find you... Tell Lupe that I tried...I tried my best... I... I'm gonna rest a little now... Yeah... got to rest." he whispered as he lay there dying.

He gave in and let it all go... All of the frustration and lost memories, he let them go and accepted the reality that he would never find out who he was. Nor would he find his way home, it was all lost to him now, taken away without rhyme or reason, or so it seemed anyway. It was something that he had no control over, it mattered not who helped him or how strong he was, it was simply bigger than he was and it was time to accept that.

He did so gladly as he felt a certain peace come over him. It was getting dark outside of the cave where he lay dying. Curiously. He started evaluating the interior of the cave, it was so open that it wasn't really a cave at all, It was more like an opening in the side of the cliff. "Does that even make sense? A cave or an opening?" he uttered. Looking back, he realized that during the fight, he wasn't able to take notice of anything other than Lee. And though he felt like he had seen it before, in his dream, he couldn't be certain that he actually had. "As long as it's dry…" he mumbled as the life force seeped from his beaten body.

He felt sleepy, "Sooo Sleeepy… I need to rest… Just for a little while, I promise, I wonnnn…" his voice gave and so did his breath, his body went limp and his eyes fought to remain open. Just as the darkness began to overtake his vision, he saw … the Light!? It was beautiful and it was illuminating the room where he lay. "Looks just like the Light!!!" he thought as he fell asleep. The darkness was always kind to him, though it was different from the "Darkness or the Shadow," that he had come to know.

This was not that darkness, this was the safety zone kind of darkness, it was a place he had come to know rather well as of late. It was a place where he could rest and recover from whatever had afflicted him, a place where at least his spirit was safe from harm. Time passed on for an undetermined amount of time, for such was beyond his ability to know. It was while he was lost in the flow of time that he heard a voice somewhere off in the distance.

It was a powerful voice, one that spoke to his soul. Almost as if it knew who he was and had access to his mind and his thoughts.

"HEEEEEYYYY!!!" the voice exclaimed, shocking him to the core.

"What the hell is happening here?" He thought… "Why do I know that voice? It sounds so familiar…" he said as curiosity tickled his mind. He focussed hard on listening to it but as he waited patiently nothing else came to him… Then, there it was again!!!

"Okay Mr. I'm gonna pour some water into your mouth so don't choke on it! OK?" Then an odd sensation took over him, while his mind concentrated on listening to the voice, he started to feel something else…It was powerful, like a rushing waterfall! Then, the darkness gave way to the light and he suddenly found himself, laying in what seemed like,"Water!?" he sat up as fast as he could and found himself sitting in the middle of a clear, shallow stream of water! He shook the water from his head and took a deep breath.

"What the heck is going on here? How did I end up here? This looks like the river we saw before we entered this place. La Vida…" he said. He couldn't help but to smile as he pulled his arms up out of the water and began splashing around like a child. The stream was so clear that he could see every rock in its bed, every plant, it was surreal. He could even see some fish swimming around near where he was sitting, they were so close he could almost reach out and grab one of them.

It was cool and soothing as it moved itself against his back and around his body, enclosing itself around him in the front. It was strange, it was like he could taste it even though he was not drinking from the stream itself. He looked down at the current as it broke around him once again and sat still, observing the element quietly. He could hear the voice speaking in the background again but he did not pay attention to what it was saying. The fresh water tempted him as he had tasted some of it as it ran around his head moments earlier. So he cupped his hands together and drank it down!

It tasted amazing, unlike any he could remember tasting before and it was much needed though for some reason, it also felt dangerous. Almost as if he were getting too much... The current changed somehow and as he looked down it no longer broke around his body... It ran through him! It was becoming him and he was joining it. He fell back into the stream and began shaking due to the force of its current.

"I won't leave you!!! I promise, I won't leave..." said the strange voice over and over again. Soon it became so loud that he began to feel consciousness return to him, as if the voice were calling him back somewhere. After a few moments the dream and its content slowly faded away from his mind, but the voice seemed to get louder, almost as if someone were there. Calling him back to the realm of pain. After the voice seized his attention, he quickly opened his eyes and looked around!

Once again, uncertain of where he was or who it was that had been calling to him. As he analyzed his body's current state, he realized that his mouth was clear, almost as if he had just swallowed down some water. In fact, his lips were still wet and so were his chin and neck. He sat up quickly and wiped them, seeing the water on his fingertips he tried to piece things together but nothing seemed to fit. He moved his limbs about, stretching like a kid who just awoke from an afternoon nap as he studied his surroundings. He felt replenished somehow and strong, not weak and near death as before.

He looked upon himself and saw that his wounds were all but gone!! "Whoa what the heck is going on here? I was torn to bits and dying a few minutes ago, how in the world am I healed up so quickly?" he wondered as he inspected his arms and legs in disbelief. He then did the same for his chest and back but found only scars. He wanted to doubt everything that happened but then he beheld the scars as they were everywhere. This he could not deny, especially the ones left by the Beast's claws when he stuck them into his chest!

That was a mortal wound, it meant that Lee was not playing around, he wanted to kill the Stranger and that is why he did what He had to do. "I can't deny the proof I guess, especially when the evidence of my battle with him is apparent." Blood still remained on his clothes and in the dirt where he was laying but it appeared to be old, not in any way fresh. "Un Freakin believable!" he said as he tried hard to discredit his memory.

"No matter how unbelievable it may be, it was true." he said as he hesitantly looked over his shoulder, to where he had vanquished the demon that had become Lee. He had to make sure he was there because if not, that would mean that he was either crazy or that the fight with Lee was not over. "Agghhh, the thought of having to go through that shit again is so not cool!" he said as he saw Its remains exactly where he left them after bashing its head in with a stone. He rolled over onto knees and then got onto his feet, though his balance was a bit off and his legs felt a little weary.

He walked a few steps over to the remains of the Demon and crouched down next to it. As He looked closer at the remains, he noticed that the body of Lee was a skeleton and not a fleshy corpse as it should be. There was no sign of tendons or muscle matter, no blood other than a stain under the body but nothing suggesting that its death was recent. "How can this be…? I mean… I wasn't out for that long was I? How could I have been?" he said as he rose back onto his feet, still confused by what he was looking at.

He rubbed his eyes thinking maybe his vision was just blurred as his eyes still struggled adjusting to being open but there was no denying the evidence. He staggered around a bit trying to get the rest of his body to loosen up, he felt stiff and tight, almost like he had been there much longer than he thought. He took note of his surroundings once again and was amazed at what he saw. The sun was shining down onto the lush little valley but once again, it was different somehow.

The trees were thicker, taller than before, making the ground much less visible from where he stood. He walked over to the edge and looked down into the valley below with a sense of sadness. No one was left but him and he wasn't even sure if he was truly alive or if he were dead also. He knew that he couldn't just sit there and whine about it forever as he still had to find a way out of this crazy place, not to mention that he still needed to find his friends. That's if they were even still alive. Just then he remembered the doorway from his dream so he looked over to the far side of the cave and there it was! It was just like his dream had depicted it.

It was an opening in the cave wall, it was natural but someone placed a wooden beam across the top of it as it looked like it was sealed off at one point. There were bricks on either side of the opening that were still pasted to the wall, left behind by whomever reopened it. He thought about what was beyond that opening and wondered if all that he had seen in his dream were true also. He was still having issues believing everything that was happening to him, it was like he was living in different dimensions and time frames at the same time. It was difficult on his mind not to mention his spirit.

"This is all just one big dream isn't it?" he thought as he looked back toward the remains of his friend and walked over to them hesitantly. He knelt down beside him once again. He peered down at it again, searching for anything he may have missed when he reached over and pushed the stone away from Lee's skull.

Once it was clear he could see that it was not human, or at least it didn't appear to be anyway. It had long sharp teeth and strange bone structure around the eyes and jaw. He inspected the rest of its body and saw that the hands were different also, each hand had only four fingers that ended with bear-like claws! Was this his friend? The man who had saved and helped him so much? It was hard to believe that it was the same man.

"This can't be Lee, I won't believe it was you Lee. Whatever happened to you, I am sorry I wasn't there for you man. I am sorry that I let you down. If you're still out there, I promise. I'll find you." He lowered his head and said a prayer for whoever lay there, before he stood up and turned toward the far side of the cave. As he turned his foot, he kicked something on the ground. He looked down at what he had knocked over and then bent down to pick it up. The moment he heard the sound the object made when it rolled on the ground, he knew exactly what it was…

He reached down and picked it up as his hands began to shake. It was a small clay bowl and it was still wet from holding water! "What the hell is happening to me? The dream… Maybe it wasn't just a dream… I mean, I remember giving… Wait a freakin minute!? I… saw a man, yeah a strange man, covered in blood. I gave him some water. I remember now! Yes but wait… If this is the bowl and I am the kid, why am I? That would mean that I am also the… There is no way that really happened… No way in hell… Right?

I mean, how could it? How could it be me?" he wondered. Though he asked himself these questions, he knew none of the answers. After all, he had no memory to compare things to so his only choice was to accept the fact that he knew nothing. "This place, it's so strange, why do I have these memories of being here before? I don't know what to think anymore, I feel... Lost. Just freakin lost!!" he shouted out in frustration as his poor mind bent like a cardboard box over the situation he had found himself in.

He turned around and walked to the edge of the cliff with the bowl still in his hand, peering down into the trees of the valley below with regret as he wondered about his friends. The feeling of being lost grew and grew inside of him as he began to feel helpless inside, despair crept into his heart as well though he tried hard not to allow it in. As he stood silent, pondering what he would do next, he saw something moving in the corner of his eye. Something through the doorway, on the other side.

He wasn't able to see through the doorway clearly as the sunlight still impaired his vision but, "I swear I just saw something... Was that what I think it was?" he wondered? He turned his head in that direction and walked over to the doorway cautiously until he arrived. He crouched down so as to try and get a better look through the smaller doorway and when he did, a powerful feeling inside of his body went off! It was that strange feeling again, the same one he felt just before being shot at, the same feeling he felt just before he was attacked by Lee.

He tried to focus on whatever it was that caught his attention through the doorway but for some reason, he could not. "I hate to say it but I hate this feeling, it always means something bad." Then, just as quickly as it started, the feeling suddenly stopped. "Whoa, that's weird.?" he thought, as he shrugged it off and proceeded to take a step toward the doorway. The moment was silent, the only sound that could be heard was the sound of the winds blowing through the cliff side opening, that was until... Boom... boom... boom!!!!

The familiar sound of a long weapon blasting through the silence of the valley followed by red hot projectiles zipping right by his head! He ducked down with a quickness to try and avoid being shot again! "Guess that boy found his rifle!!" he said angrily as holes were being blasted into the cavern wall!! He was saddened by the return of Washee and his unrelenting desire to shoot him until he no longer walked amongst the living but he was more curious about what was on the other side of the doorway.

So he rose back up robotically and was about to pass through the opening when, like clockwork, Boom... Boom... Boom!!!! Three more blasts rang out one right after the other, he knew they were coming but this time, he didn't let it bother him. He was already so tired of it all that he didn't even flinch as they flew right past him slamming into the cave wall. He ducked down and passed through the small exit when he heard a voice screaming out, "Noooooooooo!!!" Though he didn't react to the young man's scream, he thought about it briefly, how he was leaving him behind but for some reason,

he just couldn't seem to get himself to care this time around. When he passed under the doorway, it was like he had just entered into a different time... Or another dimension, it was eerie and exciting all at once.. his innards scrambled about within him, making him a bit ill, but that all dissipated when he emerged on the other side of the wall and was immediately struck by the marvelous sight of the cliffside city! "Whoa!! It's just like in my dream!" he said as he gazed upon it with excitement. It was so intricate in its design and so masterfully constructed that it was hard not to be excited about it.

He truly felt like a kid as he looked upon the amazing beauty of it all. "This can't be happening, could it? I mean, it's the same here as it was in my dream! This whole place... It's really from my dream!! Or was it a memory? Hahaha... I really don't know!" Either way it wasn't important, all that mattered was that he was there, away from Lee and Washee, away from danger. In a place that was familiar to him. "I don't know why I feel so safe here? It's like, I can't feel all of the danger or the pressure... I wonder, am I finally where I am supposed to be?" He thought as he scanned the area for movement or anything out of place.

The sky was a bright blue, not like the usual blue he was used to seeing, but a lighter version of it, almost white. It was strange somehow, too bright but not so bright that he could not see. The more he stared out into it, the more he noticed it... It resembled the sky when he was wandering the desert just before little Onley had found him. It was as if it had two Suns, not just one.

"I'm not sure that this is a good thing, something strange about this place and I can't quite explain it. It feels like the desert, almost like time doesn't exist here." Suddenly the sky became too bright for him to look upon, his eyes had a hard time adjusting to it and they filled up with tears. It was as if something didn't want him to look in that direction forcing him to turn away. He looked for as long as he could but it became too much for him to handle so he turned his head toward the valley below. He kept his eyes closed and gave them some time to rest before opening them again. When his eyes felt rested, he opened them again.

Upon seeing that his vision improved, he looked over to the trail that led to the city as he had not yet left the opening. It was ancient and had been overrun by nature, yet it was still there. He looked over to the valley and scanned it for any signs of the kid but saw none. In fact the valley itself was different once again, its like everytime he looked at it, it was different. "This place... Its almost like, its alive." he said as he finished his visual search. Even though the Kid was just shooting at him, he did not feel like he was in any danger. Once he crossed through the doorway it was like he went somewhere else...

It was hard to explain. He looked back to the trail

and sighed, "It looks like no one has walked on that trail for many moons, that's for sure." he said as he studied the details of the ancient roadway. From where he stood, it dropped down thirty yards or so and ran alongside the cliff wall for another ninety yards or so.

It was an outside trail that served as a bridge between the small opening that he had just exited and the big opening that held an entire city within its belly. By the looks of the old path, it was intelligently designed and was undoubtedly heavily traveled upon in its time. He started walking down the trail slowly at first, keeping his eyes open for any foes or possible dangers. When he looked back to the doorway and saw the world he had left behind, he compared the two. As he did, he understood that they were indeed two completely different worlds yet one and the same.

"As two worlds collide," he said. He then turned back toward the trail with an eager heart and a curious eye and pondered what awaited him there. "Whatever it is, It can't be any worse then where I came from." he thought. Then, that warm feeling made itself known in the center of his heart. When that happened, he knew that all would be well here, It was as if he had found a safe place where it could not reach him and that provided some comfort as his thoughts no longer lingered on his troubles. Rather, his mind became quiet and observant, prepared to continue onward with clarity not confusion or fear.

He lifted his head and took a step forward onto the ancient path uncertain of the outcome of his decision to go there. Afterall he didn't know what to look for nor where, all that he knew was that he saw something here and he needed to find out what it was. He looked up at the cliff walls on his left as he walked by, taking note of the small bushes and rock formations that clung to its side.

"How amazing is the work of the hand of the Creator and who can match Him?" He said out loud as he admired the scenery.By that time, He had reached the lowest point of the trail and once he was there he couldn't help but stop for a moment. He looked up at the city that lay in front of him in awe. "It seems like it's different somehow, almost like it is newer than it was in my dream... but older?" he thought as he gazed upon it.He had difficulties describing what he was looking at, even unto himself but he continued forward, ascending the road all while feeling anxious enough to puke.

The feeling was familiar and it brought back flashes of the time he walked along the same path years before, or so it seemed anyway. As he reached the top, the large path transformed from a dirt trail into a metropolitan thoroughfare that winded through the city buildings ahead. He stopped momentarily and studied his surroundings, comparing them to the images that were engraved in his mind. It was just as he had seen before, a grand and extravagant little city inside of the cliff wall!

He walked closer to the first set of buildings and looked upon them with studious eyes, they were ancient and unkempt but they were still standing solid and true. He walked over to the second set of buildings, which were different then the first and touched the walls of one of them. The feeling of the dirt bricks on his fingertips reminded him of Lupes casita, it was unforgettable. Just then, he remembered the little canals that channeled fresh water into little pools from his dream.

If his memory served him correctly, the pools were just around the corner from his present location. If he actually saw those pools there around that corner why... That would mean that he had truly been there before. Even though he had already seen sufficient evidence thus far, those pools would end the debate for him. "It can't be just a dream, how could I have known all of this if I hadn't actually been here before?" he asked. Suddenly it was as if he was afraid to continue, afraid to turn that corner and see if the pools actually existed.

It was one of the hardest decisions he was faced with up to this point and for some reason he just didn't want to make it but he did. He closed his eyes tight, still holding the little clay bowl in one hand as he brought it close to his chest. He said, "If I don't go, this whole thing is for nothing. I need to find a way through this place so that I can get Lee and Washee out as well. This is something I have to do, I have to." Once He finished speaking, he opened his eyes and started slowly toward the end of the building.

His eyes were trained like the eyes of an eagle onto the corner of the last building as it drew closer and closer. His insides quivered with uncertainty as his legs seemed to drag a little more than usual.

"Just a few more steps bro…" he uttered just as he arrived at the corner. He hesitated for a few moments and slowed down to a partial stop.He stayed for a brief second and then he walked around it with subtle courage.

When he cleared the building, what he saw made things very clear to him from that point onward. For there they were in all of their ancient glory, the little pools of water, connected by two smooth thin channels that lead up into the roof of the cliffside opening! His heart burst into pieces with excitement that he had actually found something… Something from his past, even if it seemed more like a dream than a memory, even if it were just a location. That meant that he might actually be close to his home! The idea of being home was so distant in his heart that he knew not what to think of it all.

He walked over to the little pool and knelt down next to it reaching his hand down, touching the cool water with his fingertips. The feeling of the cool water brought back flashes of his dream. A vision of his young hands filling the bowl with water, his heart pumping with adrenaline. His young mind scrambled at the situation he had found himself in as he fell back onto his butt and sat there trying to clear his mind before it exploded into a million pieces!! Soon he found himself mumbling incoherently like a madman!

Sitting in one place warring with himself over the past, present and future all at once… He lost track of himself. The hours rolled by and soon the sun was once again covered by thick dark clouds and the sounds of thunder filled the skies. He felt the cold winds blowing over his scarcely covered body but he cared little about that, nor did he care that the light of day was perishing and it would soon be dark. It was at this point that he once again noticed something strange in the corner of his eye.

He turned his head immediately and rose up off of his butt and back onto his feet. "What was that? It looked like a light…!?" he said as he set the clay bowl down next to the pool, pretty much where he had found it years before. He took a few deep breaths and then he stood up and slowly walked back over to the main thoroughfare. He kept his eyes fixed on the center most buildings as that was where he saw the light moments earlier. The buildings in the center of the city were not like the buildings that he passed on the edge of town, they were large with multiple levels that connected the cliffside opening from its floor to its ceiling.

The architecture was so intricate that it almost looked simple yet, once again, it was enough to amaze even the harshest of critics with the way the buildings were designed and placed. Everything in this small city appeared to be built with a specific purpose, it was as if the opening in the cliff wall was made specially for the former residents to live and thrive in. It didn't take long before he began imagining people, living their lives here, giving birth, loving, marrying and dying. Everyone working together toward one common goal every day in order to survive.

Everyone doing their part, like clogs in a clock, working together to make the wheels of life spin as smoothly as possible. Taking the blessings they were given by the Almighty and making the most out of every bit of them. It was an amazing thought! He could almost hear the voices of children laughing carelessly on the trails and in their homes.

The men would drop down into the valley below before dawn to hunt Elk, Deer and rabbit, then climb back up at the end of the day with the spoils of their efforts. Meat for food and skins for clothing, a beautiful existence, a dream life that once was and is no more. No matter what the present time was or how it looked, he could see them all somehow. He could feel their presence there in the cliffside, in the valley below, in his heart. Their imprint in time was powerful and it brought him to tears as he walked through the pathways of the small city as he could literally feel the emotions of the people that once resided here.

It was an emotional walk in a timeless place, the sounds of the rain falling outside echoed throughout the cliffside opening as he stopped for a few moments to soak it all in. "Why do I feel so close to this place? Is it just because I have been here before? Soo strange. And when did it start raining?" He chose to sit down instead of pursuing the light as he originally intended, onto the cold stone in silence until the darkened day turned into a rainy night. It was cold out but he wasn't bothered by it. He was lost in thought, pondering his existence, his purpose in all of this.

All of the gifts that he was given to help him on this journey were lost. Not even the stone remained, in fact, as he reached for it, he wasn't even certain when or where he had lost it. Life had truly become a labyrinth of time and space and he knew not what to do about it anymore. Even though his wounds were healed he still felt them and his reason to continue onward was getting harder and harder to see.

He needed some direction, some guidance perhaps on how to proceed from here but from where? Lee was gone, Lupe was never here and even if Washee was with him, he was just a kid. He needed real help. Just then, a realization came over him and he understood that there was only One who could truly help him but he had forgotten much and wasn't sure anymore what to say and how to ask. So, instead of just sulking, he started praying. "Almighty... I know You hear and see my struggle... I ask You to help me in this time of great need as I am lost and can no longer find my way.

The further I seem to get, the more lost I have become. I know You exist and I know You have helped me since the moment I woke up, I ask that You make Your way clear to me so that I may accomplish the things that You set out for me to accomplish... I Love You and am thankful for All of Your help thus far. I am sorry that I don't know who You are but I have seen your Light and will follow it closely." Silence ensued as the power of his prayer resonated within his heart, a peaceful feeling like he hadn't felt yet, softened his worries and comforted his mind.

The connection he seemed to have with what he started to call The Almighty was getting stronger and even though he felt lost, he knew that The Almighty would always know where to find him. "I hope you don't mind me calling you that, The Almighty... I mean, I'm not even sure where I got that from to be honest but for some reason, it feels right. Just as contentment was realized, a buzz in the back of his mind alerted him to something in the area.

His focus shifted suddenly and along with it, his

eyes moved inside of his eyelids into the direction of the mysterious presence. He then opened them and found that his eyes were fixed on one of the larger buildings in the center of the city. He concentrated on the doorway of that building for some reason and just when he did, movement! Once again, he saw what appeared to be another small flicker of light!? "There it is again!!" It was as if he had already forgotten about it, the light that is. He was overcome by the memories of the city and forgot about the light even though it was the only real thing he had seen in the entire city thus far.

He stood up and looked around at the other buildings near the center but saw nothing in them. He then returned his sights to the largest building's entrance hoping to see the flicker once again... He saw nothing. Even though he couldn't see anyone, he knew that someone was there... "Who is in there? Show yourself!! " he shouted from a distance! There was no response. "Who goes there I say? Don't be a coward and show yourself!" he shouted a second time as he stood tall and ready. "Ready for what though? Another beast? Blast crazy Washee with his deadly rifle?" he thought...

Then suddenly the darkness moved aside within the main building's entrance and revealed a figure... "Oh Shit, Is that a Man standing there!?" he asked himself in a curious manner as the figure seemed to be walking toward the light just in front of the entrance.

The building that the Man stood in was not only the largest in the city but its architecture was far more intricate than the other buildings. It must have been an important place in its time. With all of that aside, when the figure stepped into the light the Stranger could see that it was not Lee, Washee or the beast that almost killed him. In fact it was no one the Stranger had ever seen before. It was someone else entirely and he revealed himself to the Stranger as he stepped into the light. The Man was dressed in a black hooded robe and it, as well as he, looked faded somehow, ghostly even.

It was as if he were in between this world and another as he was transparent yet solid. Colorless yet filled with the traces of all colors. He suddenly waved his hand at the Stranger as if he were motioning for him to come to the building.The Stranger looked around as if there were others present with him and he wasn't sure if the man's notion was meant for him or someone else. After a few moments of awkward silence, he finally accepted the fact that the man was motioning only to him. He asked himself one last time foolishly, "Am I really seeing this? Is this really real?

This guy could be another demon or something even worse…" As the questions passed through his lips the man waved to him once again, motioning for the Stranger to come closer. "AAAggghhh… I guess I can either go find out or sit here like a dumbass. I need some answers here and this ghost might be the only chance I have at getting some."

He said while hesitating for a few moments longer. Then, "Alright, alright… Let's go find out then." he said as he finally took a step toward the building's entrance. When the other man was sure that the Stranger was coming, he turned around and stepped back into the doorway of the building, back into the darkness. "Okay, if that wasn't creepy enough to make me change my mind, I don't know what would be." he said as he continued forward. Interestingly enough when the ghostly man passed through the grand doorway, writing of some kind became visible along the doorway itself!?

Though He could not decipher its message, it was an amazing sight to see this whole place in fact! It was a glimpse into another time in history that no one who wasn't alive in those times would ever get to see. He was somehow fortunate to be able to bear witness to it, not once but twice it would seem. Though his time there so far was anything but nice, it was hard not to appreciate it for what it was. As he approached the building, the air became thick and hot. His body started tingling all over as if his flesh knew what awaited him inside the building though his mind did not.

His eyes kept searching the interior of the building for the man's figure but all that they could see was black. Anticipation took over his mind as he started to sweat and shake from it. He turned his head back toward the trail and the opening to find a red colored sky with green colored clouds. Above the valley. "What is going on here? I feel... Like I'm not real. Like, I am dreaming but somehow I can not wake myself up from it!

I'm not sure how much of this I can handle but I know that I can't turn back. I have to go on... No matter how scary it is. I have to." He stopped for a second and gathered himself again, renewing his belief that the Light was with him and that he had no need to fear. He skook it off as best as he could and then he continued forward, walking up to the entrance of the large building. He stopped and looked up at the writing that appeared around the doorway. He tried hard to memorize some of the markings though he wasn't sure why, but as he looked upon them, the writing faded out and disappeared.

He looked down into the entrance and saw what looked like an empty room filled with shadows. He felt strange about entering the old building just as he felt strange about following some ghostly man around but he couldn't let it stop him. He needed some answers and if that meant that he had to follow a ghost into a thousand year old building at the center of an ancient abandoned city, then that is what he was prepared to do! Besides, whatever was in there had plenty of time to kill him while he was lying at the edge of the city half dead from fighting off some other beast but it didn't.

As far as the Stranger was concerned, there couldn't

be anything much worse than everything he had already been through, so he lowered his chin, looked into the dark building once again, not seeing where the ghostly man went or even what was inside and he courageously walked in.

CHAPTER NUEVE

The Ancient Ones

As he passed through the entrance of the building, he lost sight of the man who had motioned for him to come near. The light was dim inside and though the entrance was decent in size, it was as if the light did not penetrate into the building as strongly as it should. He couldn't help but to feel a bit uneasy about what he was doing, afterall he had been through to this point, he had every reason to be cautious. Though as he considered his feelings on the matter, he realized that he felt no real danger there. Looking back, he noticed that just before each battle, he felt this alarming buzz inside of his core, which was not the case this time.

He felt curious more than anything and that reason was good enough for him to risk it all and walk deeper into the building. "I have nothing to fear." He said in a confident manner as he continued walking deeper inside of the ancient building. The place seemed to be all but empty of life though he had just witnessed a man walking around inside. Something was wrong though, It was as if the interior of the building was not what it appeared to be and the further into the room he got, the stronger this feeling became. Almost as if the floor could be pulled out from underneath his feet at any moment, exposing oblivion under his feet, rendering him unable to escape!

The feeling, as strong as it was, couldn't stop him from continuing further into the room though, he knew he had to go. Once his vision adjusted to the dim light of the interior, he began to notice things inside. The room was not empty of material objects as he had thought, in fact, it was decorated with amazing furnishings and art. There were intricately woven rugs hung upon the walls and hand painted pottery finely placed on shelves. By the look of things it was as if the people had vanished where they stood, leaving all worldly possessions behind along with centuries of unanswered questions.

"Looks just like the town did and the Fort, something is definitely going on here, it's too bad I don't know what it is!" he said as he looked up at the large wooden beams that made up the cieling's support. They were also intricately painted with vibrant shades of brown, red, yellow and blue. The bricks that filled the gaps between support beams were made of what appeared to be earth and straw, "Just like Lupe's casita." he whispered as he studied them closely. They were not made of hard stone bricks like one would typically find in a building of this kind; it was far more effective and probably a lot lighter to move around.

He then looked down at the floor and took note of it also,It appeared to be the natural stone of the cliffside opening. It was not carved stone, they simply built everything on top of it, adjusting their bricks according to its uneven surface. Strangely enough, there wasn't much dust inside of the old place.

It was clean and well kept compared to the other buildings he had seen so far. It was also a lot bigger than it appeared to be from the outside, with space to spare for whatever reason. He couldn't help but to become preoccupied with the place as he looked around like a child. Suddenly he saw movement again and it reminded him that he was not alone. The man whom he had followed into the building reappeared from the shadows near the doorway to another room and walked into it silently.He was motioning for the Stranger to follow again just as before and the Stranger had no choice but to once again do as he wanted.

Upon entering, he was surprised as the man he followed into the room was no longer there! It was as if he had vanished into the darkness once again. Although the Stranger didn't actually see the man disappear with his own eyes, the more he searched the darkness for him the more he realized that the man was nowhere in sight. "What's with the head games here bro?" He muttered. He began to take notice of his surroundings as he suddenly found himself standing on the threshold of an even larger room than the room he had just left behind.

He could tell by the echo that bounced around from the sound of his movements that it was big, much bigger than what he could see. He stood at the entryway, silently peering into the dark, thinking about what he should do next. He really wasn't in the mood to venture into the room blindly so he placed his fingers on the wall next to him. He turned his body to the left and walked in. The further away from the exterior light he got, the more the darkness began to reveal to him.

Silhouettes of structures in the blackness began to take shape before his very eyes, though they had been there far longer than he could have imagined. Strangely, his vision still struggled to adjust to the darkness even though he had been in the room for a while now. As he continued following the perimeter wall, his fingers could feel what seemed to be intricate carvings or writing on the walls' otherwise smooth surface. He was no mathematician nor did he traverse the entire room to verify but the room seemed to be forming into a large circle. It was difficult to determine due to the darkness but the chamber seemed to be carved straight into the solid stone of the cliffside.

He stopped and closed his eyes for a few moments hoping it would help him to see through the thick veil of blackness. "Almighty, I know you are here with me. Please help me to see that which I can not." he whispered sincerely into the dark before opening his eyes again. His ever growing belief in a Higher Power was challenged during his time in the Mesa that was certain but he knew it was still there. Guiding him, allowing him to see the things he might not otherwise have seen. Just as he had prayed for and when his eyes were opened the first thing he saw were images painted into the circular wall in front of him.

"What are these?" he asked as he readjusted his position so that he could look directly at them. They featured what appeared to be the stars, planets and the Earth itself portrayed in disc form with what looked like sublevels under or outside of it. It also appeared to have a shield or barrier over the top of it, as if it were protecting the earth from whatever danger lay outside of it.

The paintings were hard to see and they were very old but they were still there, as beautiful as they ever were! The strangest part about it is how he understood what he was seeing, the solar system and star maps, he knew some of them but how? He couldn't help but to wonder as he studied them slowly. "I feel like I've seen these kinds of paintings before but I don't remember ever being in here. Maybe I saw them someplace else, somewhere that I haven't seen yet." he whispered. After looking at the painting for a while he turned his attention back to the room behind him, as he had a feeling that it held something else for him to behold.

Some sort of information or maybe he would find a clue that would lead him back to his friends... back to his home. These thoughts passed through his mind as he stared off into the room in front of him. The entire room formed the shape of a circle, just as he had previously assumed but it seemed to drop in elevation further toward the center. It seemed that he was standing on the highest level of the room, he could see what appeared to be steps leading down toward the center.

"Not sure if those are steps or if they are benches of some kind? It's kind of like a small stadium, though I'm not entirely sure what a stadium is, but I feel like it would look like this." he said as he tried to map out a path down to the center of the chamber. As he looked to the center, it was hard to see, it appeared to be the lowest level of the chamber but he could not tell from where he stood, it was filled with darkness and shadow.

So, he started walking down the steep steps toward the center of the chamber, slowly. The sound of small pebbles popping underneath his boots sounded like weapon blasts inside of the empty chamber. Though his position was more than compromised by the sounds he made while walking down the steps he had no choice but to continue on. As he reached what he presumed was the edge of the upper level, he stopped for a few moments to observe what was there before proceeding any further.

"I wonder what this place is… It feels big, much bigger than it looks." He said as he remained still in observance. The longer he stood there the more he was able to see, though it was not like one would think. The darkness seemed to be made up of many different shadows. They all swirled around in the center of the chamber almost as if they were trying to block the Stranger's view of what was there. He concentrated on it with all of his heart, he envisioned the darkness fleeing from the power of the Light and as he did, it soon became so.

The darkness seemed to fade somehow and the more effort he gave the faster it faded, soon in its entirety.

The Stranger knew that it was the power of the Light that drove away the shadows, and in its place the Light revealed the details of the chamber to the Stranger's eyes. The lower chamber, if that is what it could be called, was big enough to be able to fit at least one hundred people inside of it and It had one circular bench that surrounded it. It looked as if it was seamlessly carved out of the inner circular wall though he could not be certain.

It then had a second bench a few feet below the first and unlike the first bench that was carved from the wall, this bench was carved straight from the stone floor itself. They were so smooth and so well designed that it was almost as if they were made by something far more talented than the hands of mere men but once again, he knew nothing. The design enabled the people to sit on both circle benches at different elevations, thus directing all their attention to whoever stood in the center.There was an opening in the circle, a narrow stairwell that connected the lower chamber with the upper and served as the entrance to the lower room.

Whomever attended such meetings in this location had to enter through the stairwell in order to sit on either of the circular benches.The upper level consisted of three more circular benches, all of which were carved from the floor and at different elevations, serving the same purpose as the two in the center circle. He looked up at the ceiling, which was painted in the same fashion as the walls, intricately decorated with star constellations and galactic scenery of all kinds. Even though it seemed like an art room to the unsuspecting eye, he couldn't help but to feel as if it were a map room of some kind, used for planning and strategy.

As he stood there observing the amazing craftsmanship of the ancient room, It didn't even dawn upon him to be fearful of the place, nor did the disappearance of the ghostly man seem to bother him as he was preoccupied with what he was looking at.

"Amazing... This place is just amazing." he whispered to himself as he turned in a circle scanning the ceiling's endless maps. "What in the world was this place? Seems like the inside of a UFO to me. Wait what? What is a UFO? Ayyyyeeee... that's all I need is more questions and no answers." As he talked to himself, out of the darkness, came a voice...

"The answers you seek are within your heart, all you need to do is look to it." The Stranger shook a little when the sound of the man's voice entered his ears but he did not fear It. He turned around to see that it was the man he saw from the path outside of the building, the man that waved him down. He was dressed a bit different than he was a few moments earlier, his dark cloak now had beautiful green colored trim along its edges and as he removed the hood from his head, a boldly decorated headdress made up of beautifully colored feathers and beads seemed to appear from nowhere.

The faded look of his being that the Stranger saw earlier was now swarming with colors, his skin was dark and reddish, his eyes were a piercing black with the Light of all Lights inside of them. The features of his face screamed out warrior with each curve and every line. He was a sight to see that was certain, and the sound of his voice was like the sound of running water, powerful and peaceful at the same time. He was not a big man, in fact he was rather short but the power he held was evident when you saw him and that made him larger than life!

He stood in the entryway of the upper chamber with a serious look upon his face. He turned to the right and walked over to the side of the chamber where the staircase was located and stopped. He raised his hands up above his head and began to sing a harmonious song and as the words passed from his lips the walls of the upper chamber slowly began to spin!! "What the hell?" the Stranger blurted out in reaction to what was happening in the chamber. He looked around at the chamber walls as the writing, much like the writing on the entrance of the building, began to illuminate the chamber.

Even though the walls that held the writing were in motion, the glyphs seemed to remain in place and the color of light that they emitted was the same color as the Light from the cave!! The inscriptions were everywhere on both the upper and lower chamber walls and were pulsating as they spun. The Stranger knew there was strategy and purpose behind every word, it was something so far beyond his understanding that he could only stand there and appreciate it all or not. So, as he stood there in silence, the song the Man sung carried on inside the chamber walls, echoing throughout the room and throughout his soul.

The man's voice was like an arrow, it penetrated the mind and resonated within the heart, the Stranger felt comfortable with it. Much like Lupe and Lee, their voices were echoes of their spirits and their spirits were close to him somehow. The same could be said about the mysterious man who was singing across from where the Stranger stood.

The walls seemed to pick up speed, spinning faster and faster the more he sang. He felt a slight wind passing over him, undoubtedly generated from the chamber's movement but it was not like a regular breeze, it was thicker somehow and cool. The words he sang bounced off of the chamber walls with a powerful melodious echo and the Stranger couldn't help but to try and hum along. When his voice joined together with the other man's voice they made a sound unlike any he had heard before. It was almost like he was tuning into the Universe somehow with their melody.

The sound waves from their voices seemed to break through the barriers of his reality, the barriers of the Stranger's very mind! Taking him somewhere he had never been before, somewhere he would never imagine going. It was the same sensation he always experienced when he traveled somewhere new yet different somehow. It was hard to explain, even unto himself, then suddenly, the man's song came to an abrupt end, the Stranger continued humming awkwardly until he realized that the man's voice was no longer audible.

He looked up at the mysterious man with the look of an embarrassed child and gave him a strange half smile along with a salute of sorts. The Man looked at the Stranger for a few moments with a sense of disbelief in his eyes, before bowing his head for a few moments in silence. He then lowered his hands and walked slowly down the narrow stairway. The feeling in the air was almost electric as the walls were now spinning so fast that it looked as if they stood still!.

The sound that the walls made while spinning was like a low steady humm in the background, otherwise silence ruled the air.The Stranger remained in place, anxiously anticipating what the man might say once he reached the bottom of the chamber floor, if he said anything at all. When the man reached the final step and both of his feet touched the stone floor at the edge of the inner circle, the ground began to vibrate and move! The Stranger was shook when he saw the floor of the inner circle begin to spin within itself somehow, clearing away the years of dust that had accumulated.

Both the upper and lower chamber walls, along with the inner floor acted as if they were separate pieces to the same puzzle and it was adjusting itself all around the benches as they remained in place. Once they came to a stop the writing on the walls dimmed down low and began to pulsate like the beat of a human heart.The man moved forward, stepping into the center of the circle and when he did the ceiling, like the other parts of the chamber, started to spin in place. It continued for a few moments, then it stopped and rapidly reversed directions, only to stop once again switching back once more.

It was like a combination lock, once the correct code was entered, the roof spun right off the top of the chamber!!! "Whoa shit!" Exclaimed the Stranger as he ducked down grabbing onto one of the benches as if he were going to be sucked out of the chamber. But there was no need, the room's atmosphere had not changed any and there seemed to be no danger so after a few moments, he let go of the bench and rose back onto his feet.

He looked up at the stars above but he didn't think much about it, as it simply resembled the midnight sky. He then lowered his head and looked around at the walls of the chamber scanning them fearfully as if he already knew what was about to happen and then... Just as he feared, the walls spun away from around the chamber and vanished into what appeared to be... The great blackness of the Sea!!! He looked around in shock and saw the vast endlessness of the waters on all sides of him! The only thing that hadn't blown away was the floor of the chamber itself and just as he found comfort in that thought...

The stone floor began fading away, turning transparent underneath their feet with the exception of the illuminated writing that continued to pulsate underneath them. The rhythm of which matched his very own heart. He couldn't help but to freak out a little but after all he had been through he was learning to control not only his fear but his reactions as well. " Whoa... that's freakin crazy!!! Never, in my life, have I seen such madness before!" He shouted as he looked about in amazement. He looked over to the mysterious Man and saw the expression upon his face, he did not share the Stranger's enthusiasm, not at all.

In fact you could say he was rather annoyed by the

Stranger's demeanor. "So much for first impressions I'd say…" uttered the Stranger under his breath as he looked down at the transparent floor that held them. It seemed like a disc that the chamber floated upon or was it that the entire chamber floated? "A person could go crazy trying to find the answers to such mysteries!" He thought they were simply beyond human comprehension.

He stood quietly on the edge of the upper level of the chamber when he noticed that the low humming sound created by the spinning walls that were no longer present had dulled out almost completely. He suddenly realized that his mind was struggling with what was transpiring and he needed to find a way to get a hold of it. He originally thought that it was the chamber's walls that spun and not him or the man in the center but the effects of interstellar or perhaps interdimensional travel that he suddenly felt in his body, proved to him otherwise. He buckled down onto his knees in pain, groaning as he hit the floor with his knees.

"Aaaagggghhhh… I hate this feeling!" He said as he held his stomach like a child with a belly ache. Even though he was in pain his mind did not dwell on it for long as he could barely believe what he had just witnessed! His mind was lost in a mixture of fear and wonder as the sudden feeling of his innards bouncing around inside of his body helped him to accept its truth rather quickly. He really seemed to understand it this time, that he had just been transported to somewhere else, not sure where but he was certain that he would soon find out.

The strong and powerful voice of the man who stood in the center began speaking once again but in a language the Stranger had not heard before. After a few minutes of struggling with them, he was able to overcome the pains in his body and he soon rose back to his feet. Taking a seat on the bench nearby, he sat quietly. His mind honed in on the energy of the Man's words as he spoke them, he sat and listened to them carefully.

It was not only the Man's words that carried weight, the man's voice, it was so strong and honest in its tone, it caused the Stranger to give him his undivided attention. He was not just a ghost nor was he a simple man, there was obviously much more to him than could be known by just looking at him. He tried hard to listen to what the man was saying, hoping to catch a word or a phrase that made sense but nothing came.The man's voice suddenly deepened with sincerity, then his story slowed down to a stop. He raised his hands up into the air above his head as he did before and then he started singing another song.

What a beautiful song it was, thought the Stranger and as the man sang it passionately, the space underneath his feet began to look blurry. It was as if a small circle was forming inside of the circular chambers floor. Like a small hurricane that whirled into oblivion, it became larger and larger until it was so powerful that the winds could be felt within the chamber! Soon the winds died down and the powerful swirl underneath the man's feet shrunk into a controlled disc of energy.

Mirror like in nature the disc came up from underneath the floor and set itself above the center of the floor about eye level. Once in position, the disc began showing images of some kind. He squinted his eyes and tried hard to focus on the images being shown but he just couldn't make them out. The sounds of people chanting in an organized manner came from the disc and as he focussed harder on what was being shown, he began to see... People!

"Other people!! Wait, they don't look the same as..." he said before stopping mid sentence to concentrate on what was happening. It appeared to be a multitude of people, filling the city streets screaming and chanting passionately about something. They looked desperate somehow, their clothes and hats were old and torn. Their faces were slim and malnourished, it was as if they had been starving and cold. His heart saddened when he looked upon their multi-colored faces. They screamed and yelled as they marched down the street, waving signs and banners in the air.

"Wait a minute? I have seen these images before!! The Darkness… It showed me things like this while I was in the cave!" he thought.Then, loud booming sounds shook the chamber with fury as he ducked down low not sure of what was happening. Suddenly, the sound of screaming voices filled the background of the chamber as the people in the disc began to panic and scramble about with haste! Then popping sounds pierced through the panicked voices as people began to fall to the ground after being hit by what he thought was a weapon blast!!

Then the wretched sound of machine wheels squeaking as they rolled over stone streets rumbled through his bones as he saw images of metal beasts filling city streets behind the people. Intense booming sounds once again filled the chamber as fire came from the spear tip of the metal beast, blasting people into oblivion as they ran away!

He saw men in uniforms holding weapons much like that of Washee's marching through the streets blasting people as they encountered them. It was all so nightmarish!! Everything that was happening was just horrible, "How could this be allowed?" he shouted!! Then, a sound unlike any he had heard up to that point broke through the chaos with a roar!!! Large birds with fire as tails, screamed past the metal beasts that were on the streets dropping some sort of containers upon them. When they hit, everything erupted into huge flames causing the disc to turn into a ball of fire itself!!

As the explosion consumed the images, the booms and roars fell silent and all that was left was darkness. There were no cries, no violence, nothing but silence. Then, the silhouette of a man appeared in the sphere, a man that was unrecognizable to the stranger's eyes. " Gosh damn it, who is that? I can't see who that is! It's just a blur." he said unto himself in frustration. Shaking his head, he turned his attention from the floor back to the rest of the chamber. He felt discouraged and emotional for some reason, "It's as if I know something more about those images than I can remember...

Like, maybe I was there or something. My heart hurts and I just don't know why..." He looked around for a few moments desperately, almost as if he were hoping to find some comfort in something but there was none to find. All the while, he couldn't help but to feel as if the man were watching him, not just his actions but his feelings also. It was as if the man could see through the Stranger, directly into his heart.

He felt exposed, like he couldn't hide himself from the vision of the ghostly man, no matter what he did. "Your heart is something that can not be hidden, young Warrior, not in this place. No one can, for we are transparent spirits, it is only our flesh that provides us with the means to hide." said the mysterious man as the fiery disc disappeared! He was caught off guard once again by the man's voice but its powerful fluidity helped him forget about the confusion and focus on where he was.

His face was solid as stone and his features were majestic and sharp, his eyes were deep black but had a light that burned bright inside of them, like the Light from the cave, it was welcoming. His headdress held some of the most beautiful dark colored feathers the Stranger had ever seen and his robe was finely woven and smelled of fresh springtime air. "I... I don't remember anything about what

I have been through, I don't even know my own name for pity sake... I am lost in this place, I lost my friends too and I just don't know what to do anymore." The Stranger looked down with sorrow in his eyes as he finished his sentence.

The Wise Man smiled and replied, " You may not remember who you were, but that doesn't change who you are, young warrior. The way in which you came is the very same way in which you must go, just keep walking with the light inside of your heart and the Great Spirit will always guide you." The words spoken by the man made no sense to him and it showed upon his face as he looked at the man with doubt.

"The Great Spirit? You mean the Light?" he asked curiously but the man did not reply, he only smiled as if he were pleased by the Stranger's question. "All of those images that I saw... I have a feeling that they weren't just random... They must be from my past but I can't remember them, any of them but I feel them somehow. Then Lee's daughter found me after I... I was being helped by a good man who didn't have to help me, he could have left me to die but he didn't and now he is lost also. He told me this place was bad, he warned me this might happen.

He said that this place was filled with Evil and that I would be tested here, but I truly had no idea how badly things would end up. He and Washee both tried to kill me, one shooting holes into my body and the other slashing me to pieces!?! I figured it was gonna be a hard trip but not like this. Now... Here I am floating around in Space with a strange man that I do not know and I am no closer to finding my way than I was before coming here." he said.

The man laughed as if he had not heard such drama in a very long time and then he replied, "Evil, like good, exists in every living being and place. Your friend was right in telling you that you would be tested, he was also right in telling you that this place is filled with evil. Though the evil that exists here is limited to the evil that you bring with you, if you are a good man then the test shouldn't be very hard but if you are not a good man then the test will be… a little more difficult." The Stranger immediately lowered his head in shame. "Does that mean that I am not a good man? I mean I almost got murdered twice!" he exclaimed!

"I am afraid that It is not that simple young Warrior, it is beyond my place to say but what I do know is that you are different and that is why you were attacked by the beast. It was sent for you once you crossed the boundary into our realm. This wouldn't be the first time you've fought that battle now would it? Remember your struggles in the desert?" he asked. The Stranger looked back on those times with confusion and was obvious as he asked, "How did you know about my struggles in the desert? Hell, I don't even know where that was, the battle with those beasts, it all seems like a dream…

Everything that has happened so far has been like one dream after another. I'm not sure I am even awake anymore. Also, is there any chance you can tell me what happened to my Sword, just figured I'd ask?"

The Wise Man replied, "The things that you were given are yours and yours alone, to find them when they are lost is but to look inside of yourself, young One."

At that point the Stranger felt like he had heard enough riddles, it was as if the Man knew every word that would, "Come from your mouth?" said the Man as he completed the Stranger's sentence.

"I was talking out loud wasn't I?" asked the Stranger with a hint of shame in his voice.

"It matters not, here, in this place there is no cover. No way to hide, we are all transparent here. I understand that all of this is hard for you but it is what it is, nothing more and nothing less." said the Wise Man.

"What do you mean in this place and who exactly are you?" asked the Stranger as he let his eyes wander for a moment toward the heavens. Upon hearing no reply from the wise man he turned his eyes back to where the man was standing and saw that he was no longer there!?

"Hey there... Sir, I didn't mean any disrespect... I just... Helloooooo??"

CHAPTER X

Legend of the Mesa

"We are the people not known, We are the guardians of the Mesa or so we think anyway. Chosen by the Great Spirit to serve his will and ensure that nothing breaks these Sacred boundaries... That is who we are." The Wise Man's voice frightened the Stranger this time causing him to turn around quickly, finding the man standing directly behind him! The Wise Man opened his arms outward from both sides, motioning to the stranger's surroundings. "The Portal."

The Stranger slowly realized what the man was referring to with his notion and he began to look around at the open space beyond the second circle. "I don't even know what to say. It's all so amazing. It's like something out of a dream. This place, you! But why did you say that you think? I mean, you are here right?" he asked.

The Man replied, "It is because we truly do not know why or how we came to be here. The will of the Creator is the will of the Creator, we are but insects before him. One day soon the Worthy One will return and we will be free to rest from our duties."

The Stranger understood what the Man meant as he himself was in the very same position as the Wise Man and his people. "I feel like I know you somehow, just like Lee and everyone else I have met since waking up in that cave."

Just then, the man stopped what he was doing, lowered his arms and asked, "Cave? You say you awoke in a cave?"

The Stranger paused for a moment before answering, understanding that what he said triggered the mysterious man somehow. "Yeah, I said cave but it wasn't really a cave cave if you know what I'm saying. It felt... Well, it felt just like it feels here.The cave was endless or so it appeared to be anyway, I dared not venture too far into it, just seemed like it wasn't for me to see so I left it alone. The exterior of the cave... It... Well it was by far more strange, it was a door carved into the side of a small red colored mountain. A door that closed on me once I was strong enough to travel but the doorway remained. It had a small hole in the center as if it were made for some sort of key. A key that I unfortunately did not have."

The Man seemed surprised by the story the stranger told him but his silence did not last for long. He asked the Stranger, "Do you know how long you were in that cave?"

The Stranger looked down into the endlessness below his feet and got a bit dizzy from the sheer enormity of it all.

"Yeah, that's some serious stuff right there, I feel like I'm gonna lose it!" He reached out and grabbed the arm of the man to steady himself a bit, almost as if they were friends, nothing less. The Man smiled awkwardly as the Stranger struggled to regain his bearings. He grabbed a hold of the stranger's arm and helped him stand on his own as he replied, "I... I am not sure how long I was in there but it seemed like forever, I mean, it took days for me to even be able to move again. God knows how long it really was."

He proceeded to tell the leader about his journey so far, about finding the Sword along with the stones, the first of which he found in the cave and the second on the body of Lee's friend. He told him how he and Lee were forced to kill two soldiers along with Lupes Grandson, a young sharp shooter named Washee, before ending up there with him. The Wise Man had his chin in his hand and had his arms crossed, he stood there and pondered all that the Stranger had told him. The Man began to whisper to himself as if he were deeply contemplating his story.

Then, the Man looked up at the Stranger and said, "The vision that came from the portal's eye was one of the future. It showed us a great many things, most of which were of death, war and destruction. We have a difficult time deciphering the future for the future is like the flowing waters of a mighty river and it is beyond our understanding. The river's destination may be certain but the challenges that the rapids bring along the way are not.

It would seem that the world is destined to meet a dark fate and there is little hope of changing it. As for you my young Warrior, I can not say what you have to do with all of this for certain but I did have a vision, three of them actually and one of them involved you. What your connection to all of this is, remains unclear but I will continue to pray on it. "

The Stranger shook his head and then said, "If you guys are who I think you are then where have you guys been for the last few centuries? It would appear that everything I have heard about you guys is true, with all of your power, with all of your wisdom isn't there something that you can do to change things? Lee said you were called, the Anasazi, that you were an ancient and honorable people, with power and weapons of light. Why can't you do something to change the direction of the world, especially since you can see what is coming?"

The Wise Man smiled and replied softly, "We have no power that isn't granted to us from above young Warrior and it is not our place to interfere with the Creator's plan for humankind. We were chosen to guard the portal and the honor has been ours but we are limited to that cause alone. In regards to your question of where we have been, long ago we were faced with a battle that we could not win. The Darkness somehow gained strength, enough of it to threaten the boundaries of the portal and in our physical forms we were not strong enough to defend ourselves from it! We were faced with a choice, one that was lasting…

I know not what you know and do not know about this world and how it was created but I will help you to understand it now. This world is not what most of humanity believes it is. The Almighty, The Father, The One True Creator, He is responsible for everything that is, was and ever will be. The intricacies of his designs are beyond human comprehension and His will is uncontestable. Though there was a time when we did not know, we did not understand who He was truly. You see We, as a people, were aware of Him but knew very little about Him though we were always giving thanks for our way of life and our homes.

It was He who allowed us to thrive as a society though we did not know how to thank Him properly. Our people lived on and around this Mesa for 800 years in relative peace and harmony, then… One day, it all changed… My Great, Great, Grandfather led our people in those times and it was said that one day a strange young man showed up. He had no people, no family, he could not speak well and he also had no memory. He had white colored skin and light colored eyes, not like anyone from the neighboring tribes, he was from somewhere else.

My grandfather and his people took pity on him and brought him into the family as one of their own. Not long after, strange things began happening around the village, animals began dying but not in the usual way. Their innards and blood were missing but nothing else! At first it was small animals, rabbits, squirrels but then… deer and elk!! My Grandfather and his Warriors began investigating the murders but found nothing, no tracks, no blood trails, nothing. It was a mystery.

He and a few others began to suspect the strange boy but had no proof so they decided to keep a close eye on him at all times. Then, one night when the moon was full a child was heard screaming off into the woods, my Grandfather and a few Warriors ran out to find the child and bring it to safety, but while they were gone two other children were taken from the arms of their mothers in different corners of the village at the same time. It was said that the screams of the mothers can still be heard on nights of a similar moon.When the Warriors arrived back to the village the young man was still in his spot with no signs of him doing anything out of place.

The mothers of the taken children could not explain what they saw, one said it had red eyes and the teeth and claws of a bear while the second mother said it was a black shadow that took hers. The next few nights were the hardest and most terrifying as the abductions continued. It was not only the children who were at risk, the elderly began vanishing and soon it was attacking grown Warriors out in the open air of the night. My GrandFather realized that there was nothing he could do to protect the people unless the beast was killed so he organized the best Warriors they had and separated them into two groups.

They then set a trap for the beast near the edge of this very city as well as at the village and they waited patiently to spring them. It was said that when the Warriors waited for the beast to appear out of the night, they were caught off guard and were ambushed by a second predator. The beast was the first, wild and maniacal.

The second was different, he appeared to be a young man, a handsome yet very dangerous young man with the ability to regenerate from his wounds. Yes, the very same young man who wandered into the village!

He tricked people into believing he was just an innocent boy but he was lethal with a knife and had little mercy for his victims. Pure evil they were. While battling the demons, my Grandfather and another Warrior were able to lure them to the cliff side where their trap awaited.

They had ropes tied to a couple of the trees and they planned to get the demons close enough to the edge that they would step into the loops and be hung up by their feet. From there the Warriors planned on burning them alive but the plan failed and they ended up falling off of the cliffside while fighting. My Grandfather was able to grab a hold of one of the ropes and it swung him from the top down into the first chamber, the very same chamber that you defeated the beast in. Both Demons fell to the earth along with the other Warrior who perished from the impact.

My Grandfather thought that it was over so he laid in the cavern and rested, injured but alive. Soon he heard the beast growling down below! At first it was said that he did not believe it so he crawled to the edge and saw it for himself! It was not only the beast with its red glowing eyes, but the young man also and they both started to climb up the wall to enter into the tunnel. My Grandfather was unable to defend himself any longer and in his moment of darkness it was revealed to him.

The Light!! He saw it through an opening in the cave and it led him out of the first chamber, down the trail outside, all the way to this exact spot. But by the time he reached this spot, the demons had already caught up to him!! He only thought of his people and how they would all suffer at the hands of these demons if he did not find a way to stop them, it was in that moment that he chose to make a stand. Not to save his own life but to save the lives of his people, sacrificing himself so that they could live, He just had to find the way to do it. In that moment he was cornered, the two demons closed in on him forcing his back to the wall.

Just as he let out his final battle cry, the Light appeared in front of him and gave him the power to defeat them both! At dawn, the Warriors who remained to defend the villages set out to find their fellow tribesmen but found only the remnants of their comrades torn up bodies all over the Mesa top. A trail of blood led them to the cliff's edge then down to the openings. Once there they worked their way to this spot, they found my Grandfather clinging to life all while holding on to one of the beast's hands as a trophy.

He said that the demons had no power over him after he became one with the Light, the very same Light that I would come to serve generations after him. It was he that showed my people that there was only One True Creator, it was he that stopped them from worshiping the earth and the elements, it was he who helped them to understand the truth. The Almighty made himself known to my Grandfather showing him great visions of the past, the present and the future, allowing him to learn and therefore to teach also.

It was through his teachings that we learned how to live properly, how to honor Him with our deeds and our lives as His servants for eternity."

"I feel like I know what you are talking about, it sits close with me, deep inside of my heart. Almost like I have heard this before." he said,

"It is quite possible that you have my young friend, it is clear that you are out of place not only here but everywhere you have traveled thus far. Indeed you are lost… Speaking of being lost, this place was not part of our civilization until that fateful night. Because of what happened here, my GrandFather built this city into the cliffside opening just as you see today. It was ingeniously designed to work with the elements to channel water in and out of the city, watering crops and providing a way to clean ourselves and our homes. This was also done to protect our people as the forces of evil seemed to have no authority here.

This chamber was built over the place where the Light appeared from, the center of this room to be exact. All of the details that you have witnessed were designs created by my Grandfather after his encounter with the light. This place is a portal. It is one of many designated passages of other worldly beings designed by the Almighty when He created the earth long ago. It turns out that the beast and the demon boy came through this very portal, set free somehow from their bondage on the other side and let loose upon my ancestors above. Once they were defeated, it became my people's mission to protect this portal, to ensure that they do not return."

The Stranger shook his head and asked, "You mean, you have been guarding this portal so that the demons do not return? Then who was it that attacked me? I fought that same beast who looked like my friend and then had to escape being shot to pieces by my other friend. A young man named Washee. These two sound alot like the two demons you just described. If your Grandfather defeated them then why are they still running around out there, killing people?"

The Man looked down for a moment in thought and then back to the Stranger's eyes, he then replied softly. "He defeated them in their worldly forms but their spirits are still free to roam the Mesa looking for others to consume. If they eat enough humans, if they overpower enough souls, they can become flesh once again. This would allow them to leave the boundaries of this Mesa and spread their evil to the nations like a wildfire and that is why this Mesa bears the legend that it does." The Stranger asked, "If your Grandfather was able to defeat them, why wouldn't Warriors from other nations be able to do the same?"

"I have no answer to this young one, my Grandfather was only able to defeat them because the Almighty granted him the power of the Light." he said plainly. "That power belongs to the Most High and is bestowed upon only those who He chooses. I have felt the power before but have not seen confrontation since my youth. I am stationed here and can not leave the boundaries of the portal as it is my duty to stand watch over it. Now in regards to the demons if they ever become flesh again, every deed that is done by them gives power to the Darkness.

The more power it gains, the more entities it is able to release from the otherside. We are here to ensure that nothing else comes out and if something does, to fight it with all the ability that has been given to us!"

The Stranger listened closely to the words that the man spoke and then replied, "I understand Sir, I am grateful for the things that you and your people have done, I'm sure it hasn't been easy."

The Wise Man smiled and bowed his head as a symbol of respect and then replied, "The Almighty is to be thanked and his Chosen One, the King. We are simply servants in this conflict and it has been our honor. Now in regards to your story, and the place in which you woke, there are portals around the world but some are few and far between. This cave you woke up in, is no doubt one of the southern portals, which is a very long way from here. How you made it from there All the way to here can not simply be an accident, it sounds like the will of the Almighty to me. There is no doubt that You are different from all of the others who have entered our home...

Here for reasons not yet known to me or even to you as it would seem." The Man said as he crossed his arms and turned toward the stairwell in thought.

The Stranger felt confused and couldn't help but to ask, "The others you say? You mean the Soldiers?" My friend Lee said that an entire Army of men disappeared in this mesa long ago.

He said they came here looking for you and your power but were never seen again. Is that true?"

The Man looked up at the Stranger, then he turned and walked around the circular room until he reached the thin stairwell. He proceeded to walk down the stairs one by one until he reached the lower level, he then replied, "Many Soldiers and many Armies have entered this Mesa hoping to take possession over the knowledge and the gifts that we have been given but none have succeeded!! The ones you speak of were exceptionally dark hearted and when they entered the Mesa, each man had to face himself and be tested. Only one of them survived, only one of them had enough good in their souls to pass the test.

Otherwise, every single man in that Army was soaked with innocent blood, the blood of the Indigenous nations they slaughtered on their way here. Each one of them became pure in their Evil deeds and felt no remorse for the years they spent slaughtering the innocent. We were prepared to defeat them in combat but in the end, the matter was handled without our help." The Stranger did not follow the Leader to the stairwell, he remained where he was on the upper level next to the bench he once sat upon though his attention followed the Man closely.

He then asked, "How did this kill them though, simply facing yourself is not lethal? I don't understand and is this your power? The power to make a person face their inner fears?"

The Man replied, "It is not Our power no no. You

must understand young Warrior, there is much that is not yet known, even unto us. The Light has its very own measure of protecting its secrets that are well beyond anything mankind can comprehend. The darkness that exists in this place is natural and has always done only its part but when those men entered the mesa, the amount of evil they carried within themselves was enough to offset the natural order of the realm.

Their Evil gave the darkness that exists here just enough power to overwhelm the boundaries of the portal, it was too much for it to contain. This is what caused the return of the defeated ones… the two demons. Until the Soldiers entered the Mesa the story of the demons had become legend but as you very well know, it is anything but. They wander the Mesa in spirit form looking for victims, yearning to escape the boundaries of this place and wreak havoc on the world outside!" The Stranger then walked around the upper level bench to the narrow stairwell where he then walked down the stairs, until he reached the bottom floor at the edge of the circle where the Man stood.

He then asked, "So they are not yet free?" with a concerned voice.

"No, they are not free, not yet. Now, It only has the ability to possess the souls of men and influence them to do its bidding but it is still confined to the boundaries of the Mesa and the spirit world." replied the Man. The Stranger frowned with concern as he thought of his friends once again, still in a state of disbelief at what transpired between the three of them.

The Wise Man looked at the Stranger and seeing the uncertainty within his eyes he said, "This may seem hard to understand but understand, you must. The beast and the boy you encountered are not your friends, you see. Either the demons possessed your friends causing them to try and kill you or they copied them. This means that the evil ones were either successful in wounding them, or unfortunately, they were able to dispose of them altogether. This would give them authority over their images and their likeness. Unfortunately both scenarios require the victim's blood. The Darkness can not copy or possess them without it.

The fact that they attacked you and that you not only survived but you actually defeated one of them means something."

The Stranger looked up and gave the Man a hard look, as if he were beginning to accept what the Man was telling him as truth. "So, what happens now? I mean, how can we stop them from getting out of here? You know, there is so much going on in my mind right now, that it's driving me crazy. How did I get involved with all of this? I mean, it really doesn't have anything to do with me does it? I'm just lost right?" he asked desperately.

"To be honest with you my young friend... I have no idea. None. I am not certain of almost anything, never have been. As a matter of fact the only thing that I am truly certain of, is The Light. The Almighty Himself. Everything else, we must learn to take with faith. He guides us across the deserts and over the seas without the need of our help but only when we let Him in, otherwise He will not.

He requires our submission, of heart, of mind, of body and soul. Nothing more... Nothing less. When we learn to surrender our hearts and our minds unto his will. As a servant, I only know what I am supposed to know and am not aware of many things. What I do know about the portal is that in order to open it, especially if you are a mortal, you have to have the keys. All of them. Though if one has the keys and the knowledge to open such a portal, depending on which portal and at what hour, during what day, anything could be set free from its boundaries. The

172

Darkness knows these laws as it was present in the ancient times when the creation of the world and the other realms was performed, by the hand of the Almighty." said the Man.

"The keys?" asked the Stranger. "Wait a minute, you mean the stones? Your'e talking about the stones that I found, right? The first one was hanging in the cave and the second was found on the body of a dead man. Though, I... I don't know where they are now, I seem to have lost them." he said with a somber tone.

The Man gave a smile and said, "There are four keys or stones as you called them, they represent the elements, starting with the Earth itself, then Fire, Wind and of course Water, then there are also two Spirit keys. One represents Darkness and the other, Light. Though be not fooled for there is a mystery that is tied to the keys and one day you will have to answer that riddle, if you do not answer correctly.

Your life and spirit will be lost in the depths of darkness for all time, for the keys were not meant to be discovered, much less carried by the hands of men." The Stranger understood what the Wise Man meant and nodded.

"Oh and what about the other man? The one who had the blue key? He happened to be an old friend of my companion Lee, he looked like he had been dead for a long while. How would, a presumed simple kind of man, get ahold of one of the keys?"

The leader held his hand out as if motioning for the stranger to calm down, he then replied. "This man you speak of, I can not tell you who he was but the fact that he had one of the keys on him can mean only one thing... Either he stumbled across it somehow and or was given it but by whom I could not say. Though if he was dead and you discovered the key on his body, then it would appear that he died attempting to protect it."

"Protect it from whom?" asked the Stranger.

"That in itself is a very good question young Warrior, one that needs an answer. It is not as if the keys are just lying around for anyone to take as they please." said the Man.

The Stranger shook his head and asked, "Why is this happening? I mean, I know you don't know but..." he paused in thought of what to say next.

"If the keys have been displaced that could mean only one thing... The War has escalated." said the Man with all seriousness.

The Stranger looked at him for a few moments while the word war settled into his heart, it was a word he had not heard in a while. Not since he had arrived here, to this place... Now he has not only heard the word but he has seen it also, inside of the sphere. "What war though?" he asked bluntly.

The Man replied in a similar fashion, "The last war of course. The war to end All wars. Don't you see, the Darkness is attempting to break its chains and assume control over the Earth. That may very well be why you are here, that may be why you found the Elements in the first place. You may be one of the Chosen, one of the Almighty's Laborers, picked to defend the light." After completing his sentence the Man extended his hand out to the Stranger in friendship. The Stranger looked at the Man's hand and grabbed ahold of it reluctantly, when he did, a flash of electricity burned through his mind!!

"Whoa... That was weird! Did you feel that?" he asked the Wise Man but he just looked at the Stranger oddly. "Ahh nevermind. Look, I don't even know who I am?! I mean, what does any of this have to do with... me? he asked.

"If the Creator allowed you to not only touch them but carry them, you must be of some importance for if not, you would be dead!" Interrupted the Man. "As far as the keys that you lost go, turn around and behold, the power of Light."

The Stranger turned around and saw the key floating above the center of the circle. As it hovered there elegantly the symbols on the floor burned bright and began pulsating as the key did. The Stranger started walking over to it as the Man said, "The key you found hanging in the portal is not an element, it is the key of Light itself! The key you found on the dead man was the element of water or the water key, as for the Sword, well... I can only assume that it was a gift. A weapon forged to help you accomplish whatever mission the Almighty may have set out for you. You must be in big trouble, there can be no other explanation."

The Stranger stood still peering at the key silently as he tried to let everything sink in. "Wait, what?! Trouble? You mean me?" he asked with concern.

"Hahaha! Yeah...." said the Man awkwardly.

The Stranger became even more confused as he did not know how to take that statement. He shook his head and asked, "If the keys are in motion as you say, what do I need to do? Do I protect the ones I have by hiding them? Am I supposed to take them somewhere? Help me out here Boss."

The Man replied, "All of the keys have been spread across the Earth and its dimensions, guarded by His Elect, to ensure the balance of things. If the Darkness gains even one key the balance that has existed will no longer hold and chaos would follow. A war to end all wars!"

The Stranger looked back at the Man and asked, "So if I really was picked by the Light to do something, does that

also mean that there is a person out there opposite of me?"
The Man looked at the Stranger with a compelling kind of
look but did not say a word... "You know, someone chosen
by the Darkness to try and stop me or maybe even kill me?"
As the words left his lips he already knew the answer to his
own question. Out of all of the questions that constantly
tore at his mind, out of all the answers that he sought with
all of his heart, this is the one answer he already had...

CHAPTER ONCE

Knowledge Is Power

"A Dark Warrior... Yes. I'm afraid that is exactly what it means. You see, we are All Creations of the same Creator yet we are torn into halves, the Light and the Dark. Many of us remain of the Light but there are some who naturally turn to the Darkness. If the Light makes a move, so does the Darkness. Right now, out there within the dimensions of the Earth, Warriors of the Dark prepare to confront the Warriors of Light. Therefore, you must prepare yourself for the times ahead, for the battle!

These Dark Warriors will be out to get the keys before you can and if they do, much will be lost. Do you understand?" asked the Man with a raised brow.

"I understand Sir. I will not doubt what I have learned here and will heed your warning." he replied respectfully.

"From this moment onward, everything that We do we must do with extreme caution for nothing is safe from the Dark, it has access to everything, even the day.

Come now... I have something you need to see." The man snapped his fingers and all of the sudden they were standing outside, in front of the building that held the portal. The Wise Man then walked away from the building to the edge of the cliffside and stood silent. He peered down into the dark valley below intently through the rain as if he were looking at something in particular.

The Stranger. curious as to what the man was looking at, decided to walk over to the edge and see for himself. Upon scanning the area below, off in the distance he saw something, a small fire! "Is that... Lee!?" shouted the Stranger! " Or... is it Washee? " he asked anxiously. The Man looked at the Stranger and snapped his finger again. Suddenly, he found himself standing in the valley a few feet from Lee who was attempting to warm himself next to a small fire.

"So this is where you've been? I've been searching for you everywhere bro, you won't believe the things I've been through!" said the Stranger excitedly but Lee did not seem to hear him. Lee's appearance wasn't the same as the last time he had seen him on the trail. It was different, tired looking. He appeared to be in pretty bad shape as his clothes were torn, he looked to be wounded as there were claw marks on his face and arms just like the one's on the Stranger's body!

"Aww shit man..." said the Stranger sadly as he knew the battles that Lee had faced against the same enemy. Though it didn't make sense at the time the Stranger couldn't help but to ponder it as he evaluated his friends' circumstances.

Lee had dug himself a decent sized hole under one of the shrub bushes and made a little shelter out of it. He used the short branches from the tree as his roof, protecting himself from the rain enabling him to get a small flame going. "Lee!" shouted the Stranger but Lee did not hear him. "Lee, hey it's me, where have you been man!?" The Stranger asked as he walked up to Lee carefully. "What the heck is going on here amigo, why won't you answer me?"

Then, the Wise Man said, "I am afraid that your friend is

unable to hear you... He is facing his own beast just as you did."

The Stranger looked at the Wise Man then back to Lee. He could see him more clearly now then before, Lee was breathing hard and aside from being wounded, he was talking to himself frantically. "I can not allow them to catch up to me, they have already taken my friends. I won't let them take me too. I am a warrior of the highest order and I will never surrender to my enemies!!" he said to himself as he tended to his wounds.

"How can this be? Didn't I already kill that wretched beast in the cave?" asked the Stranger angrily.

"Yes and No. All I can say is that it is all part of a never ending cycle of violence and murder. You can never truly destroy the enemies as long as the source still exists. Right now, in his time, your friend is fighting for his life just as you were fighting for yours. So is the young man, they both are facing the same enemy and they both will lose." said the Man coldly.

The Stranger looked at Lee and then back to the Man and asked, "What can I do to help them? After all I got him into this mess, he didn't deserve this. Aggh! Lupe and Washee! Onley and Olivia, I let them all down!!! They all are suffering because of me, it's all my fault!" he shouted with despair as he dropped onto his knees. "I am so sorry amigo, if I could trade places with you, I would!" said the Stranger with all of his heart. Then he heard another snap of the man's finger and they were back inside of the chamber except they were no longer in space, the walls and floor were present and earthly once again.

The Stranger looked around at where he was in regret before he stood up and faced the Man once again. He raised his eyes and beheld the Wise Man but was shocked at what he saw! The Man looked different, he was older with silver lines throughout his hair and wrinkles on his face. His clothes looked worn and faded, the edges of his robe were tattered and torn. In an elderly voice he asked the Stranger,

"Why did you say that you would trade places with him if you could? You don't even know him, after all your mission is far more important than one single stranger... Yes?"

The Stranger looked down and replied, "He doesn't know me, his family doesn't know me. They chose to help some freaking weirdo who was floating around in the wilderness and now they could very well be dead!! All because of me...

Lee brought me all the way over here to see his friend so that he could help me and now he and his Grand Son may be dead also. It's all my fault. None of them deserved it. I said that I'd trade places with him if I could because, I would... In a heartbeat I would!"

The Man's eyes seemed to gleam with a sharp light as he nodded his head in approval, then he said with a ghostly voice, "Come then and face yourself for it is now your turn. If you pass the test you may leave the Mesa, if you do not, then death and an eternity of misery here in this portal awaits you." The Man stepped aside and looked down at the stone floor, just then the floor turned shiny like a lake of water and the Stranger looked down onto its reflective surface...

"Look into your reflection young Warrior..." Rang out the voice of the Man. "Look into your heart and bring forth that which lies within... Face yourself, face your darkness..."

As the Stranger's eyes peered at the floor an image slowly began to appear inside of it. He suddenly gave it all of his attention and when he did the image became clearer. It was a man, though the details of his face could not be seen just yet the image seemed to be getting closer. The Stranger took a step forward and peered into the reflection with all of his energy. When he did, the floor became so bright that the rest of the existing world seemed to vanish around it, even the Man who stood next to him was no longer visible.

The image was dark and foggy but as the light dimmed out around the floor, the light of the image grew brighter. As it did, the fog began to clear away from the image and what it exposed was truly startling. He saw a young man and that young man was staring directly at him from the other side of the floor. The young man who was staring back at him had black hair and dark brown skin. His eyes were as black as the midnight sky and just like the stars shine through the blackness, so did the Light in his eyes. His face was young and soft yet filled with strength that could be seen in the way he looked back at the Stranger from the other side.

He seemed so familiar, everything about him was close, it was as if he was looking at himself from a different time, or a different dimension perhaps. The two looked into eachothers eyes and connected for a few moments and when that happened powerful feelings and memories were revealed unto the Stranger!! He saw himself in many different places with many different people, all of the images flooded into his mind and culminated with the memory of him giving a small bowl of water to a badly injured man...

It was at that moment, that the floor went dark, the image of himself disappeared and he fell to his knees in exhaustion!! The Wise Man was there as he had been before, he knelt down in front of the Stranger placing his hand on his back. "I know that what you saw is hard to understand, such things are never simple to grasp but in time you will know. A lifetime of memories flashed before your eyes and though you do not know it, your past has been restored to you."

The Stranger, still on his knees catching his breath, looked up and said, "I don't understand. I thought I was supposed to pass a test, face myself. I... I ,mean, I saw myself but not like I thought. I didn't see what I thought I was gonna see, I didn't face what I thought I was gonna face. It was just me, somewhere else! Or so I think anyway..."

The Man chuckled slightly before offering his hand to the Stranger. "My friend, you saw exactly what you needed to see, it would seem that you were here before, as a young man. Whenever you were here, you were somehow able to see and interact with yourself through the portal. How I did not see this is yet another mystery but once again, I am but a servant and as such, my knowledge is limited. The water that lies in this place is precious, it preserves the flesh and heals wounds that are usually beyond man's ability to heal. How did you know to give yourself some of it? Do you recall?"

The Stranger rubbed his eyes and grabbed ahold of the Man's hand, rising back onto his feet. He twitched at the feeling of the Man's hand, almost as if he were yet again touching a part of himself.

The man took note of this and smiled, "I believe I am understanding more and more about you with every passing moment, young Warrior." he said as he finished pulling the Stranger up to his feet. "The test is different for everyone, yet the same. Each one must face themselves, if you are presumed good then the evil in you awaits, if you are high with pride you will see yourself trodden down.

With you it was different because there seems to be almost no opposing force within you, even if you were to commit evil deeds, your spirit is good, through and through.This may be why you are here in the first place, far from perfect yet incorruptible to a measure...a true worker on behalf of the Light. Yes, that would help to explain why you carried the keys so easily and the Weapon."

The Stranger took a few extra breaths while soaking up the information he was given. "So if I passed the test, what do I do now? I need to find a way to help my friends, that is all that I care about." He looked into the Man's eyes hoping to find some sort of reassurance, some kind of sign that would give him a clue as to what he should do but he saw only Light. "That's enough for me." he thought to himself.

The Man smiled as if he knew what the Stranger was thinking and then asked, "Do you remember the images you saw on the floor, the first time they were revealed to you?" The Stranger thought back to the horrible sights and sounds that came from it and replied softly,

"Yeah, I remember... You're going to tell me that, I need to go there aren't you?"

The Man smiled and replied, "That place is not where you are going... Well, not yet anyway. It seems that it is where you come from and that means you will have to return there, at some point. You do not remember now but in time you will.

Have faith in the Creator, always believe in His guidance and you will never be lost. As for where you need to go now, I'd say... Despite wanting to save your friends, You should find your sword. A weapon like that could land in the hands of one of the Dark Warriors and if it does, then all could be lost. Your friends would understand this, they would agree."

The Stranger became frustrated with the Man's words and asked, "How do you know they would agree? I think they both would rather get back to their families as fast as possible, that's what I think they would agree to!" he said angrily. A few moments passed by with only the sound of the winds passing by the doorway to break the silence.

Then the Man said, "I know of the one they call

Jackson. I have seen his brutal use of the Darkness and it is not something one can run from. Agents of evil are escaping through every portal in this Earth and it is only getting worse by the day. The deeds of men are dark, massacres, wars, genocide, its all adding up. Building and building until there is nowhere left to build, growing and feeding until there's nothing left to eat, nowhere left to grow. By that time humanity in general will cease to exist. This is why I tell you that your mission is far greater than just one or two friends. No matter how close they are, no matter what they have done. If they knew what you know, they would make the right choice... As you must do." he said solemnly.

The Stranger shook his head in disbelief at the Man's words and said, "This can't be... It just can't be!! I mean, I can't just leave them here to die. This can't be right, it can't be!!"

The Man interrupted suddenly, "Yet it is Warrior, It is! And as a Warrior you must see the larger picture, you can not simply think of yourself and your friends. If you can find your will, you have a chance at stopping this whole thing and that would mean, saving your friends. If you choose to only think of them, you could fail and then all hope for them would be lost... For you as well. The choice is yours to make."

The Stranger paced around in circles with tears in his eyes. He whispered to himself angrily as he tried to find some way of making everything work but alas, he came to a halt. "How in the world am I going to be able to...? I mean, I don't even know where to find them. If I only had my sword, at least I could better protect them as well as myself. Last time I saw it, it was strapped to my back as I fell over a cliff! I was seriously starting to believe that it was all just part of a crazy dream!" he shouted!

"I am afraid the sword is anything but a dream. We can not tell you where it is, you are the only one who is able to do so." said the Wise Man as he motioned to the keys that were still hovering above the center of the chamber.

The Stranger turned around and stepped over to them, "Not sure why you call it a key, it just looks like a stone to me…

Though I have been known to be wrong… from time to time." he uttered as he reached up and grabbed a hold of them with both hands. Just as his palms touched the stone, the Light that shone from it suddenly went dull. The Stranger looked over to the Man with disappointment written on his face, "I don't think It likes me…" he said as he lowered his hands down to his chest to look at it. Just then, a burst of Light shot out of the stone, blinding him as he closed his eyes and turned his head to avoid looking upon it! He felt the Power but it did not feel like it came from the stone. It was far bigger than that, the Source was near and the Stranger felt Him through the Light that escaped the stones shell.

"I… am, not sure I can hold this for lo…," before he was able to finish his sentence the Light disappeared and All fell silent! He reluctantly opened his eyes to find himself standing on what looked to be… "It's … wait, it's the mountaintop from my vision! Is this really that very same spot?" He wondered anxiously as he looked back for the Man's response.

"I can not say young Warrior but it would appear that this particular location is where you must go."

The Stranger asked, "Wait… Go where, exactly? As a matter of fact, where the heck am I anyway? I feel like I don't belong anywhere, all the places that I have been to, I do not recognize but in a way, all of them along with the people I have met are so familiar. Agh, maybe I'm just freakin crazy." he said.

The Man stepped over to the wall, opposite of the Stranger and began looking at some images that were illuminated on it. After a few moments of silence, he said, "The place where you first woke up seems to have been in an alternate dimension somewhere and once you left the cave, you wandered through the under desert of Sonora for who knows how long. The Strange sights that you saw there, Have you seen a place like that since?"

The Stranger shook his head no. "That is because you are not there anymore, when you fell into the river, it carried you into the realm that you woke up in for the second time. The same dimension and time that you and your friends were in."

"Thanks. But that doesn't really answer my question." replied the Stranger sarcastically.

The Man sighed for a moment as if his patience were being tested and then he said, "Young man, if you have learned anything at all, one would think that you would learn to think before you speak. Now think… look back into your memory… Into the lives and homes of those you call friends. There you will find that which you seek. All you need to do is look." The Stranger closed his eyes and began searching his memory for clues, his mind went from the cave to the desert, scanning for anything that would help him learn the date.

"Remember young one, you must search beyond your fall into the river of time… onward onto the next awakening."

The voice of the Man helped redirect the Strangers search and as he began cycling through the memories of Lee's home, something caught his attention.

"Wait… I see something. It's a… It looks like a paper of some kind. It's on a chair across from where I sat when Lee and Olivia first fed me. It… it has writing on it! I can almost see it, It says… Wednesday August 27th 1866!! I can see it!!" shouted the Stranger excitedly! He opened his eyes and saw that the scenery had changed back into the stone setting of the chamber and the light had faded down low. "Now that I know where I am, I can…"

The Man interrupted him suddenly, "I am sorry young Warrior but you are no longer in that time frame. As I said before you have moved on now, you are here and here is not there. We are always in motion here, it is very hard to determine stopping points unless there is a specific reason."

"So, what you're saying is that my time with Lee and Washee is over? You mean, I'll never get the chance to help them and make things right? You do know there are demons on the loose out there right? I mean… Aggh!! There is so much that I haven't even told you yet, you have to help me get back there!! Please Sir."

The Man faced the Stranger and said, "Your mission is just that, my young Warrior! Yours. I can not tell you what is meant to be and what is not.

Only YOU can walk this path as it has been laid out before you alone. The mountain top you saw a few moments ago is also in a different time frame and if you have already envisioned it then it Must be part of your mission to go there. Did you happen to see your weapon in that vision at all?"

The Stranger frowned as the memory sunk in, "Yeah, it was on my back." He looked at the Man and smiled.

The Man smiled back and said, "If you saw it in your vision then it must be there. That might also be the reason why the chamber has stopped."

The Stranger looked around at the chamber curiously and then he asked the Man, "What do you mean it stopped? Stopped where?" The Man answered,

"Where it is supposed to, young warrior. Where the Most High has determined it to stop... That is how it works my friend."

The Stranger shrugged and looked around as if to let the Man know that his answer did nothing to help him in his quest to understand what was happening to him now. He then asked the Stranger humbly,

"Can you at least tell me how far from that time period we are now?" The Man reluctantly nodded and walked over to the wall opposite of the stairwell. He began reading something that appeared on the wall just like the other except this one was different somehow, it looked to be a map of some kind...

"Yes?" The Man asked. The Stranger, unsure if he had spoken out loud or if the Man could... "Read your mind?" he asked once again in the same stern kind of voice. "I can, though I choose not to... I can tell you this, from the date you saw in your memory of 1866 we have gone back and have stopped in the year of 1551." The Stranger, amazed by the Man's ability to see through him, soon shrugged it off and walked over to where the Man was standing, to get a closer look.

"1551? Why would the chamber stop here? What is so important about this date that it would bring me to it?"

The Man nudged the Stranger on the arm and said sharply, "The chamber does not act on its own. It is not alive and therefore we do not give it glory as if it were. All glory goes to the Creator and His Chosen One, nothing more, nothing less. Do you understand?"

The Stranger, being caught off guard by the Man's response nodded in agreement and said, "I am sorry Sir, yes, I understand and I won't make that mistake again... So, that's it? You have nothing else to say? I'm just supposed to walk out of here in an entirely different year and what... Hope someone else like Lee takes pity on me again? This is a nightmare, you know that right?" He

189NEGADE IN TIME - BOOK 2

shook his head in frustration as he started pacing again.

"I am sorry young Warrior, this is the way of things." said the Man coldly.

The Stranger thought back to the smiling face of the little girl who saved him and how her grandfather was going to die all alone in the wilderness with no one to help him… No one to care. He also thought of the Old Man Lupe and his charming smile. He thought about his young Grandson and how he sent him to help not knowing that he was sending him to his death also.

"We will meet again. I am certain of it, now go and do not forget your belongings, you will need them. For now that is all I can say, the rest will be revealed to you as you continue your journey." said the Man.

Shook by the Man's words, the Stranger replied, "But Sir!? What do you mean, you have nothing more that you can share with me? "

The Man sighed again and then he replied, "Evil is spilling out of its own cup and as it overflows there will be those who will kill to drink from it. They will stop at nothing until you are dead and the keys are within their grasp. I understand that this is not easy but it is what it is. There is no changing it."

"Aaaaaaggggghhhhhh!!!!!!" shouted the Stranger in frustration! "I will not leave my friends behind to die!! I need your help Sir and I need it now. How do I kill those things? If I am already out of that time period then how can I kill them demons before they can hurt… my… wait a minute. Wait just a gosh damn minute! You said that the demons were gone until that army of soldiers entered the Mesa right?" The Man smirked as if he already knew what the Stranger was about to propose.

"What if, I could somehow stop them? I mean, you said this chamber would stop anywhere as long as there was sufficient reason right? Well, saving the lives of my friends is about the best reason I can think of Sir. Can you please help me?" The Man looked up at the Stranger but said nothing as he began to fade away just where he stood. "Wait!? Don't leave! I am sorry if I said anything disrespectful... I was only trying to..." but before he could finish his sentence the Man was gone.

"The only way to defeat the demons is to somehow stop the soldiers from killing eachother, without committing evil yourself. If you fail, forever will you remain there, lost in time..." said the voice of the now invisible Man. He tried to get a grip on what was going on but he struggled to do so, he felt lost again, abandoned almost. He stood there for a few moments gathering himself together as if his spirit had just been separated from his body and mind. He shook his head as if to clear out the cobwebs that suddenly filled it and then he rubbed his eyes rigorously as if he had just woken from a long deep slumber.

As his eyes cleared out the tears caused by his hands, he came to find the chamber to be dark and empty, it was as if no one had set foot in the room for centuries. "This is creepy." he uttered as he turned around to find the stairwell up to the next level. He started walking over to it as he pondered the experience he had just gone through. "I'm not sure if this whole thing was even real, it's like I'm stuck inside of a dream and I can't seem to wake up!" he shouted!! Strange but there was no echo, nor was there any sign of life other than his own.

"I was probably standing here in the dark talking to myself wasn't I?" he asked as disbelief set in weakening his heart. He looked around at the interior of the ancient chamber saddened by the situation when a low hum began vibrating the chamber. "I don't have a good feeling about this." he said as he looked around for a clue to what was happening. The vibration seemed to emanate from the floor, it was pleasant at first as it soothed his weary joints but then it became more than a little nauseating. It had become so powerful that it felt like each one of his internal organs was vibrating on its own, within his body.

His mind even felt as if it were shaking inside of his skull. Then a low light from the floor began to engulf the chamber like flames from a fire, chasing the darkness away. It kept getting brighter and brighter until it overcame his ability to see! He closed his eyes and tried guarding his face from them but the intensity of the light grew so powerful that he could see it through his eyelids! "Aaaaaaaaaaaagggggggghhhhhhhhh!!!!!" he yelled as the vibration along with the light seemed to be causing damage! He couldn't even think straight due to the extreme nature of the environment and just when he felt that he could not take anymore, the intensity from it, turned up a hundred fold!!

He thought for a second that he was literally being fried right where he stood! The ability to yell had been removed from him and all he could do was stand there and weather the storm as best as he could. He fell onto his knees and tried to relax himself somehow but found that it was impossible as he had reached the limit of what he could take!

He began falling forward and just before his face hit the chamber floor, everything went dark. He felt his upper body and face land but it didn't hurt like one would assume, it felt more like he had fallen into... a river. Back into the everlasting flow of the current he went...

CHAPTER DOCE

Loops In Time

Just like that, with the passing of a fast cool breeze, he returned to consciousness, opened his eyes and sat up quickly! "What the hell is happening? Why won't you tell me what to do?!!" he shouted as he looked around to find that the chamber was gone!? "Wait, wait, where... Am I? Where did you go?" he asked concernedly, though there was no one there to answer. Not the Man he was looking for anyway. He shook his head rigorously as he tried to allow his mind to catch up to his body. Once he stopped, he opened his eyes again and the first thing he noticed was that the rain had stopped.

It must have happened sometime during the night as the ground was fairly dry around the little enclave. He looked to the center of the little cave, to where the small fire had burned hours earlier but had since turned to ash. Only a slight remnant of heat remained within the circle as he could still feel it with the palm of his hand. He looked to his right and saw that the young man was still sleeping in the fetal position where he had last seen him but Mr. Lee was not there. The Stranger looked around and saw that Lee had left his boot prints behind and it appeared that he had walked up the trail ahead of them for some reason but why?

"What the hell... The whole thing was just a dream? Wow, that really had me going!" he said as he tried to separate his dreams from reality in his mind. "Where did Lee go? Maybe he's looking for food or something, now that would be nice." he said to himself sarcastically. "I swear I've woken up here before..." he said curiously as he looked back into his mind for a scene from the past, but it was all blurry. He shook it off and crawled from the cave. Once he was out and on the trail he stood up straight and filled his lungs with fresh morning air, stretching his limbs out like a child would.

He looked up at the sky and it was bright blue with almost no cloud cover whatsoever. "Agh, that means it's gonna be a hot one today, mane! We should get moving now while it's still cool... I wonder where Lee is." he said as he followed Lee's tracks with his eyes as far as he could see up the little trail. While searching the horizon for a glimpse of Lee moving, he suddenly felt a strange sensation behind him. As he turned his head to look over his left shoulder his eyes caught the face of the one and only Mr. Lee standing right behind him!! "Gosh damn it man!!" he shouted angrily as Lee smiled.

"Good morning Mijo! Haha!! Such a beautiful morning for a walk don't you agree?! Did you rest well? Good... Very Good my friend. I rested well also. Let us continue on, yes?" said Lee with a childish kind of tone.

"You know something Mr. Lee, one of these days you're gonna sneak up on me at the wrong time! I'm just saying..." replied the Stranger.

"Yes, yes, the wrong time. Let us get the youngster up and atom as you say." The Stranger looked at Lee sideways for a moment or two before asking him, "Are you alright Mr. Lee? Have you been drinking today?"

Lee gave the Stranger a puzzled look and then replied, "Why yes, I have been drinking. All morning in fact. Filled up my water bag and all." The Stranger smiled and stepped over to where Washee was still asleep and knelt down next to him.

"Hey Kid, it's time to get up and get

moving." He shoved the youngster a few times until
life returned into the young man's body.

"Whoa what's going on? Where is my mom? I don't
know where they went, They left." he said half asleep.

The Stranger looked up at Lee with a saddened
kind of look and then said, "Uhhh, she isn't here right
now little bro but after we find our way through this place
we will make sure we drop you off at home okay?"

Washee shook his head and rubbed his eyes
while he yawned the last of the sleep off. "What?
What did you guys say?" The young man replied
as if he did not know what he had just said.

"Just what we needed... Issues." The Stranger
said as he stood up and turned to face the trail.

"It is time to get this show on the road homies,
yall ready?" he asked with zeal. Lee was always ready,
Washee was still getting himself up off of the ground.

"What do you mean show? Who is at homie? I really
don't know what you guys are talking about." said Washee
as he put his old hat upon his head. He then proceeded to
straighten out his clothes and place his rifle over his shoulder.
The Stranger motioned for Lee to once again take the lead,
as he stepped aside. Lee nodded with a smile and then the
three men began their ascent up the little trail hoping to
reach the top of the Mesa shortly after the morning dawn.
The trail was still wet and a bit slippery but for the most part
the cool breeze seemed to do a good job of drying it out.

"Strange that I don't hear any animals here...
Have you guys noticed that? I mean, I don't even hear
any birds. It's just weird." said the Stranger.

Lee and Washee both slowed down their

pace momentarily as they listened. "You are right my friend, I don't hear a thing." Lee said curiously.

"Yeah, me either... Nothing." Said the young man.

"Don't think we need to lose any time over it but I figured I'd mention it." said the Stranger as he motioned for the other two men to move along. Despite how strange his life has been so far, this was stirring inside of his mind.

As He looked back to all of the places he had been, there wasn't a time that he experienced this kind of silence, not since he wandered that desert anyway. That was the only other time he experienced it, in that strange desert where he was attacked by not only them flying discs but a pack of beasts also.

"That's gotta mean something, I know it. There's some sort of connection between these two places." he said.

Lee looked over his shoulder and asked, "What are you talking about Mijo? What two?"

The Stranger realizing that he was speaking out loud answered back, "The place where I woke up. The desert world outside of the cave I mean. I was silent, just like it is here. I think there is some sort of connection between the two places."

Washee, having no clue as to what the older men were talking about, asked them curiously. "What are you guys talking about? What cave? You really woke up inside of a cave?" He forgot that Washee had only been around for two days now and was not privy to all of his strange history so he decided to brief him on the situation at hand all while they continued navigating the thin rocky trail. Astonished by the Stranger's tale, Washee said, "Wow, that is unbelievable! I have never met somebody like you, Mr. I think you are,"

"Cool?! Is that what you were gonna say Little bro?" Said the Stranger, interrupting Washee's speech.

"Hahaha! Yeah, that's what I was gonna say." answered Washee happily. He smiled at the youngster from behind knowing that his story brought some distraction to his worried mind. A few moments later, the two men in front of him came to a stop. The Stranger stopped also and looked over the shoulder of Washee to see what they were looking at. The thin trail they already cautiously walked suddenly thinned out even more to the point that it had become only a foot or two wide. He moved Washee aside and stepped up next to Lee so that he could better evaluate the situation.

He looked at Lee who was already looking at Him. "What do you think, Mr Lee? Looks like we are gonna have to get skinny real fast eh?" He looked down as he spoke and took note that they had risen considerably in elevation since the last time he paid attention. "Did I miss something or did we just ascend a few hundred feet in the last hour or two?"

Lee shook his head and replied, "This place never ceases to amaze me. Yes, we have gotten quite high in a short period of time haven't we. Aside from that, this portion may be the end of us, we can not determine just how stable that ledge is. It could fail us at any moment and from that place there is no one who could help without going down also."

"How many feet across do you think that is?" asked the Stranger.

Lee crossed his arms and stroked his goatee with his right hand and replied, "I'd say 25 or 30 feet to the other side. Not impossible but definitely deadly."

"Sounds like just the kind of challenge we were looking for. I'll go first." said the Stranger as he rubbed his hands together.

"I don't think so amigo. I will go first." said Lee sharply! The Stranger was going to argue with the man but he saw just how serious Lee was about going first so he stepped aside and let him pass. Lee turned his body to face the cliff wall placing his hands against it and then he proceeded to slide himself onto the thin dirt trail.

"Gosh damn it, be careful Lee." said the Stranger in a worried tone. Washee came and stood next to Him and they both watched Lee as he attempted to slide his way across the broken trail. Dirt and small rocks fell from the trail's edge as Lees boots slid, one after the other steadily across the trail.

"You think he will make it across?" whispered Washee to the Stranger.

The Stranger looked over at Washee and nodded. "He has to make it kid, if not we won't either." They looked at eachother anxiously and then

Washee replied, "What do you mean we won't make it either?"

"What do you mean, what do I mean? It's pretty clear, Kid. If Lee can't make it across there's pretty much zero chance that you or I will make it. Know what I mean?" said the Stranger.

Washee shook his head and said, "So, your sayin if he doesn't make it we can't either but why? What makes him better at this kind of thing than us anyhow?"

The Stranger gave Washee a sideway look and said, "Kid, if I told you, you wouldn't even believe it. Mr. Lee here is a certified Ninja. That means he is one bad Mo Fo! Not to be messed with holmes. O.G. style, know what I mean?" asked the Stranger. The look on Washee's face was beyond explanation. He always looked amazed by the way the Stranger spoke but this time he was genuinely dumbfounded. The Stranger taking note, shined it on a little more by saying, "Don't sweat it kid, for reals." Washee smiled and started to repeat what the Stranger was saying to himself. Just then, the sound of Lee clearing his throat made them both turn their eyes back to him.

To their surprise Lee was standing on the other side of the broken trail smiling at them as if he were listening to their crazy conversation the whole time.

"See what I mean Kid!? There ain't No messin with this man. Right Mr. Lee?"

Lee gave a smirk and then replied, "For meals." The Stranger looked at Lee and laughed.

"Hahaha! That statement right there is not correct in any way, but it will do Sir!" exclaimed the Stranger. He then motioned for Washee to sling his rifle and step up to the trail head. Washee did as the Stranger asked and stepped up to the trail. Unlike Lee, Washee decided to put his back against the wall which required him to hand his rifle over to the Stranger before he could begin sliding along the cliff wall. "Boy are you sure you wanna do it that way? I mean, it is your decision and all but."

Washee smiled at the Stranger mischievously as he continued on across the thin trail. There were a few times where it seemed like the young man was gonna fall forward but after a few minutes of sweating bullets watching him slide across the trail the Stranger was relieved when the young man made it to the end safely! "Good work Washee, good work. Now it's my turn." Just as he stepped up to the trail head he realized that he now had the same problem that Washee did, he carried a huge rifle that greatly affected his ability to balance.

"Can you make it with that rifle, Stranger?"

Shouted Lee as he too realized the situation at hand. The Stranger gave a half smile as he tried holding the rifle different ways hoping to make it work comfortably but it was just too big. He stood on the edge of the trail and placed his stomach against the rock wall to see if it was gonna be possible but the rifle was just too heavy.

It added just enough weight to his back that he knew it was going to cause him to fall over if he had even the slightest trouble sliding across. Despite whatever efforts he could give, he knew that it wasn't going to work. Washee was pacing around in frustration as he was beginning to understand that his rifle might have to be left behind in order for the Stranger to get across also. "Aggghh!!! I'll go back across and get it, I can't just leave it behind!" exclaimed Washee.

The Stranger seeing how distraught the youngster had become over the dilemma shouted, "Don't worry Washee, I'll get it over somehow, you just take it easy bro!" After finishing his sentence He looked around for anything that he could use to help him get across with the young man's rifle but saw absolutely nothing. It was too heavy for him to try and toss it over to them, not to mention the distance from his side to the other. "Too far, shit!" he said to himself as he tried to think of something else... Anything at all but nothing. He came to the conclusion that there wasn't anything he could do, it was either he left it behind or attempted to make it across with the rifle on his back.

So he decided that aside from the risk, he was going to wing it and try getting it across. He slung the rifle over his shoulder and hugged the cliff wall as closely as possible, hoping it would work out. He began sliding his feet along the thin little trail slowly and carefully.

The added weight of the rifle didn't seem to bother him until he got about halfway across the trail as there was a portion of the wall that protruded out a few inches causing him to have to lean backward in order to pass it. That was when things got scary!! The rifle weighed a good 15 to 20 pounds and as he leaned back the rifle began to hang off of his body almost pulling him backward!! "Ahhh shit!!!" he shouted as he was no longer able to keep himself as close to the cliff wall as he needed to in order to remain where he was. That created just enough reverse momentum so that when he started going backward, he was not able to stop himself!

"Stranger, be careful! If you fall we will be l..." before Lee could finish his sentence the Stranger fell right off of the trail!!! He looked over at his companions as he fell backward but he did not yell at them, he knew keeping silent would ensure that their position was safe and so down he went. It was strange how in that moment he realized just how important his life was, not because he was about to lose it but because of his new found friends. He would now be leaving them to possibly die inside of this Mesa and there was nothing he could do about it. The look upon their faces was one of pure devastation as they witnessed him falling to his death!

"All for a gosh damn weapon?" he said to himself as he fell further away from the ledge. He could hear the voices of his companions but for some reason what they were yelling was not understandable. It was evident though in the way they looked at him that they were true friends.

He felt his heart break for them as he knew they needed his help in order to get through the Mesa alive, Lupe needed him. Onley and Olivia needed him... The thought of letting them all down did something to him. The unbearable pain that accompanied the thought of leaving them all to the mercy of the one they call Jackson was more than he had experienced up until now. His heart felt as if it were about to burst as he saw each one of their faces flashed before his eyes and all of them were in pain. "I can't let this happen!! I have to do something to remain here with my friends!!!

Almighty I pray to you, whoever you are to help me, help my friends! Even if it is only for that, I ask of you pleaseeeeeee!!!!" he shouted within!!

Lee and Washee got as close to the edge as they could without going over themselves to try and get a glimpse of their fallen companion. "It's all my fault! Oh no!!! It's all my fault Mr. Lee!!" shouted the young man as the reality of their situation sunk into his soul. Lee had no words to share with the youngster as he was in complete and utter shock also. He stared over the edge with the look of desperation evident on his face hoping to see the face of his strange friend once again. Washee stood up and started pacing around like a crazy person as tears began flowing down from his eyes.

The winds suddenly picked up again and with them came the dark gray clouds that were absent for most of the morning.

The temperature cooled down quickly and the world became a darker place for the two warriors as they mourned the loss of one of their own. As the minutes passed, they soon turned into hours and despite the weather change along with the urgency of the situation in general, the two men sat on the trail mourning their partner longer than they should have.

"We really need to get going, youngster. He would not have wanted us to remain here this way. Other lives, including your Grandfather's are in danger and we still need to protect them. Understand?" said Lee to the devastated young man. Washee nodded his head and wiped his eyes. Lee stood up and reached his hand out for Washee to grab. Just as the young sharpshooter grabbed Lee's hand,

"Hey Guys! Sorry it took me soo long but it was a long hike back up the trail there."

Lee let go of Washee's hand in shock at the sound of the Stranger's voice as Washee fell backward onto his butt and yelled out, "It's you!? It's really you!!!!"

Lee stuck in the same position for a few moments as his mind tried to process the images his eyes were sending it. "But... But... You fell. We watched you fall Mijo. Why are you not dead?" he asked in utter confusion at the sight of the Stranger.

"It;s a Loooong Story Mr. Lee. Hahaha!! Get it?! A long story?" he said jokingly as Lee and Washee both ran up to the Stranger and gave him a hug.

"It is good seeing you Mijo! We thought you were dead." said Lee.

"Yeah, I am so sorry you fell just for carrying my rifle. If you died I would have been sad for a long time Sir." said Washee with regret.

The Stranger smiled and said, "No worries my friend. It was an accident. Thank you guys for showing some concern for me. It was a scary moment for sure." Lee looked at the man's body and saw that there were no scratches or bruises, no scrapes or blood. Not even his clothes were torn or beat up in any way.

"How is it that you are in such good condition? That is a long way to fall and there aren't any other ledges or trees to grab on to. How are you not dead?"

Washee started processing everything that Lee was saying to the Stranger and he also began to question the situation. "Yeah that is really like, not cool?"

The Stranger seeing the confusion on their faces reluctantly replied, "Turns out... I can... Kinda like. Fly? I mean not that I can fly personally or anything, let's get that straight right off the bat. I prayed to that All Mighty force that seems to reside within me somewhere and it just kind of let me hit the ground... Without hitting the ground, you know what I mean?

It's a little difficult to explain guys, soooo... We should really get moving. I cost us enough time as it is" The two men looked at each other with confusion apparent in their eyes. "I'll try and explain more later, ok dudes? For now we need to get moving, it looks like it will be dark again soon." He motioned for his friends to get back on the trail and continue on but they were still very confused about what just happened and remained still. "Seriously guys, We need to get moving here, Handale, Handale!!!" he exclaimed as the two men began walking forward again.

"Oh, Washee. Here is your rifle. Keep it close!!" He handed the rifle over to the young man and then pushed him into motion as he stared at the Stranger still in disbelief. "Yep, I know Kid. I know," he said. As the two started up the trail the Stranger looked up into the sky and whispered, "Thank You." as he smiled. He then turned into the direction his amigos were walking in and followed them closely. The mood changed drastically after the accident as his companions kept mostly silent, they no doubt pondered all that had just happened to them and were baffled by it all.

The Stranger walked along behind them happily as his life had been spared yet again by the Unknown All Mighty. "That is what I am gonna call you from now on. All Mighty! It sounds pretty awesome, you know? Besides, it seems natural for some reason. I like it. Thank you." As he spoke unto himself happily he looked up and saw his companions looking at him over their shoulders as if he were a mad man.

"You doing okay, Mijo? I mean, Ok?" Asked Lee from ahead.

"Yeah Mr. Lee, as a matter of fact. I am doing

great! Life is pretty damn good right now, wouldn't you guys agree?" They both nodded awkwardly and then returned their focus to the path ahead.

The day turned to evening as the light began to fade beyond the horizon behind them. "Look! It is the top of the Mesa! We are close now, really close!" exclaimed Lee as the ending of the cliff wall as well as the rocky little trail were broken by the horizon ahead. The feeling of accomplishment fell upon them as they could finally envision life off of the dangerous little trail that almost took two of their lives in less than a day. As Darkness began to cover the sky in front of them, they hurried a little faster up the trail so that they could get to the top with enough time to set up camp. Though they were close, the trail was still very dangerous and so was the elevation they were at.

Just because The All Mighty saved him once, didn't mean that It was going to save him every time from then on. He still needed to do his part and use the common sense that he was given to remain safe and productive so that is what he concentrated on doing. Just then from the corner of his eye there suddenly appeared a glowing light of some kind. It was coming from the top of the mesa but he wasn't sure where exactly. "What in the world is that!?" he asked Lee quietly.

Lee looked ahead and saw the glow as well, "I do not know amigo but as I have said many times, people have always seen lights up here and no one knows what they are from." They crouched down and huddled around one another for a few moments to observe the phenomenon closely. They tried to understand just what it was that they were seeing but it seemed to faint and too far away for them to be able to tell for sure.

"It looks like glowing smoke but not a red glow like a fire would give. It's green...?" Washee said to Lee.

"I do not see the source as we are still a way from the top but you are right. It can not be a mere flame that is causing this strange glow. It is too big." said Lee.

The Stranger agreed with them, then he replied, "What should we do now? I know it sounds crazy but maybe we should keep moving and see what it is."

Lee nodded his head and replied, "It doesn't look like We have any other choice, my friend."

"What do you say young Warrior?" The Stranger asked Washee.

Washee spit on the ground and said, "I ain't scared ah no lights. Let's go." They all nodded their heads in agreement and then Lee stood halfway up and faced the trail once again.

He then cautiously started jogging up the trail, nice and easy. The other two men began jogging also, following close behind Lee as they steadily made their way up the last of the old rocky trail. From their current position it was difficult to estimate just how far from the top they were, it seemed as if their ability to judge distance was getting cloudy. As a matter of fact, It seemed like everything was becoming foggier by the minute! All of the sudden, the air felt thick and warm, like a mist almost except without the moisture.

The sky was dark, much darker than when they started up the trail, almost night like, though it was still evening. The trail they walked on became harder and harder to see as the glow grew brighter and brighter, blinding their vision of the earth underneath their feet. After a few hundred feet or so the hard ground suddenly didn't feel so rough, it felt different somehow. It was like they weren't really walking on it at all but they were.

"Hey guys, this whole situation doesn't seem normal.

Does this feel normal to you Lee?" The words that came from the Stranger's mouth were delayed, as if someone had suddenly slowed time waaaayyyy down... Upon realizing what was happening the Stranger tried to call out to Lee but his words seemed too slow to catch up to him. Lee, who was ten feet ahead of the stranger, didn't seem to be affected by whatever was happening to him, neither did Washee as they both continued jogging steadily up the trail. The Stranger tried to call out to them again but was unable to get the words out of his mouth fast enough for them to hear him.

The feeling was kind of like running underwater with clothes on, no matter how hard he tried to move, no matter what he tried to say, he could not do it in sufficient time to stop his friend. "What the heck is going on here? Why can't I speak? Why can't I catch up with those guys!? This is like a bad dream or something." The Stranger thought to himself as he struggled to make progress up the trail. The other two men were so far ahead of him that only a portion of them could be seen from where he was and it was obvious that they did not notice his absence or they would have come back for him by now.

"Why don't they notice that I am gone? Something is wrong here, this is not right." he thought. The Stranger stopped struggling and decided that It was time he gained control over this situation before it overcame him. He closed his eyes and gathered himself, the feeling of his feet slowly touching the ground surprised him a little but he didn't let it distract him from doing what he needed to do. He concentrated all of his energy on controlling his breathing, Letting the oxygen fill his lungs through his nostrils and pushing it all out through his mouth, one breath at a time until the feeling of being underwater subsided.

Although his eyes were closed he was still able to see the soft glow in the sky outside of them, as if it existed in his mind as well as in the physical world. The sound of Lee and Washees footsteps could be heard even though they were no longer visible as they had already put a great distance in between themselves and the Stranger.

Just then, a low humming sound filled the air. He stopped and concentrated on the sound, hoping to learn what direction it was coming from but he could not. Humming, somewhere in the background or was it in the foreground? What exactly was making the noise was unknown but it more than likely had something to do with the glowing lights above the Mesa. "That is just like the sound I heard inside of the Chamber..." Then, he suddenly realized that he could hear the footsteps of Lee and Washee no more. "Shit. That's not good, we were supposed to stay together!

They left me behind... Wait, I must be trippin, they probably stopped ahead, maybe they finally noticed that I was no longer with them or maybe... Maybe they fell!? Or... What if they were taken by them green lights up there...?" he said as he began to panic!! He started to turn around in circles searching for some sign of where he was but nothing looked familiar anymore.. All kinds of negative thoughts spun circles inside of his mind as he felt himself become enveloped in a very dark feeling.

"I need to calm down and silence these thoughts, whatever is going on with the boys, I can't do anything about it until I get myself under control. I can do this... I can do this! Can't let them get too far ahead, got to get moving again! So let's get it together and catch up to them guys before it's too late!!" he thought as he tried getting a grip on his emotions. He remained still for a few moments, gathering himself until he felt ready to proceed.

Then he opened his eyes and repositioned himself to face the top of the mesa, by this time the sky was so black that not even the stars could be seen.The lightning and thunder had disappeared along with his friends and the situation worsened while he was busy tending to himself. Though things were bad, he was determined to find his friends and get them through this place safely. The glowing portion of the sky was so bright that it was like a strange version of day up there, yet not and it seemed perverted somehow, not pure like the Light he had come to know. Just then he looked down at his chest and ensured that the Stone was still there and it was, though it was dull and without energy.

The humming sound was becoming louder with every passing moment yet he was starting to lose the ability to decipher whether the sound was inside or outside of his mind!!! "Agghhh!!! That freakin sound is gonna drive me crazy! I need to get to the top of this place and find a way to stop that sound!" Flashes of himself inside of the ancient chamber filled his mind as the sound was exactly the same! It felt as if he was unable to move forward even though he put forth the effort to do so, it felt like he was standing on a false reality, like in his visions.

The feeling of spinning out of control was connected with the humming sound somehow. It was moving him around somehow but not allowing him to move, it was the strangest sensation and he could barely stand it! The only thing that he could do in that moment was to have faith in the power he had come to know, the Light! No matter how desperate he felt inside, no matter how frightened he was.

He knew he had to do his part and take courage that his being would somehow make it through all of this in one piece. He concentrated all of his efforts on lifting his right foot and moving it forward but the mere act alone was more difficult than learning to walk all over again. It was like he was about to be birthed into another realm but had to fight to break through to the other side of reality. He began to make progress even though it was in slow motion, his foot passed the halfway point and just before it hit the trail.... The strange light atop the Mesa flashed, blinding him as he was in motion, causing him to stumble and fall to his knees!!!

He held his hands up in front of his face to block the strange and powerful light but its intensity grew with each passing moment. Winds from the sky began blowing down upon the Mesa rolling passed him as if he were but a stone on the road. He lowered himself closer to the ground so as to fortify his position against the winds but he knew if they were to blow any stronger he would be swept off the trail like a tumbleweed. The intense feeling the light exuded seemed to calm just enough for him to try and look upon it... What he saw was something that he recognized but didn't really understand until just then.

The image of a man, this man looked like a very important kind of man by the way he was dressed, he was holding something in his hands and it was causing him a great deal of pain. "It's the King... From my dream!!! Wait a minute, it's the sword!! That is what was hurting him, my freaking sword!" he exclaimed as the realization of the situation set in.

Just as he was about to try and stand up, a blast of green light came from the image and knocked the consciousness right out of him! His body hit the ground with a thud but he felt it not. The darkness had overcome his mind and laid his body down to rest once again, where and when he would wake up next...

CHAPTER EL TRECE

The Lost Battalion

"Whoa!!! What the hell is going on here? Lee, Washee, why you guys leave me!!?" he shouted out half asleep. He lifted his cheek up off the grass and opened his eyes. "Wait, where is the Man? Why am I laying in the grass, what happened to the chamber?" His mind tried hard to process what was reality and what wasn't but it wasn't able to do so anymore. "Shit, I was just with the guys right? Wait.. or was I talking to that strange Man?" he asked himself as he rolled over onto his back and sat up on his butt.

He looked around and realized that he was back on top of the Mesa. Or at least he appeared to be. He had traveled on it before when he thought Lee was with him but that must have been in a different location. He stood back up onto his feet and inspected himself for any injuries but found nothing aside from scars. This helped to ground him as he could see the evidence of his previous battles therefore he knew that most of what he remembered was true. He began turning around in circles scanning the area, hoping to see something familiar but that was not the case.

"What in the world is going on here?" he said as he struggled to understand where he was, even though he thought he already knew. "The Man... he didn't tell me anything about where I was going, is this the year 1551 like he said?" he wondered. Though he thought about it hard, he received no answers to his questions, this was something he should be used to by now but he wasn't. In fact it bothered him more and more each time it happened to him. It was no longer dark, as the midday Sun took the place of the chamber's interior ceiling. It wasn't hard for his mind to accept that his experience with the mysterious Man in the chamber was a reality and that the experience he had falling off the trail was just a dream.

Or was it the other way around? He returned his focus back to the situation at hand and that started with shielding his eyes from the Sunlight. He raised his hands to block the Sun from his eyes, once they were acclimated to the daylight, he saw that he was surrounded by trees, beautiful green trees. They were not very tall as far as tree's go but they were many in number and he was surrounded by them on every side. As he studied the area, he noticed that he was standing in the center of a small clearing and it was in the shape of a perfect circle. The trees stood around the circle as if they were guardians of some kind, forever watching the circle patiently.

As he stood there looking at his surroundings he couldn't help but to notice the amazing smell that filled the air!

"Wow, I... I think I know this smell! It smells like... Like... I guess I really don't know." he said sadly as he stood still enjoying the aroma as it filled his nostrils with delight. The ground he was standing on felt soft and appeared to be wet as if it were raining just before he arrived, though his face and clothes were dry. "It must be the mixture of the rain with the trees that created this smell!" It was a very strong and unique smell, one that a person could not forget easily. He felt strangely about how familiar it was to him but like everything else in his life, what didn't feel strange? He took a few steps forward and stopped to look around, making sure that no one was out there before he continued.

He walked over to the tree line and as he inspected the trees closely he heard a crunching sound under his feet. He looked down and saw little brown balls all over the ground. "They must have fallen from the trees." He said as he knelt down next to one of the trees and grabbed a few of them in his hand. He brought them close to his nose, smelling them deeply. The aroma brought something back to him just like the trees did, a memory!? He saw himself as a youngster again though this time he was inside somewhere. As the memories flooded into his open mind he heard voices, laughter and joking.

He looked around and saw an older woman standing a few feet from where he was sitting. She was... Cooking something. She shook the pan and the smell that came from whatever she was cooking smelled almost exactly like the little brown nuggets that he was holding.

He remembered getting up and walking toward the older woman, voices in the background laughing, talking etc. He walked up to her slowly taking note of the dress she was wearing, it was a rose colored gown with flowers of some kind on it. Her hair was short and curly and her arms were smooth and chunky. As he got up to where she was cooking he looked into the flat metal object and saw... "Pinion! Hahahaha!!!! That is what these little things are, pinon nuts! I think I have eaten these things before but I guess I'm not sure... I'm gonna have to take some for the road though." he said as he put some in his pocket. The scent of the trees, the nuts brought him back to his youth somehow though as always he couldn't figure out how or where.

He stood up and turned back toward the circle looking around at the area he was in. He kept thinking of the vision in his mind, replaying it over and over again trying to figure out if it were a memory or just a dream. Hoping that it would somehow expand, giving him more than what he saw, but nothing else came. His heart felt more than a bit lonely and his spirit sank a little every time he thought about it after that. "Ok, I need to do something, but what? I can't just walk in circles forever, Lee and Washee are out there somewhere and I need to find them."

Just as the words left his mouth a sound came from the trees somewhere. It was the sound of twigs and branches being broken as if someone were coming! He spun around scanning the area with his eyes but they caught no movement.

Just then he looked to the ground where he had been pacing earlier and saw that his footsteps transformed into a swirl inside of the circle!! It was moving in a vortex motion and as he stood there, at the edge of it, it began glowing green much like the light he saw from the trail side earlier. Then!! From deep inside of the trees somewhere, voices could be heard chattering. "What in the world is that, am I really hearing voices?" Then, the sound of clinking metal filled the air as the songs of the birds do overpowering the sound of voices. All of these sounds he remembered hearing before during his vision at Lupe's home.

What solidified them as being what he assumed them to be was the all too familiar sound of horse hooves stomping on the ground! "Horses? Here?" he asked himself as he tried to concentrate on where the noises were coming from. Then suddenly, the trees behind him started rattling, "Oh Shit!" He said as he began searching for a different place to hide. "Oh man, it's too late!" He exclaimed as silver suited soldiers much like the ones he saw in his vision began popping out of the trees all around him!! He began walking backward into the center of the circle as the soldiers soon replaced the trees surrounding him from all sides.

Once he reached the center of the circle, he stopped, knowing that there was no way out of this situation. "Guess it's time I make a stand." he said out loud as the soldiers finished filing in. All of them entered with their mouths open wide staring at the vortex that was swirling around in the circle with its dark green glow.

So taken with this sight that they hardly paid attention to this Strange man standing at the center of it all. The circle of silver suited men began to break up in one spot and the men started to move aside, just then the head of a large brown horse popped out of the crowd. As the rest of the horse's body followed closely behind, soon a man could also be seen riding upon it. He came out of the trees laying low, almost hugging the horses neck trying to avoid hitting branches on the way in. Once he cleared the tree line he sat straight up as if he hadn't the need to bow though he did and he entered into the circle. He pulled back on the reins bringing the horse to a stop as he looked down upon the circle with surprise.

The Stranger stood there awkwardly not knowing what to do when the man turned to look directly at him. "Atención hombres!" (Attention men!) He said in a loud sharp voice as all of the soldiers snapped out of their trances and stood up straight at the commands of the man.

"I've seen these clowns before." he said to himself as he waited for the apparent leader to say something else. The leader had a frightened look on his face as he looked at the swirling vortex on the ground.

He then shouted, "Padre Ortiz! Enfrente ahora!" (Father Ortiz! In front of me now!) Men were scrambling in the background as they did what they were ordered to do. A man in a dark brown robe was ushered up to the front of the circle and placed at the side of the man on the horse.The man had a strange haircut and wore a rope around his waist.

He had a satchel over his shoulder and wore a large wooden symbol around his neck that looked like an X. The man on the horse began asking the other robed man questions about what was going on, the man in the robe opened up his satchel and pulled from it, a large brown book. He began shuffling through the pages of it frantically, as if he were under a great amount of pressure to provide an answer for what they were witnessing. This, the Stranger could easily understand as he himself had been scrambling to find the very same answers these men were seeking.

The man in the robe stopped on a page and read through it until he found what he was looking for, he then looked up at the man on the horse and told him what was written in the book, pointing at it with his finger. The man on the horse reached up and removed his strange looking helmet, grabbed a rag from inside of his chest plate and used it to wipe the sweat from his brow. The robed man closed the book and placed it back into the satchel. The Stranger stood still as can be, "Do they not see me?" He said as the robed man said a few more words to his counterpart on the horse. The Leader put the rag back into his chest plate and then placed his pointed helmet back upon his head.

He motioned with his left hand toward the robed man as if to tell him to stop talking and move back, two soldiers grabbed him by both arms and pulled him back into the crowd of men. The robed man spoke angrily at the man on the horse as if he were attempting to warn him of something but the leader wasn't listening.

The man then shouted to his men, "Está círculo es del diablo! Una Symbolo de la brujerías de la gente indígenes! En el nombre de dios, estamos aquí para salvar la gente, para cambiarlos o para matarlos. Hombres, atrás! Reyes, Dominguez, Alvarez! Presentan!" (This circle is of the devil! A symbol of witchcraft, used by the Indigenous peoples! In the name of God, we have come to Save the people, to change them or kill them. Men get back! Reyes, Dominguez, Alvarez! Present yourselves!)

All of the soldiers stepped back into the trees and the three names that were called presented themselves in the flesh with a salute and a, "Si Capitan!" (Yes Capitan!) He looked down at them and said one word, "Quemalo." (Burn it.) The men gave acknowledgement then they scrambled in different directions and started calling out other names. Men presented themselves and received orders from the original three, then scrambled again back through the trees. Other men ran up with tools of some kind and began using them to cut into the bark of the trees that stood around the swirling green circle.

As the trees were being sawed into, the Strangers ears were suddenly filled with sad cries of pain and agony. He felt dizzy as the tools made a buzzing noise similar to the humming that afflicted him earlier.

"The cries... They are coming from the trees! I don't know how I know this but I can hear them, they are calling out in pain!"

The soldiers did not seem to be able to hear them, for if they did they would not have continued on, but then... They suddenly stopped! You could hear them all talking amongst themselves with curious voices as if they too began to hear the whales of agony. The Stranger looked over to the Capitan and saw that he was even more confused than his men were. He called out for the robed man again but this time he was yelling out his questions as if the man had all of the answers. The robed man was rushed up to the front of the circle once again but he was at a loss for words as he was not able to explain to the leader what was happening.

Frustrated by this the Capitan yelled out to his men, "Handale Ladrones! Son árboles y nada más, si vas a tener miedo, pueden darles una razón suficiente!" (Hurry thieves! They are tree's nothing more, if you want to be afraid, we can give you a sufficient reason!) The soldiers began cutting into the trees again and as soon as the teeth of each saw began to move back and forth through the skin of the beautiful pine trees the horrid sounds of whaling began again. The Stranger could barely stand the sounds he was hearing but what could he do?

He rose up onto his feet and looked at each one of the men as they obeyed the commands of their Leader. Just then, the motion of the Vortex began moving his insides around though his body stood still. He tried to maintain himself for a few minutes but it became too much, it was as if he were being spun in circles like a top!

He bent over holding his stomach before falling onto his knees again, this time with illness. His mind seemed to forget all about where he was as his body began to heave violently, it was obvious that he was overwhelmed by the feeling and defenseless at the moment because of it. " Uuuuggghhhh!! Uuuugggghhh!! Uuugghhhh..." he grunted as his body tried to rid itself of the contents of his stomach, which was nothing as he hadn't eaten in days. "Uuuuuuuggghhh..." one last time as he seemed to have gotten through the episode alive. "Aww man that sucked, soo bad!" He exclaimed as he spit out the last of the saliva in his mouth and wiped his face on the sleeve of his shirt.

Just then, he realized something. Everything had gone silent, no whaling, no tools and no men talking!? He looked up from the ground slowly and saw that the soldiers and their Capitan were all looking directly at him in complete shock! "Ahh shit, they can see me, can't they?!"

he asked out loud as the soldiers stood still. The look of sheer astonishment was evident on every soldier's face as they saw the stranger manifest from the swirling circle and even though he was puking at the time, it was still a sight most men never get to see. He stood up slowly and raised his hands in the air to show them that he meant no harm.

The Capitan looked over at the robed man for some sort of answer but the man once again had nothing to say. He was just as surprised and caught off guard as the rest of the men were. He looked around shrugging his shoulders with uneasiness while looking back at the Capitan for answers of his own.

"Diablo! ¡Es el Diablo! ¡Soldados, arrestar a ese brujo! Ahora!" (Devil! He is the devil! Soldier's, arrest that witch! Now!) The soldier's were hesitant, remaining where they stood fearful to engage. The Capitan shouted again, this time with anger in his voice, "Soy el Capitán y si yo digo que arrestar a este hombre, ustedes tienen que hacerlo sin cuestion! Sí no, voy a matar a cualquier hombre!!! (I am the Captain and if I tell you to arrest this man, you have to do it without question! If not, I will execute any man that disobeys!!!)

Just then a soldier from the rear began shoving other soldiers out of his way as he walked up to the front of the men. He was a large man with a sharp brown beard, his face was pale and he had deep blue eyes filled with greed and hate. He laughed at the other soldiers as he pushed his way through the final row of men and entered into the circle. He began walking around the perimeter of the circle calling them names. "Pinches cobardes, todos!!! Yo soy el que conquista!! El campeón de hombres, españoles y brujos. Hahahahaha!!!!! (Freakin cowards, all of you!!! I am the conqueror!! The champion of men, spaniards and witches. Hahahahaha!!!!!)

The look of shame was evident on their faces as

they started to shake off the fear and wonder of what they were witnessing and returned to a mindset of murder and destruction. They all encroached upon the circle and started to say the soldiers' name in sync with each other. The Stranger stood at the center of the circle with his hands in the air, knowing that the Soldier would most likely strike him down anyway. Nevertheless he stood his ground without fear.

"Maybe, just maybe, I can make some right out of this wrong, especially since I am already here. Gosh damn this is one big, ugly dude though. Not sure how I'm gonna pull this one off." he thought to himself before saying, "What's up small fry? Don't suppose you're interested in talking things over? I mean, we don't even know one another well enough to be spilling each other's blood right?"The big man looked at the Stranger with confusion on his face, then he drew his sword from its sheath and made it clear that was not there to talk. "I guess that will do, buddy. Just remember, I tried to talk this out! It was you who wanted to continue on the path of violence. Not me."

The big man replied, "Ni sabes lo que me estas diciendo brujo. Estas abborando por tu vida? Hahahaha! Andale hombre's!!" (I don't know what you're saying witch. Are you praying for your life? Hahahaha! Let's go men!!) the big man cried out in an effort to rally his fellow troops as he circled around the Stranger. He turned in unison with the big man ensuring that he did not take his eyes off of him, still holding his hands in the air yet ready for combat. He was a Strange man to the soldiers, frightening even but no matter how strange, he was also unarmed.

To men like the soldier who opposed him, that was all that mattered, who had a weapon and who did not. It wasn't the power within the enemies heart that was taken into consideration and the Stranger knew this all too well. What the big soldier did not know was that deep inside of Stranger's soul burned a flame, small at times but when the time came…

When it was needed the most, the flame turned into a wildfire! That fire would easily consume the soldier even with his shiny armor, pointed sword and evil intent. As to when the flames burned, it was never something that the Stranger could control or predict, though he had faith, as he knew no matter what, it was always with him.These thoughts filled his head as he stood silently in the circle with his arms up, calm and cool. Ready for the big man's attack, for it was clear that there would be no other way.

He no longer heard the cheering of the soldier's as he focussed only on his opponent and the moment at hand. His breathing was rhythmic and smooth, there was no hesitation or quivering, he was still and ready. The soldier had a sword in one hand and with the other hand he was motioning to his fellow soldiers continuing to rile them up before the fight. His fellow soldiers cheered him on as he returned his second hand back to his sword and focussed his attention on the Strange man standing in the circle.

Suddenly the soldier raised his weapon above his head and charged forward hastily!!! Judging by the trajectory of the Soldier's body and the positioning of his blade, it became obvious that the big man was planning on dropping his blade down into the Stranger's head! The Stranger's ability to analyze such things while under pressure came natural, as if he had lots of experience dealing with situations like this in the past. So much so, that even while this large hateful man was about to split his head into two separate pieces for no apparent reason!

The Stranger did not flinch and just as the blade of this Soldier was about to crash into his forehead… He moved his body to the right causing the big man to miss and fall forward onto his face! As he hit the ground near the

Stranger's feet he took a few moments before he understood what had just happened. He looked up at the Stranger and saw that he was standing tall and unharmed. He then looked around at the rest of the Soldiers as they stood in silence, he lifted his sword and inspected its blade in disbelief. The Soldier shook his head in shame and then rose to his feet.

He threw his sword aside as he walked to the perimeter of the circle and grabbed a large long stick from one of the men. He lowered one end and revealed a thin shiny pointed blade at the end of it. He walked into the circle again, this time holding the long weapon with both hands, eyes focussed on the Stranger who stood in the same spot. This time the Stranger didn't raise his hands, instead he found himself standing in a strange pose, half forward, half sideways.

Right hand in front of himself mid chest, left hand up guarding the left side of his body and face. His left leg was back a step or two but faced forward, heel off the ground. His right leg and foot stood a step or two in front of himself and faced forward also, it was like his body was already trained in combat and even if his mind did not remember, his instincts did. He felt powerful in that position, like an explosion ready to go off at any second, all he needed was a movement from his opponent, a sign of attack and the power would release.

"This man is angry, he wants revenge for being shamed. This makes him powerful but it also makes You stupid…" Said the Stranger aloud as the big man circled around him looking for the opportunity to strike a deadly blow with his long wooden dagger. Just as he had done before, he circled around and then suddenly lunged forward, thrusting the dagger straight toward the Stranger's body. The Stranger moved out of the way just as he had done before, though this time, he made a swiping motion with his hand grabbing a hold of the wooden pole just below where the blade was fixed.

He then jerked it toward himself pulling the weapon right out of the big man's hands. The soldier's body still moved forward due to the momentum created by his attack and as he came forward, the Stranger threw a lightning fast kick hitting the man directly in the center of his chest plate!! The power of the Stranger's kick knocked the man clean off of his feet! He hit the ground with a loud clunk sending dirt into the air as if a bomb had been dropped onto the ground. The other soldiers began cursing at the Stranger, booing as their comrade failed to subdue him for a second time.

The Stranger inspected the weapon before breaking it into two pieces over his knee. He then threw them aside and retook his position in the center of the circle ready for more. The voice of the Captain was heard cursing in frustration. He could not believe what he saw and commanded the big man to get back onto his feet. "Andale pues pinche tonto!!! Voy a castigar a toda tu familia por eso!" (Hurry up, freaking stupid!!! I will punish your entire family for this!)

The Soldier stood up and looked at his armor, there was a huge dent resembling a boot right in the center of it. He looked up at the Stranger with shame and despair in his eyes, especially after hearing the Captain's words. He turned back to the perimeter of the circle, this time grabbing a different kind of weapon from one of the other men. It was much smaller and strange looking, it was a mixture of wood, metal and what appeared to be string of some kind. Whatever it was, it didn't appear to be very dangerous.

"Come on now, you got to go for another weapon big guy? Can't handle yourself like a man!?" The Stranger said out loud to the big Soldier as he paused for a moment to listen to what the Stranger was saying. He shook his head in confusion and returned his attention to the weapon in his hands. There was a handle on one end of it and he held onto it with one hand, grabbed a thin stick-like object with the other hand and placed it in the center of the weapon. He then pulled it back against a string of some kind until it locked into place.

It was hard for the Stranger to see exactly what the weapon was but it was starting to look a little more dangerous than before. The soldier pointed it at the Stranger and pulled a small lever back with one of his fingers. It made a loud snapping sound as it launched the little stick-like object toward him with lightning speed! He watched the object come at him as if time slowed down once again, enabling him to evaluate what to do before it reached him. Though, he got a little too caught up in the evaluation process and found that he had run out of time, so he simply moved to the left and let it fly right on by!

The big man yelled out in anger and grabbed another stick, loading it into the weapon. He pointed it at the Stranger once again and then he pulled the lever, launching the stick forward only to see the Stranger snatch it right out of the air! He loaded another stick into it and charged toward the Stranger, getting into point blank range before he fired it again. The Stranger knew that he could easily move aside and allow the projectile to fly past him, so he did just that! As it whizzed by his head, he realized that someone could get hurt if they didn't see it coming.

It flew across the center of the circle so fast that most of the men didn't know what was happening and it plunged straight into the neck of the soldier standing at the opposite side!!! The man groaned out in pain before falling to his knees while grasping the object in his throat. Bright red blood squirted from the man's wound and mouth as he gurgled and choked on it. The Stranger turned halfway around and watched as the soldier fell over and gurgled no more... The men that stood next to him were in shock and neither of them did anything to help their comrade as he died right in front of them.

The big soldier hesitated for only a few seconds after the other soldier died before he dropped the smaller weapon, grabbed a second sword from one of the other men and charged at the Stranger once again with desperation in his eyes. The Stranger knew that the man would continue to fight until one of them was dead, so he made a choice at that moment, to end the competition.The big man swung at the Stranger's midsection from the right side with haste.

The distance that the big man covered was impressive as his long reach combined with his sword length, made his attack virtually unavoidable. The Stranger stepped forward and turned toward the incoming blade. While the blade was in motion, he noticed that it was angled slightly upward instead of being flush and level to the ground. Seeing this, the Stranger lifted his right leg and threw a snapping kick catching the broad side of the blade just right, breaking it in two! The big man swung around violently and fell once again to the ground in defeat as his sword had been shattered right before his eyes.

He looked around at his fellow soldiers as they began to chuckle and laugh at him calling him names under their breath. The look upon the big man's face was one of pure embarrassment as he struggled to believe what was happening to him. He stood up quickly and started tearing off parts of his armor and throwing them at his fellow soldiers in frustration! "Cobardes!! Pinches cobardes!" (Cowards!! Freakin cowards!!) He yelled. Once he finished throwing his tantrum he looked at the Stranger and seemed to challenge the Stranger to a fight, one without weapons or tricks.

The Stranger agreed to the challenge with a simple nod then he began stretching his legs and arms out, almost as if it were a ritual. The big man looked at him strangely but did not attempt to rush him. Once He was done stretching he positioned himself into that stance again, so natural, almost as if it were something that was drilled into him from a life he remembered not. One thing was certain, he knew for a fact now that it wasn't random nor was it just movement.

It was a stance that had authority, purpose. It was beautiful in its positioning and it felt like controlled fury. The big man raised his fists up close to his face and moved forward, throwing them at the stranger's head without reservation. The Stranger moved to the left and moved to the right, dodging everything that came his way effortlessly. The way he moved around was elegant, like a dance yet violent in nature, something none of them have seen before.

The big man became furious at the fact that he could not land a single blow despite his greatest efforts and he soon tired himself out. He stopped throwing punches and fell to one knee as he gasped for air, his face was bright red and sweat poured from his brow. "Brujo! Eres un Diablo!" (Witch! You are a devil!) Said the big man as he knelt in defeat. The Stranger stood in front of the big soldier with a slight look of concern on his face as he felt badly for him. He couldn't help it, the big guy looked so sad.

He moved closer to him as he knelt on the ground in front of him and began to reach his hand out as a peace offering. Just as he did, the big man pulled a dagger from inside of his chest plate and tried to cut the Stranger across the stomach! "Why you dirty rotten fool!!" exclaimed the Stranger as he grabbed the big man's forearm firmly. He then twisted it in the opposite direction and snapped it in half with a loud crack!!

"AAAGGGGHHHH!!!!!!" screamed the big man in agony!!!!!

The Stranger began to feel a sense of anger as he used

the big man's arm as leverage to get him on the ground. Once he had the big man where he wanted him, he raised his fist into the air and said angrily, "It is because of men like you that men like me become what we are... You force us into a life of fighting all because you have to have everything!! Don't you... You are the devil here white man not me and since you refuse to submit, I am going... to kill you. No more mercy!!!!" The feeling of anger became pure hatred and it began to fill his heart as he finished speaking.

Flashbacks of pain and sorrow flowed through him as he pondered the worth of the big man's life. "You should just die, all you do is kill and kill some more... If I dont stop you how many more will you murder, how many will you rape? HUH????!!!! How many have you already raped and murdered?" The big man was lost for words as he could see the Stranger's intent was changing and he had already felt some of his power. "This has to end, it has too!!!!" he yelled as he shook his fist in the air! His vision was clouded and the thoughts were racing through his mind!

He looked at the big man's face and saw that he was nothing more than a scared little man with no heart. Scared for his life, without honor, without purpose, just a helpless slug. Just then, when he was closest to striking the final blow, a memory entered into his mind.

It was far more powerful than any hateful feeling that he was inflicted with at the time and the moment he thought of it, the need to kill the big man was all but gone. It was The Light, it was there, inside of his heart like a wildfire in the darkness, it illuminated his vision clearing away the clouds and anger. It overpowered his hate and filled his heart with Love and mercy. He let go of his breath and slowly lowered his fist. He then released his grip, letting the big man's broken arm go. The big man cried out in relief and then he rolled over placing his head and knees on the ground clutching his arm tightly.

"I don't need to kill YOU!! Any of you little punks, not a single one of you. See what has happened to your champion? You all should let it go! Return home to your families before you suffer a dark fate!" he shouted as he looked into the eyes of the men who surrounded him knowing that they did not understand a word he had just spoken.The big man rose up onto his knees still holding his broken arm close to his midsection and stared up at the Stranger in awe. It was as if he had realized after being spared that he was on the wrong side.

A few moments passed as the Stranger looked into the big man's eyes and as he studied what he saw, he saw the Light deep within him!

"Perdoname Padre Dios por mis pecados..." (Forgive me Father God for my sins...) The Stranger's heart suddenly overflowed with the warmest feeling he had ever felt, it was as if the Light had shown him that anything was possible.

He learned in that moment that hatred was the true enemy and if he were ever going to succeed in his quest then he needed to learn how to Love. The Light made him aware of this and as he continued to look into the eyes of the big man he saw something that was not there previously. It was the spirit of a friend, not an enemy. Just as he raised his hand to the big man in an effort to help him up when the Stranger's spirit suddenly jumped within his body as if it were attempting to escape!! "What the hell?" he thought to himself as the feeling amplified within him.

It felt like that alarm again, the one that seemed to go off whenever he was about to be attacked. He quickly moved over to the left and just as he did, he heard a familiar snapping sound from behind!! Just then, a flying object whizzed by him followed closely by three more! The big man was hit in the chest with two of them, the third hit yet another soldier at the opposite end of the circle, this time in the leg. The Stranger turned around quickly and saw that it was the Captain and two of his men that were firing on him. He looked back to the big man just in time to watch him fall onto his face, snapping the wooden sticks off as he hit the ground.

He turned back toward the Captain and returned to his fighting stance just as the circle of soldiers began collapsing down upon him with swords drawn! The Stranger remembered The Light and even though he felt the power it gave him, he knew not to use it with anger and in that moment he decided that not one more man would die.

Nor would any of them walk away from this circle in one piece, not as long as he was able to defend himself. As the soldiers began to attack, he started punching and kicking every man that came near him! Their weapons seemed to have no effect on him though the soldiers were wielding them with deadly intent. It was unexplainable, even to him but he was able to deflect all of their attacks easily, not to mention the proximity of each soldier allowed him to use their bodies, swords and armor against themselves causing a pile up of men.

Their numerical advantage had been eliminated one man after the other as each charged at him only to end up being disarmed and tossed onto a pile of their comrades. The power he dealt out with each blow was like the power of ten men if not more. Each and every soldier was completely immobilized after taking a hit from the Strange man. The moans and screams of the soldiers could be heard at a great distance as their limbs and pride had been broken, all by a single man. The Captain screamed with fury at his men to destroy the diablo but none of them were victorious in their attempts.

Out of thirty men at least half of them were immobilized by their injuries and the other half were unconscious.

The Captain, two of his soldiers and the robed man were all that was left. The robed man looked at the Captain and then to the Stranger who had just turned back around to face them. He then proceeded to move aside putting some distance between himself and the soldiers as if to say he was not with them in their bad treatment of the Stranger.

He then started walking around the bodies of the fallen soldiers toward the Captain and his last two men. They looked at eachother fearfully and started trying to load their weapons as fast as they could. Once the sticks were set, the soldiers worked hard to pull back on the strings until they locked in place, one soldier finished faster than the other and aimed his weapon at the Stranger. He jiggled one of his fingers causing the string to fling that projectile from the mouth of the weapon with great force and as it was flying toward the Stranger he moved to the right slightly, allowing it to fly by!

"Your little sticks won't save you from your bad decisions, amigos." Said the Stranger humorously. The men looked at him with fear as the second man finished loading his weapon. The Captain's weapon was also ready to go and they both fired their projectiles at the Stranger while the first soldier began to reload his weapon for another attempt. The robed man started shouting words out loud but the Stranger took no heed to them as he was being forced once again to defend himself knocking their sticks to the ground.

He then picked up his pace lunging forward at the three soldiers with a growl! The first Soldier dropped his projectile on the ground and instead of picking it up, he turned around and fled as fast as he could! Then the Capitan's horse began to panic, bucking up and down, throwing the Captain from his saddle onto the ground!It then kicked the robed man clean off of his feet before it ran off into the trees.

The Stranger ran up to the third soldier right as he

was attempting to load another bolt and hit him with a stiff right hook to the face, dropping him onto the dirt! He then turned His attention back on to the Captain as he rose to his feet and drew his sword. "Quieres morir hombre? Es lo que vas a pasar si no corres ahora mismo." (Wanna die man? That is what is going to happen if you don't run, right now.) The Stranger said to the Captain in his own language as he approached. The Captain freaked out when he heard the Stranger speak to him in his native language.

"Eres Indio, tu salvage! Es la verdad, es la verdad. Brujos todos! BRUJOS!" (You are an Indian savage! That is the truth. Its the truth. Witches all of you! Witches!) As the Captain was yelling the Stranger launched himself forward, throwing a snappy kick to the man's face, knocking him to the ground!

"Freakin Chump!" The Stranger said as he landed back on his feet. He then looked down at the Captain who was now lying unconscious on the ground. He stood over him for a few moments to ensure that he was out before turning his attention to the robed man who was probably injured badly if not dead. He ran over to where the robed man was laying, hoping he might still be alive and when he reached him the man was whispering to himself.

"No somos de dios... Nnn, nnooo... Sssommmos, de Diosss..." (We are not of God... Www,wweee... Aaaarreeee, not of God...) Queria las armas de la Luz... De la... Luz. (They wanted the weapons of the Light... Of the... Light.)

The man mumbled to himself over and over as he lay on the ground mortally wounded from the hooves of the mighty horse. The Stranger knelt down beside him, inspecting his body to see if he was able to help him somehow.

"Senor, calmate Senor. Todo va estar bien." (Mr.,Calm yourself Mr. Everything is going to be alright.) The

Stranger told the robed man as he grabbed his hand.

The Robed Man looked over to him and asked, "Eres un sueno si? Van a regresar, los Conquistadores... Van a regresar. Quieren las armas y la fuerza ... No respetan la vida de los indígenas. Mataba millones en el nombre de... de...." (You are a dream, yes? They will return, the Conquistadors... They will return. They want the weapons and the power... They do not respect the lives of the Indigenous people. They have already killed millions in the name of... of...) Then, as he was giving his last words, the breath left his body, his head gently hit the ground and his hand let go of the Stranger's hand.

He felt badly for the man, he saw the struggle between him and the Captain over the situation and he felt that the robed man was probably a good man. He placed the man's arms and hands upon his chest and closed his eyelids.

"I pray to the Almighty that you give this man along with all of the others peace. Forgive me for having to hurt all of them, but I understand that I had no other choice."

When he finished praying the sounds of the wounded men filled his ears with their pain and though it bothered him, he had to let it go. They attacked him first, they tried hard to kill him, forcing him to hurt them the way he did, so he did his best to shake it off. He stood up and turned his attention back toward the Captain. When his eyes reached the spot where the Captain was laying they found that he was not there! He quickly scanned the area looking for any sign of him then, he saw the Captain running away through the trees, like a coward!

Shaking his head He laughed and said, "What a Punk Ass." he thought about it for a moment, debating as to whether the Captain was even worth chasing but then he realized that the Captain would be a great source of information if he could get him to talk. "I could learn

alot about where the heck I am by talking to that fool."
So onward the Stranger went, running through the tree's
after the fleeing Captain and his clinking armor. The
Captain looked back and saw that he was being pursued
and as that realization set in, he fell to the ground as if
the very life had been pulled right out of his body.

A cloud of dust rose into the air as the man hit the
dirt with a huge thud! Surprised by this, the Stranger slowed
down cautiously as he knew better than to trust these guys
when they are down. He came to a stop just short of where
the Captain was laying and as he did, the once proud leader
looked back at him in fear. He then rolled over on his back
and started babbling in his native language, begging for
his life as if the Stranger was going to take it from him.

"You aren't so tough now are you amigo?" asked the
Stranger. The leader's pleas only became louder and more
frantic as the Stranger spoke, so he was about to reach
down and grab hold of the man and help him up. But as
he reached down to grab him, the man screamed like a
woman and then he passed out right where he lay.

"Are you serious bro? I was just gonna help you up,
that's all. I swear." he chuckled to himself as he reached
down and searched the man's armor for any hidden
weapons before dragging him over to the nearest tree.
He propped him up against its trunk and then removed
the man's belt strap. He then used it to tie him securely
to the trunk of the tree ensuring that he could not get
free. After a few moments the Stranger noticed that the
man's horse had returned and was grazing nearby, it had
two large satchels on either side of the saddle and the
Stranger couldn't help but to wonder what was in them.

He stood up and slowly walked toward the horse,
careful not to frighten it. Afterall it had already killed one

man, he didn't want to be next. The horse didn't seem to mind him as he approached it so he tried his best to act normal as he got to its side. "Good girl, that's a good girl. Don't mind me little lady, I'm just gonna relieve you of some weight, that's all. Okie dokie?" he said in a soft voice. The horse was large and brown. No spots, no other colors except for some black toward its hooves. He was in awe over it. He even pondered going for a ride but he realized that it probably wasn't the best idea, not right now anyway.

"I need to find out exactly who these men are as well as where I am before I can find a way out of here." The horse remained occupied as the Stranger opened the top of one of the satchels and began to sift through the Captains belongings. There wasn't much inside other than an extra set of clothes and some water. He walked around the front of the horse talking to it as he went until he got to the other satchel. This one was tied shut, forcing him to break the strap in order to open it. Once he reached his hand inside the bag he felt only one thing, "It;s a book." he thought as he pulled it out and looked at it briefly.

He then reached back into the satchel ensuring that nothing else got missed. "You gotta be kidding me, why would he have this big ass bag and only use it to hold a single book? That makes no sense at all, must be an important book then eh?" he said as he pulled his arm out of the satchel and started to look at the book again. Just as he was about to open the cover, "Thou art the devil! How doest thou speaketh the languages of my people?" The Stranger turned quickly and found the Capitan awake and apparently not as afraid as before.

"Thou? Art the devil? Hahaha!!! Who the hell are you and I thought you only spoke Spanish? Wait, how did I know that again?" he asked.

The Capitan shook his head as if he only partially understood what the Stranger was saying. "Thou art but a peasant, how doest thou speak the languages of my people? I demand an answer, thou bag of puss!!"

The Stranger was surprised by the sudden courage of the Capitan, especially since he was tied up.

"Well now, look at you? Big ball syndrome all of the sudden yeah? I'd be a little more respectful if I were in your shoes right now homie. Now, who are you?" he asked as he walked over to the tree where the Captain was bound.

The Capitan shook his head angrily and said, "Soy el Capitán de los Conquistadores rojas! Somos los mejores guerreros de Castil y ustedes no pueden pararnos! Thou whilst not stop the empire. We whilst prevail over thou and thine forces of evil! I am Captain Dominguez, first Captain of the northern regions of Nueva Espana! The power of the Anasazi whilst be mine, the power of light whilst be mine. Y luego voy a matar a toda la gente indígena!!!! Todos!" The Stranger realized that his assumption was correct, this truly was the lost Conquistador battalion that Lupe and Lee had told him about. And this fool truly was a madman.

The Stranger stopped listening to the Captain's words as they were no longer important to him but there was something that he said that bothered the Stranger. He said, once they had the power, they would destroy all of the Indigenous people...

"Why, though? What is the beef here between them? I thought it was only about the power of Light." Just as the Stranger was lost in thought his mind was drawn away from them by a powerful sensation.

He looked up and turned his head back toward the

clearing and saw the glowing light of the vortex!!! It had reappeared and it was growing brighter and brighter by the second. The feeling that he needed to get back to it filled his heart. He looked down at the Captain and said a quick prayer for the man, "I forgive you for trying to kill me and I pray that The Almighty changes your heart back to the Light. Better hope that we don't see eachother again, now go and help your wounded." He reached down and untied the strap that held the Captain.

He then tucked the book inside of his belt and started walking back over to the clearing. Once he got through the last of the trees and was able to place his eyes on the vortex he was startled to find that it was disappearing! "Oh crap, it's closing... Fast!" he exclaimed as he ran over to it as fast as he could, He dodged the armored bodies of the fallen soldiers, trying not to hit one of them. After all, they had enough punishment for one day. Once he reached the center, he felt like he had just walked into an invisible wall as he was immediately stopped in his place.

Like jumping into a body of water laying as flat as a pancake, everything after that was slow motion. But only momentarily for once he was in the vortex's grasp, completely enveloped within its field of energy, it suddenly stopped spinning...? The light vanished just as it appeared and the only thing he heard was the sound of his own thoughts racing within his confused mind.

"Wait... This can't be good." he said as he realized that he hadn't traveled anywhere. He stood in the very same spot as he did when he entered the field and the bodies of the soldiers remained in their places though the day appeared to be late, not bright as it was. He seemed to be stuck in whatever time frame that these soldiers existed in and he wasn't sure how to proceed. He stood there awkwardly in the center of the clearing looking about like a lost little boy looking for a hiding spot. Suddenly a voice could be heard yelling in the background somewhere, he looked through the tree's for the Captain but did not see him anywhere.

Though he knew the sound of the man's voice, the voice he was hearing did not sound like his. It was higher pitched and it sounded like he was far off. "Far enough that I may be able to get out of here before there is any more trouble." Just as he started to make his way through the pile of silver suited goons, he looked up into the trees and saw a single soldier in the background holding what appeared to be a torch of some kind. The soldier did not look like all the others, he was different somehow.

The soldier moved the flame and set something on fire with it, the Stranger could not tell exactly what it was until a strange sound shook his inner ears and filled the air with its fury!! "Boom!!!" Just then, it was as if the earth itself exploded right in front of him, blasting his body into the air violently without mercy!! Everything after that went completely black!!! There was no sound, no pain, nothing but silence...

CHAPTER TRECE PUNTO CINCO

House of The Black Deer

"Aggghhh, my goodness that sucked!!" he said angrily as he woke up with a severe headache. "I'm not sure what the hell that was but it kicked my ass that's for sure!!" he mumbled as he opened his eyes. His vision was blurred and he was having a hard time seeing where he was as always. The floor was hard, smooth stone not dirt and pine needles. The fresh smell of the trees in the air was all but gone and in its place lingered a nasty stench. "It smells like ass and feet in this place, where the hell am I?" he wondered as he rubbed his eyes to clear away the clouds that blocked his vision. It was dark though there seemed to be a dim light nearby.

He pushed himself up onto his butt and then rose onto his feet. He stopped momentarily to once again inspect himself for any injuries but he found none, though his clothes felt different somehow, they were not the same as the clothes he was just wearing, even his boots were different, "What the hell, did they switch my freakin clothes or what?" he said as he tried to focus on what he was wearing instead of where he was at. Then, out of nowhere a voice began speaking to him in a language that he could not understand, he turned around quickly, startled by the sound of the voice and saw the face of a young woman!

She was standing in a doorway holding a large wooden door open and she was motioning for him to follow her. He shook his head for a moment and tried to determine whether he was in a dream or not but when the young woman called out to him again, the tone of her voice snapped him out of it. There was an urgency in her words and he definitely heard it though he knew not what she was saying..

"Timoneki nechualtepotstoka, uala notech. AxKahn! Tikpiah miakauitl, tikmonekih nik ya! (You must hurry, come with me... now! We don't have much time, we need to go!!!) she said, holding her hand out in front of her. He briefly looked at his surroundings and saw that he was no longer in a place that he recognised,

"What the hell? This looks like... a cell? Am I in jail?" he asked as he began walking toward the young woman cautiously.

She shook her head as if she did not understand what he was saying"Isiuhka, tlakui nomaiuh iuan nechualtepotstoka!" (Hurry, take my hand and follow me.) she said, as she tossed him some sort of blanket. He snatched it out of the air and looked at it curiously. She motioned with her hands for him to put it over himself as cover. She then reached for his hand and grabbed ahold of it tightly, just then, a powerful feeling came over him as if he had just touched lightning!!

They both pulled their hands back in shock at what they had just experienced and looked at one another closely. "Tlen timonekiltia?" (Who are you?) she asked concernedly. The Stranger was at a loss for words as he could do nothing but look at the young woman in wonder. It was very dark and though there was a low burning torch near where they were standing it was not enough light for him to truly see her face. She shook her head and then she grabbed him by his arm pulling him out of the cell and down the dark hallway toward an unknown destination.

"Wait, where are you taking me? Where am I?" he asked as he ran behind her through the corridor. The feeling of the floor reminded him of the hallway from his first vision. In fact, everything about this place made him feel like that was where he was. She still had a hold of his arm and as they were running deeper down the hallway, the torches they passed made him think of other lights for some reason. Strange lights that sat atop tall silver poles, he could see them in his mind lighting up what looked like roadways. It was strange the way feelings and images came to him and when.

He had no control over them nor did he remember much else about the actual images other than what they may be. Whatever the lights he was thinking of where, they were not the lights he was seeing in front of his face. Being lost in thought he was alarmed when the young woman suddenly slowed down. There was another corridor coming up and the Stranger assumed that she was making sure that it was clear before they proceeded.

As they continued on, he saw many other doors that undoubtedly housed other unfortunate individuals such as himself. The Young woman let go of his arm and picked up her pace, they came to a narrow set of stairs that led upward into another dark hallway. They ran up the stairs, through that hallway for fifty feet or so and then they turned left into a larger corridor. At the end of it was another set of stairs and once they reached them, they ascended them to the top. At the top there was a large room filled with people that they passed through to reach what looked to be another door.

As they walked through the crowd he tried not to look at the people in the room as he was afraid that he would cause alarm among them but he did notice that they were all wearing sandals of some kind. They were also wearing robes, not clothes like he was wearing.

"Wait, they look kind of like the people I saw in my vision…Yeah that's right. The people I saw in the audience, inside of the Kings chamber… Or, they resemble them anyway." he thought. He was unsure but the style of their robes and the manner in which they did their hair made him think it was the same race of people. When they reached the exit door, she opened it up exposing his eyes once again to the power of the Sun. He blocked the light from his eyes and placed his hand against the door allowing her to let go of it and when she passed, he passed through after removing his hand from it.

I swung closed with a slam! As he turned back to look at the door the young woman grabbed him by the arm and pulled him along behind her as they started walking down a stone path. "Where are we going?" he asked the young woman but she gave no reply. With each second that passed, his eyes became more accustomed to the light and once he was able to see clearly, his jaw dropped open and all that he could do was look around silently. It was hard to describe, even to himself as he was being led down a city street of some kind, filled with amazing colors and structures like he had never seen before.

Not to mention the inhabitants of the place in which they were, how amazing they all looked. Every bit just as colorful as the structures that surrounded them. It was hard for him to focus on what was going on as there was so much for him to look at. His attention returned to the young woman who was practically dragging him down the street but he could not yet see her face, just the back of her head. They turned left and then they turned right, then they turned right again and then left. After a few more turns, he had lost count of them and gave up counting them.

"It's not like I am gonna remember any of it anyway?"

he said to himself as he continued following behind the young woman. They came to what looked like a river where a small boat was waiting with two other passengers on it, both of whom had cloaks over their heads hiding their facial features. He wasn't sure if the young woman was leading him to the boat or somewhere else nearby but there was nothing else nearby, just other boats.

As she reached the boat, she stepped aboard and was given a large black robe from one of the other passengers. She put it on as she reached out for the Stranger's hand. He gave her his hand and stepped aboard the small boat with a sense of security.

The other passenger handed the woman another cloak and she then gave it to the Stranger, "Xitlatlali inin ipan iuan xitlatekipano mokuaiuh tlatsintlan." (Put this on and keep your head down.) she said. He understood what she meant though he didn't understand her words. He grabbed the cloak and put it over himself letting the smaller one fall to the deck of the boat. He then took a seat on the wooden floor of the boat, staying as low as possible to ensure that he was not seen. For this seemed to be the goal of the young woman as she snuck him out of his cell and now carried him off down a river to an unknown destination.

All this he thought to himself as the two boatmen and the young woman began pushing them out into the water. The others remained silent as they continued moving the little boat downstream. The Stranger didn't want to lift his head up as he had been told to stay low, considering the circumstances. It wasn't difficult to do what she was asking of him. Therefore all he could do was look at the floor of the boat and listen closely to what was going on around them. Just then, as if his ears knew what he was attempting to do, he started hearing the voices of others. Many others from what it sounded like. Some were close and others were off in the distance.

Some sounded as if they were aboard other boats and were now traveling past him in various directions. Out of all these sounds, the one sound that was missing was the sound of running water. He could hear the water as they rowed and as others passed but that was it. There was no rolling sound, no rapids. He could not hear the roar of the moving waters in the distance, it was odd. It was almost as if they were not on a river at all… The Stranger couldn't help but to try and sneak a peek at what was happening so he lifted his head ever so slightly and looked up.

There was a boatman to the right of him, slightly behind and it was presumed that there was another also to his left rear. The young woman was up front and she appeared to be steering the boat as the other two rowed. All he could see was her cloak, he tried looking to his right and then to his left but couldn't really make anything out without making himself seen so he lowered his head again and decided to have faith that it would all work out.

He waited silently as they continued onward without stopping, nor did they talk, not to each other, not to anyone else.The movement of the boat moving through the water was where his mind settled itself, the labors of the two boatmen as they inhaled and exhaled in stride with their rows. Finally, after what seemed like an hour had passed, they broke rhythm and started slowing down. The Stranger could also feel that the Young woman was changing the direction of the boat by the way she was moving around up front.

It didn't take long for the boat and its rowers to come to a complete stop. The sounds of the water splashing up against something and then bouncing back against the boat really stood out to the Stranger for some reason. Just then the Young Woman who was up front walked over to the Stranger and knelt down next to him.

She then whispered to him, "Tiaskh ompa. Timoneki tlatekipano mokuaiuh tlatsintlan mochinpan pa iuan nenemi notech in mitsyuki okatkah ueue? Ximitshiua asikamati?" (We are almost there now. You must keep your head down at all times and walk with me as if you were an elder. Do you understand?) she asked. The Stranger, uncertain of what she was saying, nodded and then shrugged his shoulders in agreement. The woman frowned momentarily, giving the Stranger a brief second to see part of her face. She had soft brown eyes with a certain sparkle in them, her face was perfectly round as well as oval and she had a medium sized nose that was perfectly centered on her face.

She appeared to have a ring inside of it somehow that was sky blue in color. Her cheek bones were high and her chin was a little square with a light cleft in the center. He saw what her hair looked like earlier as she was leading him out of prison through the dark hallways and it was dark brown with medium curls and she had a lot of it! Just then she grabbed his arm and pulled, signaling him to get up. He did as she said and then she started leading him to the edge of the boat.

The other two were busy tying the boat to a post that was fixed into the edge of the water way. The Woman let go of his arm and then she stepped over the edge of the boat. Once she was on solid ground she reached back for him to grab her hand, while she did this she began speaking in a strange manner to him. "Xiuala axkan kolli, nimitstlatlauki tlachi mo step. Nidont mitsneki nik kokaatiaxka oksepa amo teuan? Kiya" (Come now grandfather, come. Please watch your step, we wouldn't want you to hurt yourself again.) she told him aloud.

The Stranger did not understand why she was talking to him like she was, afterall he didn't need her help to get out of the boat, he was a strong man and could do it easily. Just as he stood straight and was about to say something the two boatmen grabbed him and forced him to crouch over a bit, then they forcefully walked him over the boat's edge. The Stranger tried to straighten himself out and almost started to push the other two off of himself but then the Young woman placed her hand on his left front shoulder and smiled kindly at him.

He looked up at her and couldn't help but to smile back. She looked directly into his eyes and nodded slightly as if to inform him that he was in good hands. He received the message that she sent and as he looked upon her soft face he couldn't help but to think of the sweet little face of a baby for some reason. She motioned for him to follow her and after a few moments the Stranger nodded and let his body loose. The two boatmen then helped him over the edge of the boat onto solid ground where he was stable.

Then, one of them pushed his head back down into a crouched position, letting him know that the time to stand straight had passed. He got the hint and realized, that particular boatman had a temper. From that point on he remained crouched over as they wanted him to be as he figured that they were trying to pass him off as an elder of some sort so he did the best he could to play the part. As they were walking he suddenly found within himself a playful side. He started teasing the two boatmen and began walking as if he truly were an elder, making them have to pull him a little from time to time.

The one with the temper could be heard murmuring things under his breath in frustration. He also pulled rather harshly when the Stranger was lagging behind and it was because of this, that the Stranger began having a little fun in his portrayal of a semi mobile elder. He swore that the other boatman reached around the Strangers back a time or two and smacked the angry one. He was overwhelmed with the sensation that he was being led around by Kids!

The further they walked the more he felt like he was gonna have to tell them to behave and to leave one another alone.

"Whoa, I feel like a Dad!" he said to himself in disbelief as he tried to visualize who his father even was. As he thought about his real father, even though he did not know who he was, the image of Lupe kept popping into his mind for some reason. He also thought of the big man and the little lady from his dream. Maybe the two were the same person somewhere, somehow.

He closed his eyes as the boatmen walked him down the street and he concentrated hard on the man from his memory. He saw the man walking next to the smaller woman… "He was a big guy with big hands… his hair was dark, and… That's all I remember about him." he thought. Then, the voice of the Young woman broke his train of thought. It seemed as if they had only walked a short distance from the water but as he took not, he saw that they had actually walked a good distance in the time that he pondered the identity of his Father. They continued on for a short time until they came to a wall of some kind.

He didn't look up much but from what he could see it was made of stone and had a wooden gate where they all came to a stop. The Woman whispered something to a man that was apparently standing guard on the other side. He responded to her and proceeded to open the gate as the Stranger and his captors awaited patiently.

"I'm not so sure about this, I mean, it could be another prison. What if this is all a trap? I mean, I do have to remember that I am not one of them. I am a Strange Man lost in yet another strange land. The sound of the large wooden door reminded him of the Army fort where he and Lee had broken into long ago. Once the door was open, they ushered the Stranger into a large courtyard filled with amazing things that he could not really see due to his hood. They came to the end of the courtyard and walked up to a large door that seemed to open on its own just as they approached it. They all stopped and waited for the door to finish opening before they proceeded through the entryway into the building.

The Stranger felt the grip of his handlers release his arms and as they did the voice of an elderly woman broke through the air. "Satepan timeetkeh in chontaltiokichtli iuikpa okse semanauatl iuan kateh axkan able nik ma kuali ualakan itlatikpa tokal. In ikal in tlilmasatl. (At last, we meet the Strange man from another world and are now able to welcome him into our house… The house of the Black Deer.) she said. As the words echoed through the room the woman who spoke them walked out of the shadows over to the Young Woman who had rescued him from the prison cell, embracing her before helping her remove her cloak.

"Kuali tlatekitl noixuihuan. Mitssemanka, tlaaniliti maluilokayotl nik mo tatah iuan inin kalli ika mo tlatekiti. Tlasokamati." (Good work my granddaughters, as always, you bring honor to your parents and this house with your deeds. Thank you.) she said as the other two walked up to the Woman embracing her also. They then removed their cloaks and revealed that they were not boatmen at all, rather they were also Young Women and apparently all three of them were sisters. The Young Woman who first pulled him from jail seemed to be the eldest of the three as she was the one who primarily gave orders and her demeanor was that of a leader.

Aside from her, the next Young Woman was taller and leaner. She was the one who was reaching over him, smacking the other sister. The playful feeling that had occupied his heart moments earlier seemed to match hers though from look in her eyes, hers was far more powerful than his.

Her hair was not as long as her older sister's and it

was wavy and wild. The color of it matched that of her eyes as they were both a deep dark brown with a hint of red deep within. Her eyelashes were long and they curled up at the ends making every blink visible from a distance. Her face was thin, thinner than her sisters anyway and it was more of an oval shape than round, her nose was longer than her sisters and she also had a ring in the center, colored red. She seemed like the quiet type though she had a certain strength about her and as she looked at the Stranger, it was obvious that she was curious about him and where he came from.

The third Young Woman looked much like the first, though she was slightly taller than her sister and bigger in frame. Her face was also round in shape though her cheek bones stuck out just enough to break the curvature of it, giving it a hint of oval. Her skin color was much lighter than her siblings' skin as it radiated a bronze tone that stood out. Her hair was a golden brown color that was somehow blended with a hint of red and it shimmered in the light as it shone. Her eyes were big and full, much like the moon and they were a light golden brown that matched her hair.

Her cheeks were rosy in color and he could tell that her smile was big, though he had not seen her smile thus far, he could tell. They were three Young Warriors and they stood before an elder, their Grandmother perhaps, with honor.

"Tikpiah okatka chiaka mouikpa, nochontaltiikniu.

Okatka amo ayoui mits ikuauakpa kaltsakualko. Nitlapopouilik uikpa amo mitsihtoka tlen otikatkahkeh chiuaka iuan uikpa amo timoh. Notoka Tepitsin pipiyollin Niin itsaki in ikal in tlilmasatl. Inin teyaochiuanimeh tikitta mitsachto noixuihuan. In ueueer ka onotsa Chikauak Se. Ka in itlatoani inin kalli iuan inon akin kikipoloa. In tlen ome ka Chipaktiyolotli. Ka se siuatli iuimachilistli iuan tlamatilistli. Iuan uikpa no tlen yeyi ixuihtli. Itoka ka Uelilismetstli, kipia nochi inon iueltiuuan tlachiua achihton kualanyotl. Nikpia okse ixuihtli yeseh kualkona texcoco. Ka in tlen ome iueueest in naui.

Nechmaluilokayotlkeh iuan inin kalli. Tinochontaltiiknui kateh ma kuali ualakan nikan. Nimitstlatlauki nechualtepotstoka uikpa tikpiah miak nik tlahtoa." (We have been waiting for you, my Strange friend. It wasn't easy getting you out of the prison unseen. I am sorry for not telling you what we were doing and for not introducing ourselves. My name is Tepitsin pipiyollin, (Little Bee) and I am the last remaining elder of the house of the Black Deer. These warriors you see before you are my Granddaughters. The eldest is called Chikauak Se, (One who is strong.) She is the leader of my house and those who serve it. The second is Yollochipahuac or (Pure heart) she is a woman of knowledge and wisdom. Now for my third Granddaughter, her name is Chicactic Metztli or (Power Moon.)

She has everything that her sisters do with a little extra. I have another granddaughter but she is away in Texcoco. She is the second oldest of the four and they honor me and this house.

You, my Strange friend, are welcome here, please follow me for we have much to talk about.) she said excitedly. The Stranger removed the cloak from his head and then took it off of his shoulders. As he stood there holding the cloak in his hands he noticed that they were looking at him in a very peculiar manner. The elder woman covered her mouth as if she could not believe her eyes and the three young women looked at each other in shock! "Why are they looking at me that way? Do I have a booger or something?" he uttered to himself as he swiped his hand across his nose just to be sure. The three younger women looked back at their elder and they all began speaking quietly in their native tongues.

"I don't mean to be rude but, I really didn't understand what you were saying there. I am not from around here as you all know." he said humbly. The women looked at him curiously as he spoke, not only did he not speak a language they understood but he could not understand them either. But for some reason, he felt like he knew them all and that was a good start. The elder woman said a few words to her Granddaughters before sending them off into the next room. She then motioned for him to follow her as she turned around and walked toward a doorway on the opposite side of the room they were standing in.

Up until that point he had not paid much attention to his surroundings as he was more intrigued with the ladies than anything. Though as he followed the elderly lady some things caught his eye, a painting on one of the interior walls showed three warriors, each with a different color of robe.

The one who stood in the center was depicted as being older, he had slight silver hair and far more feathers in his hair than the other two. His robes were turquoise and black with white edges.The first of the two warriors which was positioned on the right wore white robes with turquoise edges and was bigger than the next. The third who was positioned on the left, wore black robes with turquoise edges and must have been the youngest. It was obviously a family portrait of a father and his two sons. Further into the room another piece of art depicted a warrior wearing black robes with turquoise edges with a woman and three little one's.

He couldn't help but to walk up to it and get a closer look. The little ones turned out to be girls, "All girls? Wow, the guy had his hands full didn't he."

"Okatka tlauel imopakini isiuakoneuan kiiuan kinotetlasohtla ika imochinuan iyolo. Tirememberkeh itlasemanka." (He was very proud of his daughters and he loved them with all of his heart. We remember him always.) she said with a hint of sadness in her voice. She walked over to the depiction of the three warriors and pointed at the young man in the black and turquoise then she walked back over to the depiction of the man and his family and pointed at the man once again.

They both wore the same colors, it became apparent that she was trying to tell the Stranger that he was the same man. The father of the three daughters perhaps?

Though his whereabouts were unknown to him at the time. He nodded at the elder lady and asked, "Is that your Son, the father of the three? Where are he and his wife now?"

The elder woman seemed as if she knew his question, she looked down at the stone floor and shook her head… "Nenemi ipan nepa ohtli axkan. Kopa ika itah akin okatka notenamik kiiuan temini. To tlakah makamo kaua piltin kuitlapantli iuan tahtli opia miamaluilokayotl. Xiuala axkan. " (He walks on the other side now, along with his father who was my husband and his brother. I was left to watch over the girls and ensure that they finished their education. Our people don't leave children behind and their father had much honor. Come now.) she said as she motioned for him to follow her again.

He could see the pain in her eyes as she spoke of her lost ones, especially her Son's. She turned around and walked through the doorway, stopping as she got to the other side as if she were waiting for him to follow her. She was a beautiful lady with shining silver hair that formed one long braid down her back. She was relatively short but her presence filled the room and her strength was obvious. For some odd reason, like everyone he has met so far, she reminded him of someone… Someone especially close to the Stranger's heart and soul.

This whole existence has been so puzzling, his

life was truly one giant riddle after another. He brought his thoughts back to her as he followed her.

Her skin was dark and her face was smooth making her seem younger than she was. Her voice, though he didn't notice it at first, was like a dream. One that he couldn't put his finger on, it was hard not to get caught up in it all. So in the meantime, he just followed her as she led him through the doorway into a larger room. Once they both had entered, she motioned for him to sit down. He looked around at the room but was unable to see details of it for some reason, as he tried looking harder, the voice of the woman broke his concentration.

"Xitlapia akameh atl nimitstlatlauki." (Have some water, please.) she said as she pointed toward an incoming person who was carrying a clay jug and two bowls. The person handed each of them a bowl and then proceeded to fill it with water as they waited. She took a drink of her water and then she motioned once again for him to sit. He then looked down and noticed that the floor was covered with a large beautifully woven, multi-colored rug that was made for this reason. He saw that there were pillows and other miscellaneous furnishings in the room that would insinuate that this was a room for family gatherings.

He sat down and smiled at the woman to show that he was grateful to her for her hospitality. She began speaking to him but he could not understand what she was saying. After a few moments of listening to the woman speak he happened to look down into the bowl of water and saw his reflection. His eyes knew that he was looking at his own face but he did not recognize himself. He began feeling dizzy again, almost as if... Then without warning, the large doors bursted open!!!

He tried rising to his feet but strange men had already descended down upon him and began to club him.

COSME DUARTE

The elderly woman could be heard screaming at them but it had no effect on the men. Then, one of the men was yanked away, then another! The Stranger looked up and saw that the three warriors had come to his rescue! This motivated him to get up and fight but as soon as he moved toward that goal, his head was met with a club and everything went dark. The voices of the elder and her granddaughters could be heard fading into the black. Then, after an undetermined amount of time, he felt himself once again.

"Agghhhh... What a day!" he said as he sat up slowly. He placed his hand upon his head as it began to throb in pain from the blow he had taken earlier. He felt the area where the club had made contact with his skull and found a large knot accompanied by an even larger cut.

"Yeah that sucks bad..." he said as he lowered his hand and saw the blood on his fingers. "Where the hell am I this time?" he murmured quietly as he stood up onto his feet and looked around at his surroundings. It was a room similar to the one he had woken up in earlier that day. Though, the door was closed and there didn't appear to be anyone coming to his rescue this time around. His eyes struggled a bit to see through the murky darkness but once they did all that he saw was a dark stone room. The feeling of dried up blood gripping most of his face was strangely familiar though annoying to say the least. There was an inkling of light underneath the door, presumably from a dim lit torch in the hallway.

He wasn't sure how long he had been in there but the wound on his head told him that it hadn't been but a few hours maybe. He turned and faced one of the walls placing his hands upon it and started feeling his way around the room. He was looking for anything that might be of use but that didn't take him long as the room was just big enough for him to lay down in. His mind started racing into negative places as the realization of being imprisoned set in. His heart started pumping as if he had just run up the side of a mountain and his body began to sweat in strange places.

"Okay, ok... Just calm down man. Calm down, there is an explanation for this and a way out. Just need to be patient, that's all. Just need to remember the Light..." Just as he said the word, the light from underneath the door began to shine brighter. He concentrated his eyes on it until his ears allowed him to hear the footsteps and voices that came along with it. "Who could this be?" He wondered as the noises stopped just outside of the door. The familiar sound of a locking mechanism being manipulated, sharpened his senses as to what was happening.

The door then opened up as the light from the torches revealed the intimidating faces of the warriors who held them. Two of them entered the room holding clubs and restraints of some kind. "Mameh kuauakpa" (Hands forward!) One barked sharply! The Stranger was smart enough to understand what they were demanding of him and so he reached his hands out in submission.

The Warrior who held the bonds stepped forward and wrapped them around his wrists, ensuring that they were secure before grabbing him by the arm and pushing him out of the room into the hallway. "Xikiollini." (Move it.) said the Warrior as he and the other followed him out of the cell. There in the hallway, stood two other Warriors but these were not like the two who had just entered into his cell. They had markings on their faces, on their arms and on their legs. They also wore different robes than the first two wore. The Stranger looked them up and down just as they did to him before another man whom the Stranger did not see, walked up from behind the two Warriors quietly.

The two Warriors seemed to know that he was there because they stepped aside just as he entered into the torch's range of light. He walked directly up to the Stranger and peered into his eyes. "Tlen timonekiltia? Tleka mitspia xia? Ikexki motlakuah kateh ualtika?" (Who are you? Why have you come here? How many of your people are coming?) he asked with authority. The Stranger had not the ability to understand what the man was saying therefore all that he could do was stare right back into the Warriors eyes and show no fear. The Warriors face had similar markings on it also but his were far more intricate and colorful than the other two.

His hair was shaved all the way around but the top remained long and was pulled into a long braid that followed his head movement. He carried no weapons that the Stranger could see other than his stare and it was deadly. The Stranger could feel it.

The Warrior, seeing that the Stranger was of strong heart, smirked and then said to his men, "Inin se ka kichikauak mikis yektli no ikniuh. Xitlakui koninik. Tiuilkeh tetlanilistli ikintepan." (This one is strong, he will die well my friends. Take him to the courtyard. There we will question him.) He then stepped back and to the side allowing his men to move the Stranger down the dark hallway to an unknown location.

"I'll just follow you guys then…" he joked sarcastically as the Warriors shoved him along. After passing through a few different hallways they came to a big door, one of the Warriors opened the door revealing a beautiful night sky along with fresh air to the Stranger's body and senses. "Ahhhhhh… Thank you guys so much. That place smelled something serious you know? This is much better." he said. The Warriors groaned at him as he spoke, shoving him around a little as they brought him to the center of a medium sized courtyard where stood a pole made of stone. When they approached the pole, the warrior grabbed the bonds that held the Stranger and tied them to another strap.

That strap was attached to the pole and it made it impossible for the Stranger, or anyone for that matter, to be able to free themselves from it. "Hey guys, I'm starting to get the feeling that I am not exactly wanted around here. Is that the case, because if it is…" Before he could finish his statement the other two Warriors, followed by their boss, emerged from the doorway and approached him angrily.

Along with them a few others came out also though they were not dressed the same as the previous five. It was apparent that he was on trial for something though he knew not what that was at the moment. He turned and faced them all as they stood next to one another in silence looking at the Stranger in awe.

"How are you all on this lovely evening?" he said awkwardly.

"Ayak mitsmaka mauitstikay otl nik tlatlahto." (No one gave you authority to speak.) shouted the boss Warrior as he once again approached the Stranger.

"We gonna have another staring contest boss?" said the Stranger as the Warrior once again stood in his face.

"Nimitsotlaht olan sepa niknechmoluili mitsakin iuan kexki okachi kateh ualtika. Inin, tikmoneki nitetlaxinilis tli." (I asked you once to tell me who you are and how many more of you are coming? This, you Need to answer.) he said in the most threatening manner.

"I am sorry my friend but I do not understand what you are saying. Even if I did, I can not speak your language. What do you want me to tell you?" he reiterated. The Warrior looked back at the others as they whispered amongst themselves about the Strangers language.

The Warrior turned back to the Stranger and said,

"Kiamotlaxtl auas." (Free him.) to one of the guards.

The guard walked up to the Stranger and grabbed ahold of his bonds. He then loosened them, releasing the hands of the Stranger as he was commanded. He stepped back into position and remained silent. The Stranger rubbed his wrists with each hand as he looked into the Warriors eyes expecting an attack.

The Warrior said, "Inin ka tochan iuan titlachiuh amo tlanteyotia. Niyaoyotl ixichoka in ikal in ehekah. Nikchiua amo kimaui akin pia amo tlamaui. Nikchiua amo kimaui akin pia amo tlamaui, nitekipoloa in ueytlahtoani iuan in Mexica! Xitlachiua nechtikitta? Niamo mitsia." (This is our homeland and we do not appreciate Invaders. I am War Cry of the house of the winds and I do not fear him who has no fear. I serve the Emperor and Meshica. Do you see me, I am not afraid of you.)

He stepped up and placed himself chest to chest with the Stranger, face to face. The feel of the Warriors breath on his face was surreal, the Stranger knew that he could not show fear or the Warrior would see it. This was a moment that could change the direction of everything from that moment on, he had no choice but to rise to the occasion. This man who faced him, he was fierce and proven. He was the real deal and surely had many enemy kills to his honor. He was in no way, the kind of man you wanted to portray weakness to. Therefore the Stranger used all of the courage that he had to keep himself steady in the Warriors eyes, not to show even a splinter of weakness.

To this point in his life, this was by far the hardest challenge he has had to face. As he concentrated on holding strong he started to feel something inside of his heart, that old familiar feeling of power. Though it didn't feel as it had in the past, it was as if it were allowing him to remember that it was there but not enough for him to tap into. So he let it be and faced this awesome man with as much of his own heart as he could.

Then a familiar voice rang out! "Yaoyotl choka!! Inin ka mo chiuaka? Ken mitsuelia nokal inin ohtli? Tlen motemachti anikiya mitsixitlane mili axkan? Iuan mo temini? Intla okatkah kinikan challengekiy a tiuikpa momakteka ualis!" (War Cry!! This is your doing? How could you disrespect my house that way? What would your mentor think of you now? And your brother? If he were here he would challenge you for this betrayal!) shouted the elderly woman as she stormed into the room!

She was followed by the three younger Women that he had already met but there was another Woman with them, one that he hadn't seen before. "She must be another granddaughter." he thought as he watched them storm into the courtyard. The Warrior turned his back on the Stranger and slowly stepped toward the elderly woman. It was as if he were testing the Stranger's honor to see if he would attack him from behind. The Stranger felt that this was the Warriors intentions and remained where he stood. Though not out of fear, out of honor.

The Warrior said to the elder, "Amokiya notemachti ani iuan no temini ka kokaa ik in amokuali mitsmantin mochintin tilapia tlachiuhtli?" (Would not my mentor and my brother be hurt by the bad things you all have done?)

The elderly woman responded like a whip, "Xitlachiua amo tlatlahto nechualnik inon ohtelpochtli! Niayemo tlaxitokako. Mookichuan tlapia postehkik in nauatili kiiuan moneki ka oanilitia achto in ueytlahtoani! Axkan kaua inin okichtli iuan ya anoso ixtli in nauatili!" (Do not speak to me in that way, young man! I am still in command! Your warriors have broken the law and it must be brought before the Emperor! Now, leave this man and go or face the Law!) she exclaimed. The Warrior then called one of his men in another part of the room. The elder woman looked puzzled by the Warriors move before looking over at the man who was called. He approached them carrying some sort of object in his hands.

What the object was, the Stranger nor anyone else in the room could identify as it was wrapped inside of what appeared to be a robe. The man held it, palms up, on both of his inner forearms as he scurried to his master. The Warrior then turned his attention back to the Stranger before retaking his previous position directly in front of him.

When the servant arrived the Warrior then turned to him and said, "Tlen ka inin mitsintla amo nikan nik no tlakah niman tleka mitsokatkah?" (What is this? If you are not here to destroy my people, then why were you armed?)

The look upon everyone's face was one of intrigue as they awaited the Stranger's reply. The Stranger looked over at the man who held the object and then down at the object though he could not see what it was as it was wrapped in a dark colored robe. He looked back at the Warrior and said, "I'm sorry but I don't know what you are asking me? I don't know what you want me to do here brother, I really don't." The Stranger finished saying what he had to say and then the Warrior stepped back as did the man who held the object.

The warrior turned and faced the elderly Woman along with her troop of young Warriors. He then said, "Inin okichtli pia postehkik tonauatilua n ok otipaleui ichololistli iuikpa kaltsakualk o. Tleka? Tikpiah aik se okichtli tlasohtla inin tlapia tiseenkeh akantetlane ui se teyaochiuali stli kias.

Intla ti eliutilastli nik mitsniman oyaua kiyanon in Ohnantli. Moixuihuan kateh nik ka teopixkimeh yeseh mitskipoloh onsenka miek toteouan. In ikauiuh pia uikpa in ikal in tlilmasatl. Nitlaihto, inin okichtli uikilia miki kiuikpa. Niuil inik mo iuan tiyaochiuas kehkeh mikistli!!" (This Man has broken our laws yet you helped him escape prison. We have never seen a man like this nor have we seen such a weapon as his! If you wish to grant him citizenship then you went about it the wrong way Mother. Your Granddaughters are supposed to be priests yet they obey you more than our deities. The time of glory has passed for the house of the Black Deer. I say, this man should die for his crimes. I will allow him to defend himself and we will fight to the death!!!) shouted the Warrior with great authority!!

His men cheered a dreadful cheer as he raised his hand in might! Just then the eldest of the Granddaughters stepped forward and yelled out, "Inin okichtli ka akentenchiu ani iuan ikamo nauatlahtol ukuepa. In ueytlahtoani motlakakisn eki isasanil. Tiuil amo teyaochiua iixkich niman."(This man is innocent and has been imprisoned without trial. The Emperor needs to hear his case and until then you will not fight him! Not until then.) The Warrior sneered at her demands and began circling the Stranger in an aggressive manner.

The Fourth Granddaughter whom the Stranger had not met joined her elder cousin and proclaimed, "In nauatili kihto inon akin kitsatsayani se nauatlahtol ukuepa achto se tlahtokalistli. Ayak uel ka anoso achto niman! Amo uel teh techintimid ate yaoyotl choka!" (The law requires that anyone who breaks it gets a trial set before a council of elders and until they have that trial. No one can be executed before then! You can not bully us around War Cry!)

"Wow that little lady has got the fire doesn't she?" the Stranger said out loud as he looked around at the others in awe. Just then, more of the Warriors men walked into the courtyard and upon seeing the way the Young woman was yelling at the Warrior, they ran toward her speedily with their weapons drawn. This is when the Second and third Grand daughters jumped into action blocking the men from getting near their sister and cousin.

The second Granddaughter said, "Intla ka mitstlen tlaneki niman tikpia inko yek tlan uey okichtli!

Manel nose siuatl, nikpia ualixtlamatil istli semani teteyaotla!" (If a battle is what you seek then you have come to the right place big man. Though I am a woman, I am highly experienced in defeating simpleton soldiers.)

The third Grand daughter chimed in and said, "Tleka tika tlasohtla inon? Mitsokchiua tlachiua inon tlahtolyotl ako anoso itlah? Kisohtla mitstlen tlaihto, san tlachuia mosemiluit ekiuh iuan ka kaktok."(Why are you talking like that? Did you just make that whole speech up? Like he cares what you say, just do your job and stay quiet.) she said as she stood partially behind her sister ready for combat.

"Tlen? Ka kaktok mitsuilmits? Tlasemanka anilitika ako ipan in kauitl." (What? You be quiet!! You're always bringing weird stuff up at the wrong times.) replied the second eldest.

Then, the voice of the eldest granddaughter rang out, "Mitsuil omeixtin ka mitskaktok! Techkichiua ya tlachi amokuali!" (Will you both shut up! You're seriously making us look bad.)

The Warrior laughed as he paced around the Stranger. "Se teh siuah mochintin. Mitssanima n uil itta tlamantin nooh. As uikpa inin kiokichtli, uetsi,s nik no uil anoso noteyaochiu alis." (You are a bunch of women, that's all. Soon, you will see things my way. As for this man, he will fall, either to my will or to my weapon.)

The voice of the elderly woman rang out once again, "Tikpia okatka yaoyotl choka!! Axkan anmoh iuikpanikan mitsachto tetlachiuilist li uehka ompa itlakoltilistli nik mosenyelis maluilokayo uh." (You have been warned, War Cry!! Now remove yourselves from here before you cause further harm to your family honor.) The Warrior looked to his men and then commanded them to attention. He then walked over to the servant who carried the object and placed his hands on the robe ever so gently.

He waited there for a few moments and then he said, "Intla moeliutilas ka nik tlakui iachto in ueytlahtoani, kiniman yas achto in ueytlahtoani. Okichtin, tlakuepa kiinik iuan xitlachi iachtika!" (If your wish is to take him before the Emperor then he will go before the Emperor. You have my word. Men, return him to his cell... And watch him closely!) He then lifted his hands off of the object and watched his men as they secured the Strangers wrists. One of them began acting unreasonable as he was struggling to properly fasten the bonds and when the Stranger pulled his hands back, the guard struck him on his already open head wound, knocking him to the floor.

The other guards, assuming that he was resisting, rushed over and began stomping on him and beating him with the ends of their spears. The shouts and yells of the women could be heard but not for long as his consciousness had turned off... Silence ensued...Then,

"Ahhhhggghhh... That could have gone better." he joked as he returned to life. Or so he thought... It only took a few moments until he realized that something was wrong... There was no light nor was there any sound, it was completely silent. "I don't even feel my own heartbeat, I must be dead... Right?" He asked but strangely no sound came from his mouth, he said it again but he did not hear his voice. "I know that my eyes are open yet I can not see. I know that I can hear but my ears do not hear, not even the sound of my own voice!!" He shouted but once again, he heard nothing.

Then suddenly, a voice that was not his own infiltrated his ears, one from the past... One that he had longed to hear but hadn't nor was he sure that he ever would again. "Your eyes will see only what you want them to see my Love. Your ears, they hear my voice yet can not perceive who I am... Your heart... It is the only one that knows me... The Light, let it guide you through the realms, all the way back to me. Back to your love, your life... Find me!"

"It's you isn't it? The woman from the desert, why can't I see you? Why can't I touch you?" he asked but heard no reply. He stood still and tried hard to envision her face, her eyes, her smile. But for some reason he could not no matter how hard he tried. It seemed like he had waited for days to hear her speak again but to his heart's dismay, he heard nothing.

Just as he was about to give up hope, the voice said, "It is because I am no longer in bondage...

You have freed me. Now I need you to come back to me... No matter how hard it may get... Come... Come back." And just as the voice came, it also went. Floating upon the winds if there were any inside of this darkness...

"No, don't leave, please! I mean, I've been alone since I saw you and all that I am really trying to do, is find you..." Silence ensued. "No... please don't leave... I ..." he shouted as he fell to his knees in heartbreak, sobbing as he realized how much he loved her. He raised his head up and cried out, "Who are youuuuuuuuuuuuuuuuuuuuuuuuuuuAAAAAggggghhhhh!!!!!!!!!!!!" he shouted!!!! His voice carried on into the darkness along with his broken heart until his mind once again went blank....

CHAPTER CATORCE

Demons of War

"Despiértate kabron brujo!! Despiertate ahora mismo!!!" (Wake up you goat, witch!! Wake up right now!!) yelled out a voice from the dark, then suddenly, the sensation of cold water being dumped over his body shocked him to his core,

"What the hell is going on around here?" he yelled out as his mind and body finally aligned in a manner that brought him to his senses. As the water fell away from his eyes and his vision cleared, he could see that it was no longer day, the night had taken over and it was cold out! There was a large fire nearby but he could not feel its warmth. Though it enabled him to see that he had been taken prisoner! "How in the hood did I get myself caught up in this mess?"

Not only did he get caught but ironically it was by the very same Captain he had freed earlier. He had many men with him as if they were all healthy again but they were not the same men from before. These men were new and did not witness the events of the day as the Captain did.

"Atención hombres!!! Este brujo, es el hom," (Attention men!!! This witch is the ma,)

Just then, abruptly interrupting the Captain, another

voice rang out from the background, "Basta!!!!" (Stop!!!!) it was a sharp voice, catching the Captain and the men off guard. The Captain looked back quickly as if he knew he was doing something wrong while the men who were with him, all stood straight up at the sound of the other man's command! Putting their arms at their sides and their feet together, they made a loud clanking noise for a few seconds as the men were getting into their positions.

They then turned and faced each other taking a few steps back, creating an opening through the crowd as the Stranger looked on. Once the silver suited men were clear, the Stranger saw a man standing at the other end of them, another Captain perhaps or possibly someone superior.

"I got a bad feelin about this guy…" He said to himself as he turned his attention to how he was tied up and to what he was tied up against. Turns out he was tied to a tree, though not with a strap, not even with ropes but with chains. "Ahhh the irony of it all." he said as he remembered tying the Captain up to a tree earlier. Just as he chuckled at his situation, it suddenly reminded him of the position he was just in. He became preoccupied with the memory of being tied to the pole as the Warrior was questioning him.

"Whoa it's like, everywhere I go, I am in some kind of trouble.." As he was lost in his thoughts, the man had already walked himself up to the Stranger and stood before him silently.

"Atención brujo!!" (Attention witch!!) yelled the cowardly Captain, catching the Stranger's attention. He snapped out of it and looked up to find a tall, slender man standing before him, wearing the same type of armor as the others but slightly fancier with some golden edges. His face was thin and long, he had blonde hair that fell at his shoulders and his eyes appeared to be a sharp blue color.

He had a thin mustache that was curled at each end and a pointed goatee that didn't look to be natural. He had a sword on his side but for some reason, it didn't seem like a sword.

It was strangely designed in the most intricate way and it appeared to be made of gold. He was wearing black gloves over his hands, much like the Military commander called Jackson that he saw a few nights ago. The man noticed that the Stranger was peering at his sword so he grabbed a hold of it and turned his body to the side as if he were guarding it. He looked down at it and then back at the Stranger in disgust,

"De donde vienes brujo? Eres de la tribu? Dime lo que sabes y no te voy a matar. Si no... Vas a morir, pero no tan fácil. Vas a quemar en el fuego de dios! Ya Capitán, muévase!!!" (Where are you from, witch? Are you from the tribe? Tell me what you know and I won't kill you. If not... You will die, but not easily. You will burn in the fire of God! Move it now Captain!!!) yelled the man as he stepped aside allowing other men to rush over to the Strangers position and attempt to hold him down while others loosened the chains.

"Tienen caución, este hombre lo mataron todos mis soldados con la fuerza del diablo! Tienen mucho cuidado con el." (Use caution, this man killed all of my men with the powers of the devil! Use extreme caution with him.) The Captain's tone was so sincere that he almost convinced the Stranger that he actually had killed all of his men but he knew that it was not the case, he simply disabled most of the Captains men. It was actually the Captain and two of his personal guards who killed a man, not him. Once he felt the tension of the chains break he felt like making a move, afterall he was able to defeat multiple soldiers earlier, why not do it again?

He thought, but after a few moments passed, he realized that if he reserved himself, he could learn more about what was going on. "Maybe, just maybe, I can find a way to stop these guys from fulfilling their destiny... I mean, what did the man in the chamber say about them?" he thought to himself as he tried to recall the man's words.

"He said that when they entered into the Mesa and had to face themselves, the evil that existed within them overpowered them and in the process it caused them to commit deeds of unspeakable evil to each other. So much so, that the two demons were able to manifest once again into our realm to hunt and torture those who entered this place." The words he recalled gave him the chills as he sat there against the tree wet and cold.

"So, why would I be sent here? To this particular time and place? What good could I possibly..." Just then, interrupting his train of thought, he was yanked up onto his feet by his hair!! "AAAGGGGHHHHHH!!!!!!!!" he yelled out in pain as five soldiers surrounded him from all sides! He then felt the points of their swords press into his flesh, ensuring that he didn't make a move. Aside from being chained to the tree, his hands were also chained together with shackles around his wrists. Though he felt like lashing out, especially after they pulled him up in such a manner, he chose, once again, to play along with them for truth's sake.

Besides, the last thing he wanted to do was to lash out in anger, he could feel it filling them. They walked him cautiously over to a large pole that was placed into the ground like a post and proceeded to tie him to it. "Well wouldn't you know! A pole, and you're gonna what... tie me to it? Haha, How original is that?" he said aloud as they proceeded to chain him by the head, the chest, just above the knee and then by the ankles to the pole. Once they were finished, the men began placing small pieces of wood all around the pole just as they would if they were about to light a fire.

The Stranger looked at them curiously as they

performed their duties as commanded. "This must be the order of the new Boss man on the scene." he thought as he watched the soldiers closely. Just as he thought of him, the man appeared from the back and as he made his way toward the Stranger, he smiled eerily.

"Atencion!!" (Attention!!) yelled out the Captain as his apparent superior was once again in the area. The Soldiers all jumped into their positions wherever they stood and became silent. "Ya sé que eres un diablo, pero lo que yo quiero saber es, porque lo mataste a mis soldados? Lo mataste sobre 20 hombres sin tener misericordia… Dejaste solo el Capitán vivo, ni El Padre vivió. Porque y mas importante, como?" (I already know that you are a devil but what I want to know is why you killed my soldiers? You killed over 20 men without mercy… Leaving only the Captain alive, not even the Father lived. Why and most importantly, how?) he asked in a condescending manner.

The Stranger thought about what the man was saying and it occurred to him that he was being accused of murder, "Wait, what did you say? Ummmm, Uh, que me dijiste?" asked the Stranger curiously… The soldiers all began to speak under their breath as they realized he could communicate with them. The Commander stepped forward and without warning reached back with his left hand and then let loose swinging his hand forward slapping the Stranger across the face with the back of his hand! "Dónde prendiste mi lengua brujo!? Eres un diablo y estas culpable por matar 20 soldados de Nueva Espana y vas a pagar!!!"

(Where did you learn my language witch? You are a devil and are guilty of murdering 20 soldiers of New Spain and you are going to pay!!!) shouted the commander with a certain pitch in his voice that struck the Stranger familiar.

"Wait a minute,,, This guy sounds familiar!? His voice,

his thin build, where have I seen him before? Thought the Stranger to himself as he looked at the man's face in wonder.

"Donde handa su gente eh? ¿Dónde está tu tribu de diablos kabron? Quieren sus vidas, quieren sus armas, quieren todo y no voy a parar hasta que tenga todo!! Si tu quieres vivir, vas a decirme lo que quiero saber!! ¿A quien te dio sus poderes? Dime ahora porque si no, lo voy a quemar… ¡Handale Sargentes!" (Where are your people eh? Where is your tribe of devils, you goat? I want their lives, I want their weapons, I want everything and I will not stop, until I have everything!! If you want to live, you will tell me what I want to know!! Who gave you your powers? Tell me now for if not, you will burn… Lets go Sargeants!) he yelled out sharply!!

Just as the words left his lips three men ran up from the back with torches light! They stopped just in front of the Stranger and anxiously awaited their orders. As this was going on, the Stranger was busy thinking about what he was going to do. It was obvious that the men whom the Captain had commanded was just a small portion of the soldiers that were in the Mesa. It was also obvious now, that the man who was speaking was the real commander of these soldiers and he wanted answers. Answers that the Stranger would not give to him even if he knew them!

"At this point, I think it is safe to say that these are most definitely the fools that Lee and the Man in the chamber had spoken about. Still not sure what to do about it though, I mean, how can I change things without making them worse? Not only that but I think he's saying that I killed all those men? I did not kill them, I only hurt them, disabled them even but I never killed anyone. Right?" he asked himself again even though he already knew the answer. He looked into the eyes of the men holding torches then back to the Commander just as he began to speak again.

"Porque mataste a mis hombres? Dime la verdad!!! Voy a darte una chansa mas y si no me dices porque mataba mis hombres, si no me dices donde andan su gente... Vas a quemar..." (Why did you kill my men? Tell me the truth!!! I am going to give you one last chance and if you do not tell me why you killed my men, if you do not tell me where your people are... You will burn...)

The Stranger looked him dead in his blue eyes and said, "¡La única persona que vas a quemar es tu!" (The only person who is going to burn is you!) Now, let me go or I will be forced to thrash you!" said the Stranger in a tone that seemed to silence them all. The Commander sneered and nodded his head, giving the order to light the fire beneath the Strangers feet. The three men looked at each other and then at the Stranger, the three of them hesitated and for that the commander pulled out a strange weapon from his belt and pointed it at the nearest soldier.

Not one moment later a blast of flames came out of the end of the weapon, entering into the head of the soldier and exiting the opposite side. Blood and brain matter sprayed both of the other two soldiers as they dropped down to the ground in fear!! Everyone who was in attendance was shocked at the sight of what had just transpired but the Stranger knew that it was coming.

"It's happening, just like it was supposed to. I can feel the evil welling up within all of you and soon you will turn on one another. Soon, you will all be dead and no one will know what happened to you. May the Almighty bless your," Just as he was about to bless the Commander, he dropped the weapon he was holding and pulled his sword from its sheath. He then pointed it directly over the heart of the Stranger and began pushing it into his chest!

"Uuugghh!!!" said the Stranger as the point of

the Commander's blade began to pierce his flesh. It was then that he realized that the Commander's saber wasn't like any other blade, it was different somehow, perverse in its nature. He began to sense that his end was near, the blade caused pain unlike any pain he had ever felt and it was growing, like a sickness.

"En frente de dios, eres condenado a muerte por fuego!" (In front of God, you are sentenced to die by fire!) he said just before he pulled back his saber and then swiped it across the Stranger's face!! The blade opened a nasty cut on his left cheekbone and on his head! The Stranger winced in pain but made no cry, nor did he moan, he simply looked at the Commander smiled and then said,

"I know who you are… Yeah, I've seen you before. Now, I understand…"

The Commander sneered once again as he watched the blood pour down the Strangers face onto the ground below. He then turned to the two soldiers that held the torches as they were still crouching down fearful for their lives. The Commander swung his sword in a back hand motion smacking one of them directly in the mouth with the side of his blade. "Whack!!" The blade undoubtedly knocked the young man's teeth in as his head flew backward violently before falling on the ground!! The remaining soldier quickly snapped to and leaned forward with his torch, lighting the sticks underneath the Stranger's feet.

Once the sticks caught fire, the Commander once again swung his saber in a swift powerful manner and removed the third soldier's head from his shoulders! The other men who stood in the back looked at one another in shock, then out of nowhere, the Capitan started laughing uncontrollably. The Stranger began to see something as he looked around at them all, it was dark. Like a cloud of black smoke inside of a dark room it floated along through the soldiers bodies like it was dancing. From one soldier to the next it passed, until it came to a certain young man.

The cloud seemed to just pass over him as if it were not able to infect him as it was doing to the others. He noticed that the soldier was not the same ethnicity as the others, he was darker and his eyes were thin like Lee's.

He was kneeling down next to some kind of weapon, cleaning it as if it were his own. It was clear that he was highly uncomfortable with the situation at hand and that he was separating himself from it. "Wait!! That's the little guy I saw just before I got blasted! I remember him alright, something is definitely different about that guy. The shadow stays away from him... That is most interesting indeed." he said. On the other hand, everyone else began acting like maniacs in the way they were responding to their Commander's actions. It was becoming a dangerous situation all the way around.

The Stranger, so caught up in what he was witnessing, almost forgot that he had just been set on fire and was now probably burning from his feet to his waist. Just as his mind realized this, he looked down and saw that the flames were indeed reaching up to his waist but strangely, he was not being burned by them... Somehow, someway, not even his clothes were being scorched by the heat of the fire! "What in the world is happening to me!? It's as if someone or something were protecting me." he said in amazement. Just as the words left his lips he remembered the Light!

"It has to be!! There is no other explanation than this, how can there be?" As the truth sunk into his heart, he felt the power building up inside of himself once again. The kind of power he had no way of describing, it was so much more than he could comprehend and it was blessing him with its presence!!! With this new found confidence he looked up at the Commander and smiled once again.

The Commander, having seen that the Stranger was untouched by the flames, raised up his saber and lunged forward as if to stab him in the chest with it! Just as the tip of his sword was about to reach the Stranger's flesh it was knocked away by the sword of the cowardly Capitan himself!

"El es mio para matar!! Yo soy el que manda aqui, no vamos a seguirte Comandante Morales!!" (He is mine to kill!! I am in command here, we will no longer follow you Commander Morales!!) The Commander, surprised by this maneuver, laughed as if he were already expecting this to happen. He looked down at his sword and then over to the Captain with an evil smile. Just then, the Stranger saw it! The eyes of the Commander... They turned blood red right in front of everyone and smoke seemed to rise from his mouth! The Captain saw this and laughed like a madman once again but he did not back down.

The two officers began to circle one another as their Soldiers made a larger circle around them in an effort to watch the duel. "This would be a very good time to get out of here." he said to himself as the soldiers were all preoccupied with the fight. As he stood there, tied to the pole, surrounded by flames, he thought to himself about what he would do next. His face was bleeding badly and the soldiers wouldn't be occupied for long. "I really need to come up with a plan here." he said as he tried to free himself from the chains. "RRRRRRRrrrrrrrrrrrrrrr!!!!!!!!" he grunted as he tried with all of his might to break loose from their grasp but was unable to do so.

The harder he tried to break them, the tighter the chains seemed to get, not only that but it seemed that his ability to remain burn free was fading. The heat from the fire was beginning to burn the soles of his feet and the

272

wounds that he received from the Commander's saber were now infecting his body with something!! He calmed himself down and tried centering his spirit as he had done in the past but the situation was proving to be a bit too much for him. Though he was able to feel the power of the Light within him, he wasn't able to access it and that was a problem considering his current circumstances.

He tried repeatedly to steady himself but the heat and the overwhelming presence of evil was getting the better of him and his concentration would not hold. The terrible feeling of panic began to set in as he tried harder and harder to get free from the chains but was only tiring himself out! He looked over to where the Commanders were squaring off and saw that they were indeed fighting each other! The Cowardly Captain sure wasn't acting like himself, he was fighting the Commander with such fury, such hatred, that any evil leader would be proud of him.

The Commander was the same, it was as if two separate forces battled each other for control over the men, and the Stranger. "Muuueeeerrrrtttteeeee!!!!!" (Diiiieeeeeee!!!!!) cried a voice from the crowd of men as a soldier rushed into the circle with an axe preparing to strike the Captain from behind, when another soldier saw him and ran his sword through the attacking soldier's stomach.

This caused an all out riot as the remaining soldiers began fighting amongst themselves, slashing and stabbing each other without mercy. The Captain's eyes and demeanor had changed dramatically just as the Commanders had and the manner in which he fought, it was as if his cowardice was all but a memory. The Commander's anger matched his rivals and as they battled one another for the right to kill the Stranger and rule the men, he was still tied to the pole lost in thought.

"How did the Captain get so powerful all of the sudden?

I just don't understand, he was such a weenie!" he thought. Just then, a vision crept over him. His mind rewound itself to a few hours earlier when he noticed that the vortex was closing. This was the last time he saw the Captain or so he thought. He freed the man and then ran over to the vortex but when he stepped into it, it seemed to stop working but that was not the case. Upon entering the circle he felt its motion but it did not seem to take him anywhere and when he noticed this, he tried to escape but ended up being captured instead.

This was because he was briefly stuck in between two different time frames and while he was there a horrible thing happened. He suddenly saw a vision of the Captain walking cautiously through the trees after he witnessed the Stranger disappear into the vortex. As he approached, a dark shadow came to him frightening him onto his knees.

The Captain began to beg for his life but was stopped from speaking. There were a few moments of silence but by the way the Captain was acting it was as if the Shadow had been speaking to him, offering him a deal of sorts. The Captain looked around strangely at all of his men before rising to his feet... He then bowed his head to the Shadow and grabbed the first sword he could find. He then walked over to one of his wounded men, who was begging the Captain for help. Once he reached him, the Captain lifted his sword shaking like a scared little boy, tears began pouring from his eyes...

"Aaaaaaaagggggghhhhhh!!!!!" he screamed out like a pained animal and as the soldier lifted his arms in an effort to protect himself, the Captain ran his sword through the soldier's chest plate taking his life!! He pulled the sword from the soldier's lifeless body and cried angrily! Like a madman, he looked around enraged by the situation... He then proceeded to stab and slash the rest of his wounded men in a devilish episode. His men screamed and tried to fight, some tried to escape but they were unable to do so. The Captain's personality changed with each death, he became more and more comfortable with the evil he was committing with every swing.

The shadow grew so large around him that it seeped into his body and encircled it from the exterior. The Stranger couldn't believe that this was happening while he was right there, even though he really wasn't. "That is how he became so brave, freakin punk! He tried to blame me for all of that murder and now he wants to finish me off but I won't let him... I can't.

One thing I want to know is how did they capture me? What was that blast that knocked me out?" He thought back to when he tried to run from the circle as he heard others coming. "Wait, how did I not see all of those men dead? It's like I didn't even notice them. Poor bastards." he thought. Then, inside of his mind he saw that he was hit by a weapon much larger than any he had seen previously, it was the very weapon that the strange soldier was cleaning! "It was that little black thing on wheels? That little dude hit me with that thing and that is how I ended up here...

Yeah, I remember now, but why were the shadows avoiding him if he is one of them? I just don't get it?" Being lost in all of these thoughts kept him from paying attention to what was now happening around him but something told him to look up and when he did, he saw the Commander charging directly at him, saber ready, eyes fixed! "Oh great, here we go again!" he thought as he braced himself for a final blow, knowing that he was weakened and vulnerable. He had survived many battles already but wasn't sure that he was going to make it through this one.

As the evil Commander charged toward him with his glowing red eyes, he looked up into the sky and gave thanks to the Light, to the goodness of the world, to the Almighty Creator for all of His help through the dark times. He thought of the poor soldiers who he had hurt earlier and how they would never return home to their families because of his deeds.

He prayed for forgiveness for all of his wrong doings and as he finished, a sense of peace came over him and he was ready to die...

CHAPTER QUINCE

Sacrifice of Oneself

Just then, he looked back down at the Commander as he continued his charge toward the Stranger and closed his eyes… Just as he prepared himself for the final strike, a loud boom followed by a shock wave shook the camp, throwing soldiers in the air like toys. Including the Commander!! "Whoa shit!!!" Shouted the Stranger as he opened his eyes just in time to see the commander hit the dirt with a thud!! The Stranger kept his eyes on the man expecting that he would get up onto his feet at any second and just as he thought of it, the man started coming back to life. He got up onto his hands and knees and started rubbing his head with one hand.

"I really need to learn to stop visualizing things like that. It clearly doesn't work out in my favor." he said as the Commander shook his head, clearing out the damage done by the blast. He then took note of the Stranger who was still securely fastened to the pole and then he snarled like a beast as the red in his eyes began to burn bright once again. He looked around and saw his sword lying nearby and as he reached for it with one hand, a figure came running from out of the shadows and kicked the commander right in the face!!!!

"Son of motherless goat!!!" shouted the Stranger,

As he saw the head of the Commander shoot backward

COSME DUARTE

like a ball instantly knocking him unconscious. "Ahhh that had to hurt hahahahaha!!! I hate to say it but what goes around comes around homie!" The figure stood over the Commander ensuring that he was out before reaching down and picking up his sword. The fire from the explosion raged on, burning nearby wagons and trees alike. Ash and embers floated in the air like fireflies in the darkness as the Stranger tried hard to focus on the face of the man who saved him.

The man turned and looked at the Stranger, he then began walking toward him with the Commander's sword in hand. He was one of them as far as the Stranger could tell, afterall he was wearing the suit. "This is not gonna end well is it?" he said out loud as the soldier quickly approached. He got close enough for the Stranger to see his facial features and once he did, he recognized him immediately. It was the soldier who was cleaning the weapon, the one that the shadow ignored!

He reached the Stranger and as he did he made certain that he looked him in the eyes as he stuck the Commander's sword into the dirt and then proceeded to pull something from his belt. He looked down in amazement at the man's body and clothing as the flames burned underneath him yet he himself did not. After a moment of hesitation the Young Soldier moved around the Stranger to his rear and then he proceeded to unlock the chains that held him to the pole. One by one the Stranger became free from the pole and once his legs were loose, he leaped away from the pole in happiness.

He turned to look at the Soldier and when he did the Young man was already motioning for the Stranger to follow him. He grabbed the sword from the ground and turned back into the direction that he came from. The Stranger didn't hesitate as he started running behind the young soldier with haste! There were silver suited goons everywhere, some on the ground, some scrambling to put the flames out, others fighting amongst themselves without care.

He did the best that he could to navigate his way through the madness without being noticed and so far, that didn't appear like it was going to be too difficult to achieve.

The young soldier was obviously the man who was responsible for the massive explosion and release of the Stranger but why? "Who could this guy be and why would he risk everything to help me escape? It simply doesn't make sense but I am not going to argue, not right now anyway! If he is willing to help me out then I am willing to take the chance on accepting that help." Just as he finished his thought the sound of a familiar voice rang out through the chaos!

"Eeeeexxxtttrrraaaaannnnnoooooooooooooo!!!!!!" The Stranger and the young soldier stopped and looked back toward the flames. What they saw was disturbing to say the least. It was the Commander screaming at the top of his lungs with fire burning through his eyes. He was barely visible from where they were but they could see him as he began screaming and yelling at his troops! It was hard to believe that all of that madness may have been created by the Darkness but he saw it with his very own eyes making its way through the crowd of men.

Even though the young soldier amplified the craziness with his explosive stunt, the evil was already turning them against each other long before he chose to intervene.

They looked at each other in disbelief and then the young soldier said, "Followeth closely behind me, let us continue forth without reserve!" The Stranger dropped his jaw when he heard the young soldier speak, it was as if he were not real. The young man turned back around and ran away from the camp into the tree line as the Stranger followed suit. The trees were thick and he was losing track of where the young man was going, he searched the darkness for his shiny suit but did not see it. It was only the sound of his armor that enabled the Stranger to keep up with him. After they had put a good deal of distance between themselves and the fires, they slowed down until they came to a stop.

It took a few moments for them to catch their breath but once they did, the sounds of horses and soldiers could be heard off in the distance. "They're searching for us..." said the Stranger as he looked around through the trees in an effort to see where the soldiers were. "Thank you by the way" he said to the Young Soldier as he realized that he had not yet thanked him for the daring rescue.

"De nada Estrano." (It was nothing, Stranger.) Replied the young soldier with a slight smile upon his face. It was at that moment that the Stranger got to look upon the face of the Young Man up close.

His hair was dark and short, his eyes were thin and just as dark, his skin color was dark also, almost like the Strangers but a shade or two lighter. He was about the same height as the Stranger though a lot thinner in frame. It was weird but, the young man reminded the Stranger of Lee for some reason. He was the same ethnicity that Lee was, which was strange considering all of the other soldiers were white but beyond that, there was something about him that was Lee. Just then the sound of horses headed in their direction turned the Stranger's mind back to the situation at hand.

Both men ducked down and hid behind a tree so that they would not be seen as the riders were getting too close to the tree line for their comfort. Just as they reached the trees they stopped. The Stranger cautiously looked around the tree that he was hiding behind and saw that there were four riders in all. Two of them dismounted and drew their swords from their sheaths. One of the riders said something to the two and they nodded in agreement as if to acknowledge the orders given them. They then turned toward the trees and began to infiltrate the forest in search of the Stranger and his new found friend. He looked over to where the young soldier was hiding and saw that he was no longer there!?

"What the heck, where the hell did he go?" he thought as he looked around for a few moments in search of the youngster while the two soldiers were quickly approaching. "It's almost like they saw where we went or something, how are they this close if they didn't?" he wondered anxiously as he waited for the soldiers to get close enough for him to attack them, if he had to that was.

Somewhere off in the distance he could hear what sounded like the Commander screaming and hollering, no doubt furious over the fact that the Stranger escaped. He kept his eyes on the two soldiers as they were now close enough for the Stranger to hear their hearts beating.Then suddenly one of them gasped as if he had just seen a ghost but before he could mutter any words he was violently knocked to the ground with a slam!! The Stranger jumped forward with a quickness throwing a kick at the second soldier that sent his helmet flying in the air and his body to the earth!

"Handale Indio!" (Go Indian!) Said the young man as he witnessed the Strangers skills. The Stranger looked over at the Youngster and smiled.

The two riders that waited on the outside of the tree line began to shout out for their comrades, "Marcos… Juan!? Handale ladrones antes que venga el Comandante!!" (Marcos… Juan!? Hurry up thieves, before the Commander comes!!) The Stranger and the Young Man knew that they didn't have long before they were discovered, they looked at each other and nodded in agreement. They both crouched down and started moving toward the two riders to attack them before they gave their positions away. As they maneuvered their way through the trees the horse of one of the riders must have sensed that they were coming because it began to squirm around and buck in fear.

The soldier tried to get it to settle down but it only got worse the closer they got to them.

The second rider was confused as to what was happening and he was trying to help the other soldier calm his horse. This gave them the perfect opportunity to attack without being seen. The first rider could not hold onto the reins any longer and he was thrown from the saddle in a bad way landing on his head. The second rider jumped off of his horse and as he ran over to his fellow soldier the horse that had lost control kicked him in the back knocking him to the ground also. The Stranger and his new partner cleared the tree line just as it happened and as a result they slowed their run down to a stop!

They looked at each other in disbelief as their objective of subduing the two riders was accomplished, before they could even reach them. "The Light sure works in strange ways! Thank you Almighty!!! I could not have asked for better help than what you have sent me." he proclaimed as he reached the rider who had been thrown first. He kneeled down next to the soldier and rolled him over gently, he then went to place his fingers on the man's neck so that he could verify that the man was still alive for he heard no breathing.

When his fingers touched the man's neck they were met with a protruding bone that had snapped when the soldier landed on the cold hard ground. "Awww... This guy's dead." he looked over to his companion who was kneeling down next to the second soldier that was kicked. The Young Man shook his head and then gestured to the Stranger that he was injured badly.

"May the Almighty bless you amigo, though you may not have been the best of men..." he said as he left the soldier alone. He turned his attention to the other man who the Young man was tending to, the soldier was groaning badly as he lay there on the ground. He got up and walked over to them slowly, for some reason he felt emotional about the loss of life this time around. Deep inside he could feel that there was good in these men though it was being driven from them.

"He whilst not liveth for a period of time for he hath damaged rib bones." The Young Man said as the Stranger knelt down next to them both. The Soldier was undoubtedly in a massive amount of pain and there wasn't much that the Stranger could do for him.

"I don't know how to help him, if his ribs are broken, that is beyond my ability to heal partner." he said to the Young Man with sincerity. The Young Man looked down at his fellow soldier and thought to himself about what they should do. The soldier was lying on his stomach and was not able to see who was kneeling next to him. Considering just how much pain he was in, he probably didn't even notice that someone was there until they started talking about him. When he did realize that he was not alone he began trying to scream out for help though he was unable to due to his injury.

The Young Man's eyes filled with a certain sadness for the Soldier as it suddenly dawned on the Stranger.

The Young soldier undoubtedly knew who the man was on a personal level. They were probably even buddies. The Stranger asked concernedly, "Was he your friend... Tu amigo?"

The Young Man answered gently, "Si, el es mi amigo." An awkward silence ensued,then, for some reason the Stranger felt how much the Young Soldier cared about his friend and he could not ignore it. Just then a reflection of steel caught the corner of his eye and as he looked over to the Young Man, he saw that he had pulled his dagger from his belt and was prepared to put his friend out of his misery. To add to the situation, the rest of the Soldiers had seen the runaway horses of their comrades and were now headed directly over to the escapees.

He could see the glowing red eyes of the Commander in the center of the horde of silver suited goons headed straight for them. "Oh man we are in for it this time bro. All of your homies are coming this way, our only chance is to take off now while we still can. Back into the tree's!" he said as he tried to gauge just how much time they had until the Soldiers reached them. He looked back to his companion and saw that he was still considering taking the fallen soldier's life though it was apparent that he did not have the strength to do so. He was torn and it was gonna cost him far more than he understood at that time.

But for some reason, the Stranger knew... He knew all too well that this moment would forever change the destiny of this good hearted Kid.

"I can't let him hurt himself that way, I can't make him leave his friend either but if we get caught he will be tied to a pole right next to me. I don't think there are many more like him in this battalion of goons that would stand up for what is right... He saved my life, that's for sure." It was at that moment that he realized something... He could force the Kid to run so that they could live and risk breaking his heart, he could let the Kid take his friend's life and risk ruining his heart for life. Orrrr... The last option, well it wasn't so simple as it required him to do something that didn't make much sense but he knew that it was the right thing to do.

He wasn't going to leave either of them behind, nor was he about to allow this heroic Young Man to soil his soul by having to either leave his friend to suffer or by taking his life. Even if it were for mercy's sake. He looked back toward the Soldiers and saw that they had spotted Him and were now not far off. The Commander screamed for the Stranger as he rode as fast as his horse would carry him with all the evil he could muster. The time for thought was up!! He turned back toward the Young Man and caught his hand just as it was dropping the blade down onto his friend. The Young Man looked at the Stranger in shock.

"You must flee for the wrath of the commander is near, doom followeth! Go Strange man, run!" shouted the young man with tears in his eyes!

"Watch out little buddy, let me see him!" said the Stranger as he let go of the Young Man's hand and pushed him aside.

"Aye que correr, Señor! Para salvar tu vida, corre ya!!!" (You need to run Mr.! To save your own life, run now!!!) repeated the Soldier but the Stranger would not listen.

The Stranger looked at the Young Man and said, "Somos amigos jóven, si él es tu amigo pues… es mio también." (We are friends, Youngster, if he is your friend then… He is mine as well.)

The Young Man smiled wholeheartedly before moving into a helping position, giving the Stranger more room to do whatever he was going to do. The Stranger, knowing full well the consequence of his actions, decided that the best thing that he could do for the man was to lay his hands upon him and pray.

"I don't know why I have this sudden urge to do this but I trust in you Almighty One with all of my heart! If there is anyone that could help this man it it You! I ask you in all of your wisdom and kindness to heal this man of his wounds and grant him the gift of life!" he said as he put his hands upon the back of the soldiers head and neck gently. The Young

Man sat there in silence, though, not with a sense of fear. He knew, just as the Stranger did, that his decision to stay with his friend was going to cost him his life. Not only for the lives of the two riders but for his actions against his comrades when he decided to betray his battalion to help the Stranger.

None of that stuff mattered, what did matter is that two men cared more for someone else's life than they cared for their own.

The air had gone from cold to hot in a matter of seconds as the Stranger worked hard to concentrate on his connection with the Light.

"I pray to you my Maker... I know that I don't know these men and I know that I am supposed to be trying to find my friends so that I may finish whatever it is that I am supposed to finish concerning them. They are my friends, proven through words and through deeds. My loyalty to them is all that I am and if I let them down, I could never forgive myself for it. They gave soo much for me and it is my duty to do the same for them. Lupe and Olivia... Sweet little Onley and her protective heart. I just want you to know, as my maker, as my guiding Light, that I would never let them down unless I had no other choice. I have fought and given up my own blood to try and be there for them but...

This Soldier right here... He risked everything to free me from that evil Commander and well, his friend is hurt. I can not leave them behind. Not to save myself, not to save my friends. I trust them unto your will... I surrender myself to your will and I ask once again, that you heal this Soldier of his wounds. I ask in the name of the Chosen One whom the Man in the chamber spoke of. In the name of your Son."

Just then, the Stranger's body began buzzing with energy!!! So much so that he could barely think straight as he tried hard not to let go of the injured

Soldier. The energy could be felt seeping into the man's body and after a few moments the Stranger could actually feel the man's ribs snap back into place!!

The Soldier screamed out in pain like the Stranger had not heard before!! The energy was so powerful that it began to glow through the Stranger's body making him visible to the oncoming horde. The Young Man who sat next to the Stranger was pushed over by the field of energy and he was so amazed by what he was seeing that he rubbed his eyes and tried to refocus them a time or two, to no avail.

"Que estas pasando, Dios mio!!!" he exclaimed as he laid on the ground in absolute awe over what he was bearing witness to. The Injured Soldier suddenly stopped squirming around and lay silent and still. The energy had returned back to where it came from and the glow died out leaving its essence in the air as the Commander along with his men reached the escapee's with weapons drawn!!!

"Para te asesinos, manos arriba!! Si te mueves, mueres. Soldados, agárralos ahora mismo!!! (Stop assassins, hand up!! If you move, you die. Soldiers get them now!!!) The men did just as they were commanded and put their hands in the air.

The Young Man looked over at the Stranger and said, "Lo siento amigo mio… Pero gracias por quedar conmigo. Gracias por no dejarme solo." (I am sorry my friend… But thank you for staying with me. Thank you for not leaving me alone.)

The Stranger smiled at the Young Man and said, "Aint easy having Pals!" then he started laughing as the Soldiers grabbed his hands and began to tie them up.

The Young Man said in return, "Pals." Then Soldiers grabbed his hands also and violently threw him to the ground, punching and kicking him without remorse.

"Hey that's my homie right there!!" He shouted as he tried to stand up and help the Young man. This was when his already bloodied head was met with some sort of blunt object and before he could do anything else, he fell to the earth with a slam!

"Vamos a celebrar mañana mis Conquistdadores!!! Con carne y hueso de Indio y sangre de traidor!!!!!" (Lets celebrate tomorrow my Conquistadors!!! With the meat and bones of traitors!!!!!) screamed the Commander as his men were cheering along with a victorious spirit. These were the sounds that his ears heard as the darkness took over him. Just as his mind was turning off his eyes saw something amazing... The Injured soldier sat up!!!

CHAPTER SIXTEEN

The Way I Came

The sound of the winds whirling around brought him back to life as he suddenly felt his body ache with discomfort. He lifted his head off of the ground and opened his eyes.The area was dark and his eyes were filled with something crusty but he did not know what it was. He placed his hands on the floor to help himself up and that was when he realized that he was not outside where the silver suited goons captured him, he was in a room of some kind with stone floors. He pushed himself up far enough to where he could sit on his butt so he did.

He reached up to rub his eyes when, "Gosh damn that's smarts!!" he shouted upon touching the wound on his face!! "I must have forgotten about that one." he said as he checked the other wound on his head. "Those guys dont play around do they?" he said as he cleared his eyes of the dried blood that covered them as best as he could. Once he was able to see he looked around at where he was but for some reason it wasn't making sense to him.

"Wait... This can't be right?" he said in disbelief as he rose onto his feet and beheld the ancient chamber in all of its awesomeness. "How did I get back here? I mean, those guys, they caught me didn't they?

And what happened to the dude and his homie?" he

thought as his mind spun in circles. He was standing in the very same spot where he stood when the Man disappeared and the chamber started to vibrate. It was as if it were all just a dream, well except for the wounds anyway.

"Hellooo!!! Is anyone here... Sir!? Hey, not sure if you remember me but, I am back and was wondering if you could tell me what the hell is going on? I mean if it's not too much trouble that is" he said nicely. After waiting around for a while with no reply, he tried again, "Hola... Is anyone there? Was anyone ever there?" he wondered as silence ensued.

"Maybe I should get going. After all, my friends are still out there somewhere... though I don't know where exactly... Now that I think about it, I don't even know if I am even in the same era as they are, the Man said that I had already passed them. Hell, I don't even know how I got here... Shitty." he said sadly. After a few moments of pondering, he visually located the stairway and walked over to it. He proceeded upward though he did so hesitantly, as if he were waiting for the Wise Man to appear once again and help point him in the right direction but he did not. In fact, the chamber had never felt this lonely.

He reached the final step and when he did the exit was just around the room. He looked over to the doorway with a certain dread, "What am I gonna do now? Where am I gonna go?" he whispered into the stillness of the air. The questions filled his mind and weighed heavy on his heart.

He looked down and saw the stone hanging from his neck but did not remember seeing it the whole time that he was tied up.

"So strange, it's like the more I learn, the less I know," he thought. He returned his focus on what he was going to do next and as he was thinking he began walking to the exit door. He passed through the doorway of the chamber back into the room of the building where he first entered and looked around. "I just don't know what to do from here, I don't even know how to get off of this Mesa. Why won't the Man tell me something, anything?" he said grudgingly.

"You know what... I don't need direction from him or anyone for that matter. I have You to guide me don't I?" he said as he looked upward, referring to the Light. He then looked toward the exit door and walked through it. The Sun was fresh in the eastern sky which allowed him to see the valley below clearly. Once again, it looked different somehow though not like it usually did. It looked the way it did when they first entered, "If that makes any sense at all." he said to himself as he thought of where to go next.

It was then that he remembered when the Wise Man took him from the chamber and brought him outside showing him Lee's location. "Wait just a minute, that's right, he brought me out here first. Right over here in fact. I know its a long shot but maybe just maybe I can find my way to his camp." he said as he stepped over to the ledge where the Wise Man had shown him Lee's position.

He looked over into that direction and decided that it was the best info he had to work with so that's where he was gonna go.

He couldn't help but to think about his friends and how he would never see them again. It had become the focal point in his life thus far, his friends. He knew their sacrifice for him and it was far too much for to bear. He fell onto his knees in regret and shed a few tears for them while he could. He also prayed unto the Almighty and asked Him to bless them and their families. His heart was heavy and he wasn't sure if he was going to be able to make it through. Not because of some beast, though he knew that he needed to remain cautious of that, but because of the weight of his regret.

The Wise Man told him that he had already passed their time frame and was not going to be able to help them. He knew that already but for some reason, he walked out of that chamber feeling like he was back.

"What year did he say it was, 1549? I think that's what he said but I'm not sure. Anyway, it must be true, I ran into that Lost Battalion and that's something I can not deny... Right?" he wondered. "The Wise Man also told me that there was a possibility of helping my friends by stopping the soldiers from committing all the evil deeds that they had committed. But did I do that? Was it enough to change the course of things, to weaken the two demons enough for my friends to escape? I guess, I can't be sure, I wasn't even sure of how I had gotten away from those soldiers in the first place.

If not for the Young soldier I would not have gotten away, I wonder what happened to him and his friend. I pray they made it, I pray Almighty that You allowed them to get away from those madmen, just as You allowed me to. Otherwise, it's a mystery... One big mystery..." he said sadly as he felt his courage draining down into the stone underneath him.

It was a dangerous time for him and he knew this all too well as he thought of giving in and letting go. But no matter how much he tried to lure himself into that dark place of defeat, his heart just wasn't built that way and so he pulled his feelings back up from the stone floor and used them to fill his heart to its capacity. He then burned them all up inside of the flames within his heart,the flames of goodness and positivity, the flames of dedication and of Light!!

"I can't just sit here and cry like a baby about the things I can not change. I should make good use of this day and get going…" Just then as he turned his head back toward the city he saw something… It was something he never thought he would see, not there inside of the city anyway.

"I… Is that what I think it is?" He asked even though he already knew the answer… He rose up onto his feet and walked over to an object that was half buried with dirt as if it had been there for a very long time. It sat directly across from the building he had just exited though he did not see it for some reason.

He reached the object and knelt down next to it in awe… It was one of the Soldier's silver helmets! What it was doing there was yet another mystery, "What the hell is this doing here? I thought the Wise Man said that no soldier had ever entered this city before but obviously that was not accurate." he said as he pondered the situation. He looked into the reflection cast on the helmet and saw the city inside of it, how surreal it was in a strange way to see it like that.

Opposing forces within a singular entity, "Not sure why that strikes me so, but it does. I almost don't want to touch it but there may be a clue as to who it belonged to and why it is here." So he reached down and grabbed the helmet by the brim, lifting it off and out of the ground. The first thing he noticed was that it had a slash in the brim, right in the front. It looked pretty bad, not sure what kind of weapon could have done that but had to have been something special. Just as he thought about it, the odd looking sword that sliced a line into his face suddenly came to mind.

"Hey wait a minute now… That sword, it was most definitely odd. Come to think of it, when I first noticed it, the Commander turned aside as if to block me from looking at it… But why? What is so special about that swor…. Wait a freakin minute!! Dude, what is wrong with you? The sword from the statue in the cave… It looked just like that?!!" he stopped momentarily so that he could search his memories to see if he could truly match them and even though he wasn't one hundred percent certain... He was pretty certain.

"He must be the bad guy!? Lupe and the Wise Man both warned me about this... My enemy that is. It must be him and maybe that's why I am here. Not to save my friends but to try and stop that fool from wreaking havoc on the people?!! Nah, I can't be that important. Whatever it is, I'm sure that the way will be shown to me in time. Just need to make sure that I am ready when it is." He flipped the helmet over and inspected the inside of it for any clues as to whom it may have belonged to but saw only a number engraved into it.

"Thirty Seven... Must be a serial number or maybe even a soldier's ID... But who's?" After inspecting it closely for a few moments he placed it back on the ground where he found it and rose back onto his feet.

"Who could have made it this far into the city if not the Young Soldier? How that could be possible is beyond me but then again, I am here right? For now, I guess I'll just move forward and have faith that the Light is guiding me in the right direction." he looked around and took a deep breath. "I haven't had a drink in a while, now that I think about it, I am pretty thirsty. Hopefully there is some water in those pools." He said as he turned toward the city and began making his way to the watering pools.

As he approached the buildings that hid them his heart started thumping as he wasn't sure that there would even be any water in them.

"This day is really going to suck if there's no water," he said sincerely.

Once he cleared the corner he was shocked to see something else that did not belong there, it was definitely the sign that he was looking for. He walked over to it and knelt down. He looked at it for a few moments before he reached out and grabbed ahold of it.

He brought it up to his face and gazed upon it closely before he said, "It's his knife...The soldier who saved me, it's his knife! I recognize it from when he was about to kill his friend... That means... That means that...? Hell, I guess I don't really know what it means!" he said as he thought about it. "He made it out right? I mean those guys never found this city, at least it doesn't look that way but maybe he did. But how?" he wondered. He was so lost in thought, questioning and re questioning himself about the situation, that he nearly forgot about his need for water. He looked down at the pool and remembered just how thirsty he was.

"Ahhhh, thank the Light for this water!" he shouted as he saw a small amount of it at the bottom of the little pool. He set the knife down and lowered his face into the pool, careful not to get his blood mixed in with the water and slurped away. The second the water hit the interior of his body he felt like a new man! It was hard to explain but it was true. He didn't drink very much as he felt that his body had reached its limit and though he didn't drink but a few swallows it was more than enough. He filled the palm of his hands up and brought them up to his face and splashed his wound with it in an effort to clean it up a little. When he did his flesh was met with an indescribable feeling.

"Wow that stings!!!" he shouted as the water seemed to be burning his flesh somehow!? He took the pain as best as he could for a few moments but then he shouted out, "Gosh damn that freakin hurts!!!!!" He stood up and danced around like a kid until the pain began to die out. "Awww man, I'm glad that is over whew!!" he said as he pulled his shirt up to wipe his cheek off. Suddenly, that warm energy began to burn inside of his face and to his surprise, the open wound began to close!! He lowered his hands and stood still while his flesh began grafting itself back together.

"This is the weirdest feeling ever..." he uttered as his wound closed up in a matter of seconds. The warm energy then dissipated leaving his face healed and good as new! He shook it off for a few moments before stepping back to the pool, he knelt down next to the remaining puddle and looked at his reflection. Sure enough, his wound was healed. He then cupped his hand and dipped it into the pool one more time and filled it with the precious liquid. He then raised his hand carefully up over his head and then he poured the water onto his head wound hoping for the same result.

Sure as the Light shines, his head began to sting and buzz with pain. "Aaaaaggggggghhhhhhh... That sucks so bad!" he grumbled as the cut on his head burned closed. He remained still for a few more seconds to ensure that the miracle has been completed before he touched his head with his hand. "I know its all because of you, thank you once again." he said as he looked up.

He then reached over so that he could pick up the Soldier's blade and tucked it into his belt. As he looked around unwittingly, his vision came across the small clay bowl that he onced used to give himself water with and he smiled. This reminded him of the other large opening where he had vanquished the beast before so he walked over to the edge of the building and looked down the ancient path that led to it. He was shocked at what he saw for the doorway, it was sealed off!? "Why is that doorway closed? I remember when I first passed through it, It did look as if it were sealed off at some point but it wasn't at that time.

Hmmmm.... Maybe I'm not where I think I am." he said as he thought about it all. He looked back in the direction where he saw Lee and decided that he would head that way and see what he could find. He walked over to the opposite edge of the city and started making his way down the cliffside, careful not to fall down onto the cacti that covered the lower portions of it. Once he got to the valley floor he marked the direction he wanted to travel in and started making his way through the trees as quickly as possible. It was hard, not knowing where he was going or what he was supposed to do.

Sure he had been in that position before but it was different this time. He had learned so much since then, he had friends, people he cared about. When he left the cave, it was just him there was no one else, as far as he knew he was the only human on earth and that made things simple.

"Now all that I can think about is letting them down. Just sucks that things had to go this way." he said as he continued weaving through the trees of the mysterious valley floor. After an hour or two he reached a rock wall of sorts so he decided to stop and take a break while he found a way to climb it. "Strange, I didn't see this from the city. It looks natural, not man made but I'm not sure. There's something about it that's not right though." He thought as he inspected it as best as he could. After a few moments of looking, he was surprised to see what appeared to be writing.

He moved some of the branches and weeds away from the wall and tried to see what it was exactly but he could only see a portion of it due to the foliage that had grown over it. "I can't see what it says but it looks like there's lots of writing on this wall, must have been visible at one time but it sure isn't now. Hmmm… Guess if it were important enough for me to uncover I would feel it but I don't. Just feel the need to get the hell off of this Mesa. Whatever it is, it wasn't meant for my eyes to see it. Not this time anyway." he said as he found a way to get up the wall.

He started climbing it as best as he could focussing

only on getting to the top without falling or slipping as he sure didn't need anymore injuries. Once he got to the top he was shocked to find, "It's a fire ring!!" he shouted as he pulled himself up over the edge of the wall and onto his feet. He ran over to a small clearing approximately 25 feet from the wall's edge and knelt down beside a small circle of rocks.

"Is this where Lee was camping?" he wondered as he searched his memory for clues. He remembered seeing him huddled into a makeshift shelter and he was dug in tight. It looked like he had actually dug a hole in the ground underneath one of the trees and then built up branches and stuff around him.

That is what his memory showed him and unfortunately It took only a moment to determine that this was not the same place. There was no makeshift shelter nor were there any holes dug near the trees, "Hmmm. By the looks of it, no one has been here in a very long while. Even if this is the same spot there's no evidence of him ever being here. Where oh where can I be?" he sang melodiously as he scanned the area for clues. After a quick search he rose onto his feet and walked over to the edge of the wall that he had just ascended.

He looked down at the valley that he had just traversed and then up to the city that he had just left and to his surprise, it looked different. "Every time I look at that place it looks different!" he said with a sense of surprise. "Hmmm, guess I need to concentrate on where I am going and not where I have been…" he thought. With that being said, he turned around and looked at the trees in front of him with wonder. "Where should I go now? he thought as he looked into the forest ahead. This portion of the valley, he did not see from the city. It was higher in elevation and he was not able to tell what direction was best for him to take so he just started walking. He was about one hundred yards into the forest when something caught his eye up ahead…

"Looks like the trees are thinning out up there... or they are disappearing altogether. Great, more desert adventures coming up!" he said sarcastically as he continued walking forward. It wasn't long before all of the trees had disappeared from his path, not because of drought, not because of fire, it was because he had finally reached the end of the Mesa!!!! He ran to the edge of the Mesa like a child running to the finish line of a race and when he reached it, he dropped onto his knees and said, "Thank you All Powerful Light, thank you so much for allowing me to make it through that place!!

I started thinking that I was never going to find my way through there. I truly thought that it was going to be the end of me. YeeeeHaaaaaaa!!!!!!!!!" he shouted with all of his heart!!! Even though he had gotten through the Mesa his life had changed drastically in a very short amount of time. In the beginning, he lacked knowledge and his ignorance was his bliss but that was only for a short time. His enemies had made themselves known to him at almost every turn whether he understood that or not and now he knew for a fact that he was being hunted. He had no idea who it was or when they would strike, all he knew was that it was going to happen.

He once looked upon the scenery with childlike eyes, as if everything was new but now things were different... He had no time for wonder or exploration. He could not afford to let his Enemies get the jump on him, he was in a race against the forces of Evil and that was all he needed to concentrate on from there forward.

He had to be cautious every second of the day, he must not trust anyone unless they were sent by the Light, "Even though I don't know who is who in this battle, I will do my best to be patient. I just need to let the Almighty take me where He wants me to be." he said as he took a few deep breaths.

"Life is like a river, the destination may be certain but the course is full of rapids and danger." The words of the Wise Man as best as he remembered them. "I get it now." he said as he thought of the Wise Man's advice. The Sun was behind him now and the evidence of it could be felt on his neck as the heat from its power soaked into his skin. Just then, he realized how late it had gotten. He had been walking all day through rough terrain and lost track of time.

"Whoa the day really passed me by. I haven't taken a break or even had a drink since the cliffside city. Yet I'm still not thirsty, not like I should be anyway." he said as he evaluated his body for signs of dehydration. His lips were not chapped nor did his body feel the usual effects from the lack thereof. "It must be the water, It truly is blessed!" he thought. He then remembered the Wise Man had told him that the water had healing power.

"Thank you once again Almighty One for the help!" he said as he returned his thoughts to the land below. From where he was standing, it seemed like he was on top of the world, he had to be at least a thousand feet up! He could literally see as far as his eyes would allow him to, it was breathtaking!

He stood in awe as the evening light accentuated every color one could imagine on the earth below sending chills up his spine. It was as if he had never seen something so beautiful before. He thought about making camp right there and spending one more night on the Mesa but he felt in his heart that he needed to get off.

His time there was done and he needed to get moving before dark. The way down was perilous and it was steep. His heart wanted to try and find Lupes casita but he didn't know the way, not to mention the fact that he was no longer in that time frame. "1549... Fifteen Forty

Nine… Why does that seem so off? If it were 1549 why would the helmet and the blade look like they had been there for a long time, it's even a bit rusty. How then, could this be true?" he asked curiously. "I guess I'll just have to find Lupe's casita and if it is there, then I will know, if not… I guess I'll get an answer either way won't I?" he uttered.

That sounded like a solid plan but it wasn't as easy as that, especially since he really didn't remember what direction he and Lee had come from. From the Mesa top he could see that there was a mountain range with white capped peaks off to the north and a desert with barren lands as far as the eye could see to the south. He sat down for a few moments and tried to remember anything that Lee may have said about the short cut that could give him a clue as to which direction to walk in when suddenly, he remembered his journey in the wagon with Lee.

They passed over the grand snow capped mountains to the south of where Lee lived and after a few days of high mountain passes and freezing cold nights they dropped down in elevation. "Down into the desert! Yes that's right, we went from the mountains down into the desert and then after some hills we had to climb another Mesa and then, we arrived at Lupe's place. Now if I recall correctly from Lupe's house, we rode west for three days to get to the ghost town and another half day to get to the Fort. We left the crime scene and rode one day back eastward, straight into the Mesa.

If I made it straight through the Mesa and am now on the other side, that would mean that I am looking at the very same mountain range that Lee and I traveled over to the left." he said as he scanned the range closely. "Then, just a few miles away from there is a smaller Mesa… Looks just like the Mesa that Lupe's casita was built next to to me! If we would have returned the same way that we came then I would have to go around the North side of this Mesa

in order to get back to the trail to Lupes casita and that
would take me to that very Mesa over there...It has to be
the one." He finished speaking to himself and then began
searching the edge for some sort of a trail leading down.

As he walked along it, the Sun began to set low in the
sky and he would soon be in the dark. He pondered the wisdom
of trying to get down the Mesa at night when suddenly,
another sign!!! It was another fire ring, this one was right next
to a big boulder that sat right next to the edge of the Mesa.

Strange that there are no other tracks, no footprints
leading from the fire circle to any particular location,
just a ring of rocks in the dirt. "Hmmmmm... this is
just another community ring isn't it? There seems to be
alot of these in odd places. At least I know that I wasn't
the only person who made it this far." he thought.

He couldn't help but to question if Lee had ever made
it off the Mesa, silly as it may be. For all the Stranger knew
Lee was already dead and so was Washee, long ago. Hopefully
that was not the case but only time would reveal the mystery
of what happened to Mr. Lee and the young sharpshooter.
He cautiously walked over to the small trees and saw a
thin trail leading down the mountain in a very dangerous
manner but it looked like he could make it if he had to. As
he turned back and looked at the fire ring he felt that it was
wiser of him to stay put for the night as the darkness was
falling fast and the trail down the cliffside was treacherous.

"What should I do? " he questioned himself, "It
would be nice to be off of the Mesa as soon as possible but if
I take a fall down that cliff its game over mane!" he thought.
After a few moments he reluctantly decided to stay for the
night and play it safe just for once. He started combing the
area for firewood and was successful in that mission as
there were branches and twigs everywhere. He felt secure

for the time being, not like before where he felt the eyes of something upon him in the darkness. It was nice for a change though he didn't assume that it would last long.

He gathered a good amount of wood and began organizing it inside of the stone ring. He used his fire starting skills and soon a thin line of white smoke began to rise up into the darkening sky.

He was able to get it going just as the darkness overcame the light, just as the sounds of the night revealed themselves unto him. The crickets rubbing their legs together, rabbits or squirrels scurrying about in the woods, gnats buzzing by the Strangers ears. All familiar sounds to him as he had lived this way ever since he woke up in that amazing and mysterious cave. There was so much for him to think about, all of the things that Lee and Lupe shared with him, now the Wise old Man added so much more to it all with his words.

It was hard to imagine what life was like before he went to sleep in the cave. However he came to rest there, he couldn't see himself as he was before. He had come to know himself better as a Stranger than as any kind of person he could think of and he was beginning to like it that way. That is what he told himself anyhow, as he sat and watched the flames from the fire reach for the sky only to die off into the air. He started getting tired and as the battle between his eyelids and his will to remain awake began, it didn't take long at all for his will to lose the war as he laid over onto his side and fell asleep.

The sounds of night time creatures and the crackles of the fire were interrupted by something. It was as if the sounds that so freely floated off into the night air were now muffled somehow.

Even though he was asleep he could feel that something was off and after a few moments of struggling to return to the living he finally woke up with a sudden jerk!! "Whoa what the hell!?" he shouted as his body jolted awake from its slumber! "Who are you and what are you doing here?" he shouted as he opened his eyes and found a dark figure standing across the fire from him! The figure said nothing as it stood there observing him.

He stood up quickly and positioned himself in his fighting stance as the figure began moving toward him. "I'm warning you, if you come any closer I will kill you…" he said with all seriousness.

"Young warrior, is this how you address an old friend?" said the figure as it neared him.

"I don't know you shadow, show yourself and stand down, or prepare to die!" he shouted as he lunged forward and threw a vicious kick to the figure's head! As his foot neared the figure's head it moved like a ghost causing the Stranger to miss completely! He fell to the ground and jumped back onto his feet as fast as he could. "What the hell are you? Are you here to play tricks or are you here to fight?" shouted the Stranger as he began throwing combinations of punches and kicks without ceasing until he realized that none of his attacks were landing.

Frustrated by this he stopped and tried catching his breath while the figure stood still.

"Are you finished?" asked the figure as it reached up and pulled its hood back revealing the face of the Wise Man!

"It's you? Hey, it's just you?!!! Hahaha… I was starting to think that you didn't exist, where have you been?" asked the Stranger passionately.

"I have been where I am supposed to be my friend, nowhere more, nowhere less. I see that you have successfully made it to the boundary of this realm, well done young warrior, well done. Tell me, now that you made it, what did you learn?" asked the Wise Man.

"I don't know if I can give you an answer to that question Sir... I am still not sure what is real and what is not. I mean soo many things have happened to me since the last time we spoke. I found that lost battalion and was almost murdered not to mention tied to a stake and set fire to. That reminds me, the Commander, he was familiar to me. Not sure why but he was and The Darkness was definitely there, I saw it moving through the soldiers, growing in power with every evil deed that they committed. I didn't think I was going to make it out of there but then this Young Soldier saved me.

I tried to do the same for him but was caught and then... I woke up inside of the chamber with no one around. Outside, I found a soldier's helmet and then at the watering pool, I found this." He pulled the knife from his waistband and showed it to the Wise Man.

"It's the Young Soldiers knife... What do you think that it means? And why is it so old looking, same as the helmet. I mean, did he make it also?" asked the Stranger softly.

"Reality is never what one thinks it is for only the Most High determines what is reality and what is non. I would say, leave it to Him to decide. What is most important for you is that you continue onward with the mission that has been given to you. The Master has said, The path that leads to destruction is wide, the path that leads to salvation is narrow. Do not turn left, do not turn right. Keep your heart focussed on the will of the Most High and you will never fail. The enemy though they are crude, they are faithful to their Master. They will die for him. This gives them the advantage over anyone who is not willing to do the same for the Light. Be the Light my Son... Let the Light be you."

The Stranger nodded as if he understood. He then opened his mouth and was about to ask, "Your question has already been answered Young Warrior, it is only you that does not accept it. Soon you will though... Soon, you will see and you will know... Until then..." As the words of the Wise Man left his mouth, his being began to fade away right before the Strangers eyes.

"Wait, wait a minute! Don't leave yet, I still have so much to ask you... Like, where am I? Is this 1549? How do I know where to go? Please don't leave without saying something!!!!" shouted the Stranger in despair!

"Every night that you settle down to rest, what brings forth warmth? Hmmmm? More importantly, what brings light to the darkness?" asked the Wise Man.

"A fire?" replied the Stranger.

"A flame that comforts at night and smoke that leads by day... Behold the smoke, Young Warrior... Behold it." said the Wise Man as his being dissipated into the air like vapor.

"Wait, that doesn't make any sense Sir! Will I ever see you again?" shouted the Stranger as the vapor floated off into the valley of the Mesa. He followed it as far as his eyes would allow him to see and then he looked down at the fire in front of him and sat down. "This whole thing, it makes no sense." he said as he repeated the words of the Wise Man over and over in his mind until he laid down and fell back to sleep.

Suddenly the sounds of early morning birds filled the air with their songs as did the passing winds. He opened his eyes to see the sun had not yet risen but it was informing him that it was well on its way as its glow lit up the Eastern horizon. The fire was long gone, leaving only a few small embers on the bottom of the ash, glowing red with heat.

He sat up and looked around, surprised that he slept so well considering all that he had been through recently.

"What a dream that was..." he said as he rose to his feet.

He adjusted the Soldier's knife in his belt and checked his chest to verify that the key was still around his neck, which it was. He then searched around for evidence of his encounter with the Wise Man but there were no footprints in the dirt, nor was there any sign that someone other than himself had been. He decided that it was just a dream and though the decision was an easy one to make, the words of the Wise Man stuck to his bones like sinew. The Sun would rise soon and right along with it, the unforgiving desert heat.

He knew he had to move fast if he wanted to reach the second Mesa by the end of the day, for if he didn't chances were not good that he would survive. After all he hadn't had a drink in close to twenty four hours and he was lucky the water kept him hydrated for the whole day, not sure he would be so lucky this time around. "I'm not even sure that I know where I'm going even though I think I have figured it out. This whole thing could end up being a really bad decision on my part. I guess I don't have much of a choice though, I just wish I had some kind of verification that I was going the right way.

Like a sign or something you know? Is that too much to ask? Ahh well, best shut my mouth and get my ass moving." he said as he grabbed a few handfuls of dirt and threw them onto the warm embers, ensuring they were extinguished properly. He slapped his hands together a few times dusting them off and then he turned around and began walking toward the trees next to the cliff. Just then, as his eyes met the horizon he saw something. Something that made his heart sink into his boots...

Off into the distance on the other side of

the second Mesa where he presumed Lupe's casita to be, rose a column of dark black smoke!!!

"What the hell could that be? If this isn't the same year that Lupe exists in then why would there be smoke rising from that exact same place? I have a real bad feeling about this!" he said as a shiver suddenly crept up his spine. The notion that he may not be in the time frame he thought he was in had become a normal feeling but this time it was different. Even though he was told that he was no longer in the same era as his friends, his heart was telling him something else and it was scaring the shit out of him!

As he stared off into the distance, the Sun's rays had not yet broken the horizon and as he looked directly at the dark column of smoke a familiar dark green light exploded lighting up the area around the Mesa like a star! It was the very same light he had seen near Lee's home when he and Lee were first setting out on their journey, it was the same light that those discs emitted when they were searching for him in the desert. It was the light of Darkness and instead of being right behind him as it had been up to this point...

It now illuminated the path ahead of him and he knew that it was time to confront it!

TO BE CONTINUED IN...

R3NEGADE IN TIME
Book 3
Warriors of Light.

Made in the USA
Monee, IL
03 August 2025

21875219R00174